This was it! The moment everything about her life would change!

She would enjoy great new experiences. Get back to the basics of medicine and enjoy some survival training.

Plastering a huge smile on her face, Beau opened the door and scanned the room full of faces, ready to say hi.

The smile froze on her face as she realised who was in the room with her.

A man whom she'd hoped *never* to see again.

The smile left her face and unconsciously she let her hand grip the door frame to keep her balance, wrong-footed suddenly by the shock of seeing him. Her centre of gravity was distorted by the backpack, but also by this imposter—the image of the man who'd broken her heart—standing in front of her.

Of all the parks in all the world, he has to be in mine.

Dear Reader,

The only times I have bumped into my ex-boyfriends—only two, I promise!—I have managed to ignore them completely. Rather successfully, too, whilst pretending I was having a fabulous time, laughing and chatting with my friends. I have never been in a situation where we were forced to spend time together, and if I had I don't think it would have gone very well!

Beau and Gray have to spend a week together, and I wanted to explore what would happen when two people who have completely different versions of past events meet and have to get along. Have to rely on one another for their very survival. Would the past get in their way? Would they be able to overcome their difficulties, their prejudices and their hurt and allow the other person back inside their heart?

It was fun to explore this possibility—and to place the story in one of my favourite destinations in the whole world. The glorious Yellowstone National Park. I do hope you enjoy their adventure!

Happy reading!

Louisa xxx

HQ122217

SEVEN NIGHTS WITH HER EX

BY
LOUISA HEATON

MILLS & BOON

First published in Great Britain 2016
By Mills & Boon, an imprint of HarperCollins*Publishers*
1 London Bridge Street, London, SE1 9GF

Large Print edition 2017

© 2016 Louisa Heaton

ISBN: 978-0-263-06688-3

Our policy is to use papers that are natural, renewable and recyclable products and made from wood grown in sustainable forests. The logging and manufacturing processes conform to the legal environmental regulations of the country of origin.

Printed and bound in Great Britain
by CPI Antony Rowe, Chippenham, Wiltshire

Louisa Heaton lives on Hayling Island, Hampshire, with her husband, four children and a small zoo. She has worked in various roles in the health industry—most recently four years as a Community First Responder, answering 999 calls. When not writing, Louisa enjoys other creative pursuits, including reading, quilting and patchwork—usually instead of the things she ought to be doing!

Books by Louisa Heaton

Mills & Boon Medical Romance

The Baby That Changed Her Life
His Perfect Bride?
A Father This Christmas?
One Life-Changing Night

Visit the Author Profile page
at millsandboon.co.uk for more titles.

To my husband, Nick, who offered to take me
to Yellowstone Park as a research trip.
(But we never did get there…sigh…)

CHAPTER ONE

WOW! THIS PLACE is amazing!

Dr Beau Judd drove her hire car into a vacant space outside the Gallatin Ranger Station in Yellowstone National Park. Silencing the engine, she looked out of her window and let out a satisfied sigh.

This was *it*. This was what she'd been looking for. A return to nature. The vast open expanses of the American wilderness. Huge sweeping plains of golden-yellow wild flowers, ancient stone outcrops, forests of pines and fir trees, beautiful blue skies and the kind of summer weather that people back in the UK could only dream of.

She grabbed her guidebook and flipped through the pages, determined to take every moment that she could to learn about where she was. Those golden flowers—bursting skywards like mini-sunflowers—what were they called? Beau flicked through to the flora and fauna section of her book and smiled.

Balsamroots. Perfect.

Her gaze fell to the text beneath the picture and her smile widened.

Native Americans would often use the sap of this plant as a topical antiseptic.

Now, wasn't *this* what she was here for? To learn? And that plant was a perfect start to her new learning experience on the Extreme Wilderness Medical Survival Course. She'd spent too long cooped up in hospitals, on wards, in Theatre. Standing for hours, operating in the depths of a patient's brain, gazing for too long at X-rays or imaging scans, stuck in small rooms passing along bad news, living in a sterile environment, never seeing the sky or enjoying the fresh air.

Her *life* had become the hospital. She'd even begun to forget what her flat looked like. There'd been too many nights spent sleeping in the on-call room, too much time spent with patients and their families, so that she hardly saw her own. Hardly had any friends apart from her work colleagues. Hardly saw anyone she cared about at all.

This next week would all be about Beau reclaiming *herself.* Getting back to grassroots medicine. Getting back to hiking—which she'd used to love, but she hadn't worn a set of boots for years. Not unless they had a heel anyway.

She was one of the top neurologists in England. Had spent years building up her reputation, skill set and repertoire.

Now was the time to take some time out. For herself. Regroup. Do what she loved. Learn and hike in some of the most beautiful country on the planet.

Beau got out of the car and sucked in a lungful of fresh mountain air. Then she popped the boot so she could get her backpack out. She'd bought all new kit—tent, clothes, equipment, walking poles. All colour-coordinated in a gorgeous shade of red. *Matches the hair,* she thought with a smile as she tied a bandana around her head to keep her long auburn hair off her face.

The first day's hike started today. She wanted to be ready. She didn't want anyone having to slow down because of her. Here she would make friends—hopefully for life—and with this experience under her belt perhaps she could start thinking about doing that season at Base Camp, Everest. Her ultimate goal.

She slung the backpack over her shoulders, adjusting the straps, then closed the boot, locked it. Lifting her sunglasses, she strode over to the ranger station, ready to check in and meet the other hikers. Hopefully she wasn't the last to arrive. She'd left Bozeman a whole hour earlier than she'd needed to, but still… She'd find out when she got inside.

It took a moment for her eyes to adjust to the interior of the log cabin, and then she noticed the receptionist standing behind the counter.

'Hi, there! I'm Dr Judd. I'm here for the Extreme Wilderness Medical Survival Course.'

'Welcome to Yellowstone! And welcome to Gallatin. Let me see here…' She ran a finger down a checklist. 'Sure. Here you are.' She ticked Beau's name with her pen. 'The others are waiting in the back. Go on through and help yourself to refreshments. They'll be the last you'll see for a while!'

Beau smiled her thanks and headed over to the door, from where she could already hear a rumble of voices in the next room.

This was it. The moment everything about her life would change! She would enjoy great new experiences. Get back to the basics of medicine and enjoy some survival training.

Plastering a huge smile on her face, she opened the door and scanned the room of faces, ready to say hi.

The smile froze on her face as she realised who was in the room with her.

A man whom she'd hoped *never* to see again.

Gray McGregor.

How was he even *here*? In this small ranger station? In Yellowstone Park? In America? What the heck was he doing? Why wasn't he back in Scotland? In Edinburgh, where he was meant to be?

This had to be some sort of double. A doppelgänger.

We all have one, right?

The smile left her face and unconsciously she let her hand grip the door frame to keep her balance, wrong-footed suddenly by the shock of seeing him. Her centre of gravity was distorted by the backpack, but also by this imposter—the image of the man who'd broken her heart—standing in front of her.

Of all the parks in all the world, he has to be in mine.

The real Gray she'd not seen for… She thought quickly, her mind stumbling as much as she was, over numbers and years that suddenly wouldn't compute. Her brain had flipped in a short circuit. Frozen. The ability to add up basic numbers was beyond her at this terrible moment in time.

And the clone just stood there, the smile that had been on his face before he'd become aware of her presence disappearing in the same way that clouds covered the sun. His eyes widened at the sight of her, the muscle in his jaw clenching and unclenching.

It is *you.*

The noise in the room quietened as the other backpackers sensed a change in the atmosphere, but then rose again slightly as they all pretended not to see.

It was all flooding back! All of it. The day she'd dressed in white *for him*. The hours spent getting her hair done at home, giggling and laughing excitedly with her hairdresser. Then the hour spent with the beautician, getting her make-up looking perfect. Putting on *that dress*, attaching the veil, taking hold of her bouquet and glimpsing herself in the mirror before the photographer had been allowed in to take pictures.

The joy and excitement of the day had been thrumming through her veins as with every picture taken, every smile she gave, every pose she stood for, she had imagined walking down that aisle to be with him. Anticipating the look on his face, the way he would smile back at her, the way they would stand side by side in front of the vicar...

Only, you weren't there, were you, Gray?

The *heartache* this man had caused...

He looked a little different from the way she was used to seeing him. Back then he'd been fresh-faced, his dark hair longer and more tousled. Today his hair was cut shorter than she re-membered, more modern, and he had a trim beard that was as auburn in colour as her own hair. And he was staring at her with as much shock in his own eyes as she was feeling.

But I'm not *going to let you see how much you hurt me!*

Deliberately she tore her gaze from him, tried to ignore her need to hurry to the bathroom and slick on a few more layers of antiperspirant, and walked over to one of the other hikers—a woman in a dark green polo shirt.

'Hi, I'm Beau. Pleased to meet you.'

She turned her back on him, sure that she could feel his gaze upon her. Her body tensed, each muscle flooded with more adrenaline than it needed as she imagined his gaze trailing up and down her body.

Resisting the urge to turn around and start yell-ing at him, she instead tried to focus on what the other hiker was saying.

'…it's so good to meet you! I'm glad there's another woman in the group. There's three of us now.'

Beau smiled pleasantly. She hadn't caught the woman's name. She'd been too busy trying not to grind her teeth, or clench her fists, whilst her brain had screamed at her all the horrible things she could say to Gray. All the insults, all the toxic bile she had once dreamed of throwing at him...

All the pain and heartache he'd caused...she'd neatly packaged it away. Determined to get on with her life, to forget he'd ever existed.

What was he even *doing* here? Surely he wasn't going to be on this course, too?

Of course he is. Why else would he be in this room?

Months this trip had taken her to plan and organise. Once she'd realised that she needed a change, needed to escape that cabin fever feeling, she'd pored over brochures, surfed the Net, checking and rechecking that *this* was the perfect place, the perfect course, the perfect antidote to what her life had become.

It was far enough away from home—from Oxford, where she lived and worked—for her to know that she wouldn't run into anyone she knew. Who did she know anyway? Apart from her family and patients? And her colleagues? How many of *them* had planned a trip to Yellowstone at the same time as her? None. The chances of *him* doing the same thing, for the same week as her... Well, it had never even crossed her mind.

Why would it? She'd spent years forcing herself to not think of Gray McGregor. The damned Scot with the irrepressible cheeky grin and alluring come-to-bed eyes!

Eleven years. Nearly twelve. That's how long it's been.

Eleven years of silence. Why had he never contacted her? Apologised? Explained?

Like I'd want to hear it now anyway!

Outwardly she was still smiling, still pretending to listen to the other hiker, but inwardly... Inwardly a small part of her *did* want to hear what he had to say. No matter how pathetic it might be. Part of her wanted him grovelling and on his knees, begging for her forgiveness.

I'll never forgive you, Gray.

Beau straightened her shoulders, inhaled a big, deep breath and focused on the other hiker—Claire. She was talking about some of the trails she'd walked—the Allegheny, the Maah Daah Hey.

Focus on her, not him.

'That's amazing. You walked those trails alone?'

'Usually! I think you can take in so much more when you've just got to entertain yourself.'

Was he still looking at her? Was he thinking of coming over to speak to her? Beau stiffened at the thought of him approaching.

'What made you come on this course?' she asked.

'Common sense. A lot of walkers I meet on trails are...shall we say, *older* than me? And when I was walking the Appalachian, this guy collapsed right in front of me. In an instant. I didn't know what to do! Luckily one of his group was an off-duty responder and he kept the guy alive until the rescue team arrived. You never know when you're gonna be stuck in the middle of nowhere with no medical assistance!'

Beau nodded.

'What about you, Beau? What made you come on this course?'

'I just wanted to get out and about, walking again. Somewhere beautiful. But somewhere I can still learn something. I want to work in the hospital tent on Everest at some point.'

'Oh, my Lord! You're braver than me! Are you a nurse, then?'

'A doctor. Of neurology.'

'My, my, my! You'll no doubt put us all to shame! Promise you won't laugh at my attempts to bandage someone?'

Beau didn't think she'd be laughing at anyone. The mood of her trip had already changed. Just a few moments ago she'd been carefree and breathing in the mountain air, assuring herself that she'd made the right decision to come here. But now...? With Gray here, too?

She would make him see that she was not amused by his presence. She wasn't *anything*! She had no energy to waste on that man. He'd been given more than enough of her time over the years and her life had moved on now. She was no longer the heartbroken Beau whom he had left standing at the altar. She was Dr Judd. Neurologist. Recommended by her peers. Published in all the exclusive medical journals. Award-winning, innovative and a leader in her field.

She would have nothing to do with him this next week, and if he didn't like her cold shoulder, then tough.

Beau slipped off her backpack, put it to one side and went to make herself a cup of tea at the drinks station. It would probably be the last decent cup of tea she'd experience for a while, and she didn't want to miss having it. They had time before they set out.

She kept her back to the rest of the room, studiously ignoring Gray.

He would have to get used to it.

Yellowstone National Park. Over three thousand miles away from his native Edinburgh. He'd travelled over the North Atlantic Ocean, traversed mile upon mile of American soil to make it here to Wyoming, this one small spot on the face of the *whole planet*, and yet... And yet somehow he had managed to find the one small log cabin in the huge vastness of a national park that contained the one woman he could not imagine facing ever again.

Why would he ever have expected to find her *here*? This wasn't her thing. Being outdoors. Hiking. Roughing it in tents and having to purify her water before drinking it. Beau was an indoors girl. A five-star hotel kind of girl. Life for her had never been about struggle and survival. This should have been a safe place to come to. The last place he would have expected her to be. Wasn't she a hotshot neurologist now? Wasn't she meant to be knee-deep in brains somewhere?

Seeing her walk into the room had almost stopped his heart. He'd physically felt the jolt, unable to take in oxygen. His lungs had actually begun to burn before he'd looked away, breaking eye contact, his mind going crazy with questions and insinuations as heat and guilt had seared his cheeks.

You broke her heart.

You never told her why.

You deserve to suffer for what you did.

And he *had* suffered. Hadn't he?

If only she knew how much he longed to go

back and change what happened. If only she knew how much he'd hated himself for walking away, knowing what it would do to her but unable to explain why. If only she knew of how many nights he'd lain awake, thinking of how he could put right that wrong…

But how to explain? It was easy to imagine saying it, but actually having her here, right in front of him… All those things he wanted to say just stuck in his throat. She'd think they were excuses. Not good enough. Was she even in the right frame of mind to want to talk to him?

Beau had turned her back. Begun talking to another hiker. Claire, he thought she'd said her name was.

He took a hesitant step forward, then stopped, his throat feeling tight and painful. He wouldn't be able to speak right now if he tried. She clearly wanted nothing to do with him. She was ignoring him. Spurning him.

I deserve it.

Other people in the room were milling about. Mixing, being friendly. Introducing themselves to each other. Gray allowed himself to fall into the crowd. Tried to join in. But his gaze kept tracking back to her.

She still looked amazing. Her beautiful red hair was a little longer than he recalled, wavier, too. She'd lost some weight. There were angles now where once there'd been curves, and the lines around her eyes spoke of strain and stress rather than laughter.

Was she happy in life? He hoped that she was. He knew she was successful. Her name had been mentioned in a few case meetings at work. He'd even suggested her once for a family member of an old patient. His own work in cardiology didn't often give him reason to work with neurology, but he'd kept his ears open in regard to her. Keen to know that she was doing okay.

And she was. Though she had to have worked hard to have got where she had. So had he.

He watched from a distance as she mingled with the others, placing himself in direct opposition to her as she moved. The room was a mass of backpacks, hiking boots, men slapping each other on the back or heartily shaking each other's hands as they listed their posts and achievements to each other. Two women at the back of the room sat next to each other, their backpacks on the floor as they sipped at steaming cardboard cups. The last taste of civilisation before they hit the wilds of America.

But all Gray could concentrate on now was Beau. And his own overwhelming feelings of regret.

Would simple words of apology be enough?

Would telling her about the many times he'd picked up the phone and dialled her number even be adequate? Considering that he'd never followed through? He had always cancelled the call before she'd had a chance to answer. And all the emails he had sitting in his 'Drafts' folder, addressed to her, in which he'd struggled and failed each time to find the right words... The times he'd booked to go to the same medical conference as her, hoping to 'accidentally' bump into her, but had then cancelled...

She'd just call me a coward. She'd be right.

He had been afraid. Afraid of stirring up old hurts. Afraid of making things worse. Afraid of hurting her more than he already had...

Time had kept passing. And with each and every day that came and went, it had become more and more difficult to make that contact.

What would have been the point? He could hardly expect forgiveness. Or reconciliation. An apology would mean nothing now. He'd broken things so irrevocably between them. How could he fix them now? He had nothing to offer her. Not then and certainly not now. He was broken himself. And even though he'd known that, years ago, he'd still asked her to marry him! He'd forgotten himself and what he actually was in the madness of a moment when he'd felt so happy. He'd believed anything was possible—got carried away on the *possibility* of love.

But he didn't expect her to understand that. They'd come from two separate worlds and she'd known nothing of his family life. Of what it was like. He'd deliberately kept her away from his poisonous family. Kept her at a safe distance because she was so pure, so joyful, so full of life, believing in happy-ever-after.

She still wasn't married. And that puzzled him. It had been all she'd ever wanted back then. Marriage. And children. It was what she had thought would complete her. After all, she'd said yes to his proposal and then just weeks later had started talking about children.

That was too much. That smacked the reality right back into me.

That was when the full force of not having thought through what he'd done had come to the fore. That was when he'd realised he couldn't go through with it.

For a man who was an expert in hearts, he'd sure been careless with hers.

And it had almost killed him to know that he was doing it.

The tea wasn't great. But she kept sipping it, swapping hands as the heat from the boiling hot water burned through the thin cardboard cup.

She was beginning to get over the shock and was now feeling calmer. She could even picture in her mind's eye dealing with him quite calmly and nonchalantly if he decided to speak to her. She'd be cool, uninterested, dismissive.

That would hurt him.

Because Gray liked to be the centre of attention, didn't he? That was why he'd done all that crazy adrenaline-junkie stuff. He'd passed it off as doing something for charity, but even then he'd wanted people to notice him, to say he was amazing or brave. That was why he'd done Ironman competitions, bungee jumps, climbed mountains and jumped out of planes. *With* a parachute, unfortunately.

He had always succeeded. People had *always* clapped him on the back and told him he was a great guy and he'd thrived on that. Had lived for that, doing more crazy things despite her always begging him not to. Had he listened? No.

So her ignoring him? Choosing not to notice him? That would have to sting a little.

Gray was an attractive man. Usually the most attractive man in a room. And he wasn't just a pretty face, but a brilliant cardiologist, too—getting his papers published in the most prestigious medical journals, trying out new award-winning surgeries, being the toast of the town.

He could at least have had the decency to fail at *something*.

And not once had he called, or apologised, or explained. Even his family hadn't had a clue— not that they'd spoken much to her. Even *before* the wedding. Perhaps that had been a clue?

Beau risked a quick glance at him, feeling all the old hurts, all the old pains, all the grief that she'd tried so unsuccessfully to pack away come pouring out as if they'd had the bandages ripped from them, exposing her sore, festering wounds.

She swallowed hard and looked away.

I will not *let him see what he's doing to me!*

A rage she had never before experienced boiled over inside her and she suddenly felt nauseous with the force of it. She turned away from him, her hand trembling, and took another sip of her tea. Then another. And another. Until her stomach calmed and her hand grew more steady.

She let out a breath, feeling her brain frazzled with a million thoughts and emotions.

This course was meant to be an enjoyable busman's holiday for her. Could she do it with him here?

There's thirteen of us, including the guide. Surely I can just stay out of Gray's way?

Beau had been looking forward to this adventure for ages. This was the moment her career and her life would take another direction and lead her to places she had never dared to go.

She'd thought about it carefully. Planned it like a military exercise. She'd excelled in her hospital work and was top of her game in neurology. Other neurologists who felt they could do no more to help their patients would suggest *her* as the patient's next course of action. She was very often someone's last chance at life.

And she excelled, knowing that. She lived for it. The staying up late, the research, the practice, the robotic assistance that she sometimes employed, the long, *long* and challenging surgeries. The eye for detail. The precision of her work.

Awards lined her office walls at home in Oxfordshire. Commendations, merits, honorary degrees. They were all there. But this...

This was what she craved. A week of living by her wits, experiencing medicine in the wild, using basic kit to attend to fractures, altitude sickness, tissue injuries, whilst hiking through some of the most stunning scenery on the planet.

Forget technology—forget the latest medical advancements. There would be no security blanket here. No modern hospital, no equipment apart from a few basics carried in a first aid kit and what she could find around her.

It was perfect.

Even if *he* was here.

High grey-white mountains, lush expanses of sweeping green and purple, firs and shrubs, thickets of trees hiding streams and geysers. It was a vast emptiness, an untamed wilderness in all its glory, and *she* would try to beat it. No. Not beat it. Work *with* it, around it, adapt it to her needs so she could succeed and get another certificate for her wall. Another trophy so that she could think about applying for Base Camp, Everest. So she could work at the hospital there.

That small medical tent, perched on the base of one of the world's greatest wonders—that was her real aim. Her next anticipated accomplishment.

And there was no way she was going to let all that be ruined by the one man she'd once stupidly fallen in love with and given her heart to. The one man who had broken her into a million pieces. Pieces she still often felt she was still picking up.

She was still trying to prove to the world that she *did* have value. That she was the best choice. The only choice. His rejection of her had made her a driven woman. Driven to succeed at everything. To prove that he'd made a mistake in his choice of leaving her behind. To prove her worth.

Because I'm worth more than you, Gray. And I'll prove it to you.

'Yellowstone National Park is a vast natural preserve, filled with an ecosystem and diverse wildlife that, if you're not careful, is designed to kill you.'

Mack, the ranger leading their group, tried to make eye contact with each person standing in the room.

'There is danger in the beauty of this place, and too many people forget that when they come here and head off-trail. They're so in awe of the mountains, or the steaming hot geysers, or the dreamlike beauty of a wild wolf pack loping across the plains, that they forget to be *careful*. To look

where they're going. We are going to be travers-
ing land millions of years old, trying to be at one
with nature, but most of all we are here to learn
how to look after one another with the minimum
of resources. Yes, this could be done in a class-
room, but...' he paused to smile '...where would
be the fun in that?'

There was some laughter, and Gray noticed
Beau smile. It was exactly the way he remembered it, lighting up her blue eyes.

'Each of you will be issued with a standard
first aid kit. When you receive it, you need to
check it. Make sure it's all there. That's *your* responsibility. Then we're going to buddy up. The
buddy system works well. It ensures that no one
on this adventure goes anywhere in the park
alone and that there is always someone watching your back.'

The likelihood of Gray being paired up with
Beau was remote. And he certainly wasn't sure
if it was something he wanted. But he caught her
glancing in his general direction and wondered
if she'd thought the same thing. Probably.

Mack continued. 'Today we're going to be hiking twelve miles across some rough terrain to reach the first scenario, where we will be dealing with soft tissue injuries. These are some of the most common injuries we see as rangers, here or at the medical centres, and we need to know what to do when we have nothing to clean a wound or any useful sterile equipment. Now, one final thing before we buddy up... We will *not* be alone in this park. There are wild animals that we're all going to have to learn to respect and get along with or stay out of their way. I'm sure you all know we've got wolves and grizzlies here. But there are also black bears, moose, bobcats and elk, and the one animal that injures visitors more than bears...the American bison.'

He looked around the room, his face serious.

'You see one of those bad boys...' he pointed at a poster on the wall behind him '...with his tail lifted, then you know he's going to charge. Keep your distance from the herds. Stay safe.'

Gray nodded. It wasn't just bison he'd have to watch out for, but Beau, too. She didn't have horns to gore him with, but she certainly looked at him as if she wanted him dead.

She was angry with him, and for good reason. He had walked away from their wedding and it had been one of the hardest things he'd ever done. Knowing that she would be left with the fallout from his decision. Knowing that he was walking away from the one woman who'd loved him utterly and completely.

But life had been difficult for him back then, and there was a lot that Beau didn't know. All she'd seen—all he'd *allowed* her to see—was the happy-go-lucky, carefree Gray. The cheeky Scot. But the man she'd fallen in love with hadn't existed. Not really. It had been a front to hide the horrible atmosphere at his home, the problems within his own family: his father's drinking, his mother's depression, the constant fights...

Gray's parents had *hated* each other. *Resented* each other. His mother had been trapped by duty with a man she detested. With a man who had suffered a tragic paralysing accident on the *actual day* she'd decided to pack her bags and leave him.

Being in the same house as them had been torture, watching and listening as they had systematically torn each other apart. Each of them trapped by marriage. An institution that Gray had vowed to himself *never* to get involved with.

'Love fades, Gray. Once that honeymoon period is over, then you see your partner's true colours.'

He could hear his mother's bitter words even now.

So why had he ruined it all by proposing to Beau? He hadn't wanted to get married—ever! And yet being with Beau had made him so happy.

The day he'd proposed they'd been laughing, dancing in each other's arms up close. Her love for him had been beaming from her face, her sapphire eyes sparkling with joy, and he'd wanted... He'd wanted that moment to last for ever. The words had just come out.

Will you marry me?

'We've got one hour before we're due to depart, so take this time to check your pack, check your first aid kit, use the bathrooms, freshen up— whatever you need to do before we set off. Let's meet back here at one o'clock precisely, people.'

Mack headed out of the room and a general

hubbub began as people began to talk and check their bags and equipment.

Gray had already checked his bag three times. Once before he'd set off from Edinburgh, a second time when he'd arrived in America and a third time when he'd first arrived at the park. He knew everything was as it needed to be. There was nothing missing. Nothing more he needed to do.

Technically, he could relax—and, to be quite frank, he needed a bit of breathing space. He headed outside to the porch of the ranger station and sucked in a lungful of clean air before he settled himself down on a bench and took in the sights.

It was definitely beautiful here. There was a calmness, a tranquillity that you just didn't find inside a hospital. Hospitals were clean, clinical environments that ran to a clock, to procedure, to rules and regulations. As busy as a beehive, with people coming and going, visitors and patients, operations and clinics.

But here...here there was peace. And quiet. And—

The door swung open with a creak and suddenly she was there. Alone. Before him. Those ice-blue eyes of hers were staring down at him. Cold. Unfeeling.

He got to his feet, his mouth suddenly dry.

'I think it's time I made some rules about the next week.' She crossed her arms, waiting for his response.

'Beau, I—'

'First of all,' she interrupted, holding up her hand for silence, 'I think we should agree not to speak to each other. I appreciate that circumstance may not always allow that, so if you *do* speak to me, then I'd prefer it was only about the course. Nothing else. Nothing personal.'

'But I need to—'

'Second of all…you are to tell no one here what happened. I will *not* become the subject of idle gossip. And thirdly…when this is over, you will not contact me, you will not call. You will maintain the silence you've been so expert at keeping for the last eleven years. Do you understand?'

He did understand. All too keenly. She wanted nothing to do with him. Which was fair enough.

Except that he felt that now she was here, right in front of him, this week might be his chance to explain everything. Forget a pathetic phone call or a scrappy little email. That had never been his style. He had seven days in which to lower her walls, get her to accept his white flag of truce and ask her to listen to him.

But he didn't want to become the subject of gossip, either. He didn't want to fight with her. Nor did he want to share so much that she found out about his injury. But time would tell. They had a few days to cool down. They'd get to talk. At some point.

'I do.'

Her lip curled. 'You see? That wasn't too hard to say, was it?'

Then she pointed her finger at him, and he couldn't help but notice that her hand was trembling.

'Stay out of my way, okay? I want nothing to do with you. *Ever.*'

He nodded, accepting her rules for the time

being, hoping an opportunity would present itself to allow a little bending of them.

They would have to talk eventually.

Beau checked her first aid kit against the checklist—gloves, triangular arm bandage, two gauze pads, sticking plaster, tape, antiseptic wipes, small scissors, one small saline wash, a safety pin. Not much for a medical emergency, but she guessed that was part of the challenge. The other part of the challenge for her was going to be a mental one.

Ignore Gray McGregor.

How hard could it be?

She retied her hiking boots, used the ranger station bathroom and then grabbed something to eat, forcing herself to chat pleasantly with some of the other hikers. No one else had a medical background, it seemed, apart from her and Gray. The others were experienced walkers, though, used to long treks and mileage, so she hoped they could all learn something from each other.

At one o'clock precisely Mack came back into

the room, followed by another ranger. 'Right, everyone, gather round. I'm going to issue the buddy list. Now, remember, your buddy is more than just your friend. They're your safety net, your lookout, your second brain. You don't go anywhere without your buddy, okay?'

He awaited assent from the group.

'Now, we've tried to divvy everyone up equally and pair people with similar interests, so here goes.' Mack picked up his list. 'Okay, let's see who we have here. Conrad and Barb—you guys are married, so it makes sense to buddy you guys up... Leo and Jack—you guys are both from Texas... Justin and Claire—you guys mentioned you've met before, walking the Great Wall of China... Toby and Allan, both ex-Forces personnel...'

Beau shifted in her seat. There were only four of them left to name: her and three guys, one of whom was Gray.

Please don't pair me with Gray!

But what did she have in common with the other two? They were brothers, and surely Mack was going to pair brothers. Which meant... Her heart sank and she began to feel very sick.

'Dean and Rick—brothers from Seattle, which leaves our UK doctors, Beau and Gray. Welcome to America, guys!'

Beau couldn't look at Gray. If she looked at him, she'd see that he was just as horrified as she was about this.

Was it too late to change her mind and go home? Go back to the hotel in Bozeman and stay there for a week?

No! You've never backed away from anything!

Looking around the small room, she saw that everyone was pairing with their buddy, shaking hands and grinning at each other. Reluctantly she let her gaze trickle around the room until she locked eyes with Gray. He looked just as disturbed as she was—uncomfortable and agonised—but he seemed to be hiding it slightly better. She watched as he hitched his backpack onto his back and came across the room to her, looking every inch the condemned man.

Staring at him, she waited for him to speak, but instead he held out his hand. 'Let's just agree to disagree for the next week. It should make this easier.'

Easier, huh? He had no idea.

She ignored his outstretched hand. 'Like I said, let's just agree not to talk to each other *at all*. Not unless we have to.' Her voice sounded shaky, even to her own ears.

'That might make things difficult.'

'You have no idea what *difficult* means.' She hoisted her own backpack onto her shoulders and tightened the straps, turning away from the muscle tightening in Gray's jaw.

'I think I do, my lass.'

Her head whipped round and she glared at him. 'Don't call me that. I am *not* your lass. You know nothing about me now.'

'You want me to talk to you like you're a stranger?'

'I don't want you to talk to me at all.'

'I'm not going to be silent for a week. I'm not a monk.'

'Shame.'

'Beau—'

She glared at him. *Don't say another word!* 'Let's get going…*buddy.*'

He took a step back, sweeping his hand out before him. 'Ladies first.'

Beau hoped her stare would turn him into stone. Then she followed Mack and the others out of the ranger station.

CHAPTER TWO

BEAU MARCHED ALONG at the front of the pack, as far away from Gray as possible. She knew he would be lurking at the back. She walked beside Barb, her nostrils flaring and her nails biting into her palms.

She was beginning to get a headache. Typical! And it was all *his* fault. And she had no pain-killers in her first aid kit. No one did. She had to hope that it would pass soon. The whole point of this course was to make her think differently. To use what was around her to survive.

Beau thought that she already knew quite a bit about survival. About not giving up when everything was against her. About not allowing herself to succumb to the void.

Since the day Gray had left her standing at the altar, she'd become a different person. Stronger than before. Driven. Her eyes had been opened to the way men could hurt her.

And to think that I solemnly believed that he wouldn't do that to me.

She'd allowed herself to feel safe with Gray. Secure in the knowledge—or she'd thought so at the time—that he loved her as much as she loved him.

Beau ground her teeth. Perhaps she'd been naïve. Perhaps she'd been cocky. She'd told everyone back then how Gray was her soulmate, her one true love. That he was the most perfect man and she was so lucky because he wanted *her*. There had been one time she remembered sitting in the kitchen with her mum, waxing lyrical about how wonderful he was, how happy *she* was and how she couldn't believe she'd found a man who wanted all the same things she did.

Her mum had listened and smiled and rubbed her arm and told her daughter how happy she was for her. How this was what life was all about. Finding love, settling down, creating a family of your own. That it was all anyone needed.

Beau had almost not been able to believe how

lucky she was herself. But she'd believed in *him*. Almost devoutly. Her faith in their love had been undeniable, and when Gray had asked her to marry him, she'd been the happiest girl in the world.

She'd thought no one could be happier than her. She'd thought she was going to marry the man she was head over heels in love with and that they would have children and a brilliant life together, just as her parents had done. They'd be strong together, united, and when the time came for them to be grandparents, their love would continue to grow. It had all been mapped out in her mind's eye.

But then he'd destroyed everything she'd believed in and she hadn't even got an apology! Not that it would mean much now. Too much time had passed. The time for an apology had been eleven years ago. Not now.

But there was nowhere for her to escape him here. They were stuck together. Buddied up, for crying out loud! She must have tutted, because Barb turned to look at her as they slowly marched up a steep, rocky incline.

'Mack mentioned you're a doctor?'

Brought back to reality, she tried to push her anger to one side so that she could speak politely to Barb. 'Yes, I am.'

'Do you have a specialty?'

She nodded and smiled. 'Neurology.'

'Ooh! That sounds complicated. They say there's so much about the brain that we don't know.'

'Actually, we know a good deal. Technology has advanced so far nowadays.'

'You know, I think I saw a documentary once where there was a brain operation and they did it with the patient wide awake! I couldn't believe it! This poor man was having to identify pictures on flash cards whilst the surgeons were sticking God only knows what into his brain!'

Beau smiled. 'It's called intraoperative brain mapping.'

Barb shuddered. 'Have you seen it done?'

'I've done it. I'm a surgeon.'

'Ooh! Con—you hear that? Beau here's a *brain surgeon*!' Barb grabbed her husband's arm to get his attention and Conrad nodded at Beau.

'Well, let's hope we don't need your services during this next week, Doctor.'

She laughed, a lot of her anger gone. The married couple seemed nice. They were both middle-aged, though Conrad's hair was already silvery, whereas his wife's perfectly coiffed hair was dark. They reminded her slightly of her own parents. Happily married, easy in each other's company and still very much in love.

Despite everything, it made her smile. 'How long have you two been together?'

Barb glanced at her husband. 'Thirty-five years this August.'

'Wow! Congratulations.'

'Thank you, dear. I have to say it's been wonderful. We've never had a cross word and we've never spent more than a night apart.'

'How do you do it? Stay so happy, I mean?'

'We pursue our own hobbies, but we also make sure we follow an interest together. Which is why we're doing this. We both love walking and seeing the country. Though last year Con had a few heart issues, so we thought we'd come on this course. Combine an interest with a necessity.

Sometimes you can be out in the middle of nowhere and it can take hours before you get medical attention. We both thought it a good idea to
get some medical basics under our belts.'

Beau nodded. It *was* a good idea. For a long
time she had thought that basic first aid, and especially CPR, ought to be taught in schools. So
many more people would survive accidents or
sudden turns of events in their own health if everyone was taught the basics.

'Good for you.'

'What made *you* come on this course? This
kind of stuff must be old hat to you.'

Beau looked across the plateau they'd reached,
at the glorious sweeping plains, a patchwork of
green, grey and purple hues, and the mountains
in the distance. The open expanse. 'I got cabin
fever. Needed to get back to nature for a while.'

'And the other doctor? The Scottish one? It
looked like you two know each other.'

There was so much she could have said.

*Why, yes, I do know that lying, conniving, hor-
rible Scot...*

'Briefly. A long time ago. We haven't seen each other for a while.'

Barb peered at her, her eyebrows raised. 'Parted on bad terms, did you?'

She smiled politely. 'You could say that.'

'Aw…' The older woman patted her arm. 'Life's too short for holding on to anger, honey. When you get to our age, you learn that. Our son Caleb, bless his heart, always jokes that Con and I are *"on the coffin side of fifty"*!' She laughed out loud. 'And he's right—we are. People waste too much time being angry or holding on to resentments and it keeps them stuck in one place. They can't move forward, they can't move on, and they lose so much time in life, focusing on being stuck in the sad when they could be focusing on being happy.'

Beau appreciated what Barb was trying to say, but it didn't help. There was still so much anger inside her focused on Gray. Suddenly she realised that until she heard some sort of explanation from him, she didn't think there was any way for her to move forward. She knew an apology wouldn't help—not really. But maybe she'd like to hear it, see him wriggle about on the end of his hook like the worm that he was.

Gray McGregor owed her *something*, and until she heard it, she wasn't sure what it was. But she wouldn't let it bother her. She told herself she didn't care. Even if she *was* still trapped in the past when it came to Gray. She might have grown up, found herself a stellar career and proved to her peers that she was one of the top neurologists in the country, but in her heart she was still a little girl lost. Hurt and abandoned.

Her heart broken in two.

And there was only a certain Scottish cardiologist who might be able to fix it.

Gray replayed in his mind his recent words with Beau. He kept his gaze upon her, walking far ahead of him, wondering how she was feeling.

Those dark auburn waves of hers bounced around her shoulders and gleamed russet in the sunshine. He could see her chatting amiably with Con and Barb and wished she could be as easygoing with him. It would make the next week a lot easier for both of them if they could put the past in the past and just concentrate on enjoying the hike and the medical scenarios.

But the sweet, agreeable Beau he'd once known seemed long gone, and in her place was a new version. And this one was flinty, cold and dismissive.

He wasn't sure how to handle her like that, and he'd already been feeling enough guilt about what he'd done without her laying it on thick to make him feel worse.

I know I owe you an explanation.

So many times he'd thought about what he needed to say to her. How he intended to explain, to apologise. Always, in his own mind, the conversation went quite well. Beau would listen quietly and attentively. Most importantly, she would understand that the decision not to turn up at their wedding had hurt him just as much as it had hurt her.

But now he could see just how much he'd been wrong. Beau would not sit quietly and just listen. She would not be understanding and patient.

Had *he* changed her? By walking away from her, had he changed her personality?

So now he chose to give her space. Letting her walk with Barb and Conrad, staring at the back of her head so hard he kept expecting her to rub the back of it, as if the discomfort of his stare would become something physical.

And he worried. There was strain on her face, a pallor to her skin that reinforced the brightness of her freckles and the dark circles beneath her eyes.

Surely *he* wasn't the cause of that? Surely she'd just been working too hard, or for too long, and wasn't getting enough sleep? He knew she worked hard. He'd kept track of her career after medical school. She was one of the top neurologists in the country—maybe even in the whole of Europe. That had to take its toll, right?

But what if she's ill?

A hundred possibilities ran through his mind, but he tossed them all aside, believing that she wouldn't be so silly as to come out on a trek through the wilderness if she was ill.

It had to be stress. Doing too much and not eating properly.

He hadn't seen a ring on her finger. As far as he

was aware, she wasn't married, and the hours she worked would leave hardly any time for dating. Unless she was seeing someone at work? There was always that possibility…

He shifted at the uncomfortable thought and tugged at the neckline of his tee shirt, feeling uneasy. Hating the fact that the idea of her being with someone else still made him feel odd.

Yet she was never mine to have. I should never have let it get so far in the first place. I was wrong for her.

'Here you go…have a pull of this.' Rick offered him a small flask. 'It'll keep you going. Always does the trick for me at the start of a long hike.'

Gray considered the offer, but then shook his head. 'No, thanks. Best to stick to water. That stuff will dehydrate you.'

'What do you think I've got in here?' Rick grinned.

'It's a whisky flask, so I'm guessing…alcohol?'

'Nah! It's just an energy drink my wife makes. It's got guarana in it. It's good for you!'

Gray took the flask and sniffed at it. It smelled very sweet. 'And how much caffeine?'

'Dunno. But it tastes great!'

He passed it back without sampling it. 'Do you know that some energy drinks can trigger cardiac arrest even in someone healthy?'

Rick stopped drinking and held the flask in front of him uncertainly. 'Really?'

'If you consume too many. The high levels of caffeine mixed with other substances can act like a drug, stimulating the central nervous system to high levels when consumed in high doses.'

'You're serious? I thought all that pineapple and grapefruit juice was *good* for me.'

'It can be. Just don't add all the other stuff. Do you know for sure what's in there?'

Rick shook the flask, listening to the swish of the liquid inside. 'No. But she spends ages in the kitchen making it for me and it always seems to help.'

Gray grinned. 'I'd stick to water, if I were you.'

'How do you know all this?'

'I'm a cardiologist. I've operated on a fair few people who've ended up in the ER because of too many energy drinks.'

Rick began to pale. 'Wow. You think something's good for you...'

'Sorry to be a party pooper.'

'Nah, you're all right.' Rick tipped the flask upside down and emptied the juice out onto the ground. 'Doesn't make sense to carry the extra weight, does it?'

Gray looked up at Beau and considered all the extra emotional weight he was carrying. 'It doesn't. It doesn't help you at all.'

They'd been walking for a steady hour, and by Beau's reckoning—not that she knew much about these things—they'd walked about three miles into the park, all of it uphill. Her calf muscles burned and she was beginning to feel sore spots within her new hiking boots. She hoped she wasn't getting blisters.

The hillside had produced a plateau, a wide expanse of grasslands, and eventually they'd passed through a grove of lodgepole pine trees—tall and slender, the bark looking almost white from a distance, but grey up close.

Mack stopped them as they got near. 'You'll see

a lot of these throughout the park. They're a fire-dependent species, and the seeds you can see, once fallen, provide a natural foraging source for grizzlies as we pass into fall. So you see this tree, then you look for the bear that goes with it. Luckily there isn't one here today.'

He smiled as everyone looked at each other and laughed nervously.

'But this is one example of always needing to be prepared. If you're walking in a new area, know the ecology, the flora and fauna—it can help you stay safe. Today there's no reason not to know. The Internet can tell you in an instant. There are books. Read. Research. It could save your life. Medically, indigenous tribes have used the lodgepole pine for many ailments—they steam the pine needles and bark to help with lung issues, and they also use it for bronchitis, fever and even stomach ache treatments. You can make a pitch from the pines and use it as a plaster for infections, burns and sores.'

Beau looked up at the canopy of the tall tree and was amazed. Working in a hospital, with the technology and advancement that came in the present day, it was easy to forget that all medicine originated from the use of plants, trees, shrubs and flowers. But it was important and not to be forgotten. She got out her compact camera from her pack and took a picture.

Mack walked them on and the plateau soon began to dip down towards a narrow rocky stream. The sound of running water was refreshing in the day's heat and Mack encouraged them all to take in some liquid refreshment and eat a small snack.

Beau perched on a large stone and nibbled on a flapjack she'd brought, avoiding Gray's glance and hoping he would stay away from her for a while longer.

Irritatingly, he sat down opposite her.

'How are you enjoying this so far?' he asked in his lilting Scottish burr.

'It's wonderful. Especially when I don't have to look at *you*.'

He glanced down at the ground. 'There's no need to attack me all the time, Beau. I feel bad enough as it is.'

'Good.'

He let out a heavy sigh, looking out across the stream bordered by rocks and grassy banks. 'I suppose you want me to go away?'

She didn't look at him. 'Or just be quiet. Either would do.'

He pulled some trail mix from his pack and offered it to her. 'Nuts?'

She glanced at him to see if he was making fun of her or being insulting. 'No. Thank you.'

'You know you're stuck with me, hen?'

She put away her flapjack, annoyance written all over her face, and refastened the buckles on her backpack. 'I'm not a hen.'

'Sorry, lass.'

She stood up and heaved the pack onto her back. 'Wow. An apology. You *do* know how to make them, then?'

Gray looked up at her, squinting in the sun. 'Aye.'

'*And...?*'

'And what?'

'Where's my *real* apology? The one you should have made eleven years ago?'

He cocked his head to one side and pulled his sunglasses down over his eyes. 'I'm saving it.'

'Saving it? For what?'

He looked about them before getting to his feet and leaning in towards her, so that his face was up close to hers. It was unnerving, having him this close. Those moss-green eyes staring deeply into her soul and searching. His breath upon her cheek.

'For when you're actually ready to listen. There's no point in me trying to explain whilst you're like this.'

'I'm not sure it's important, anyhow. Too little and too late.'

'And that proves my point.'

He walked away to sit down somewhere else.

Beau began to breathe again. Their brief conversation had unsettled her. Again. Plainly the way she was reacting to him was not working. Open hostility towards Gray was like water bouncing off an umbrella. It made no difference to him at all. He quite clearly was not going to apologise to her unless she got herself together.

Irritating man!

Most irritating because she was stuck with him for a week!

She had to be realistic. They were here. Together. And, worst of all, they were *buddied up* together. She knew from the itinerary for the trip that there would be paired activities where they would have to work with each other away from the main group. Orienteer themselves to another part of the park. Which meant time alone.

They had to start working together. Whether she liked it or not.

She turned to look for him and saw him standing with Mack, chatting. Beau headed over and plastered a charming smile onto her face. 'Excuse me, Mack, could I have a quick word with my buddy here?'

'Absolutely. Glad you're here, Gray.' He slapped Gray on the arm before walking away.

Gray looked at her curiously. 'Yes?'

'You're right. We need to be working together for this next week and, as buddies, we need to be strengthening our working relationship. I'm not prepared to fail this course, and with that in mind I'm willing to put our past to one side in the spirit of cooperation and…peace. What do you say?'

She saw him consider her outstretched hand. Saw the question in his solitary raised eyebrow, saw the amiable smile upon his face before he reached out and took her hand.

A charge shot up her arm as her hand tingled in his. The strange yet all too familiar feel of his hand on hers was electrifying and thrilling. Her instinct was to let go. To gasp for oxygen. To rub her palm against her khaki trousers to make it feel normal again. But she did none of these things because her gaze had locked with his and she'd stopped breathing anyway.

Who needs oxygen?

Gray's leaf-green eyes bored into hers with both an intensity and a challenge, and Beau felt as if she'd been pulled back through time to when they'd first met on a hospital rotation.

They'd been so young, it seemed. All the students had been fresh-faced and eager to learn, eager to start their journeys. The girls smartly dressed, professional. The boys in shirts and ties as yet unwrinkled and sweat-free.

She'd noticed him instantly. The gleam in his eyes had spoken of an ambition she'd clearly been able to see. And had held a twinkle that had spoken of something else: his desire to stand out, to be noticed, to be cheeky with their lecturers. The way he'd pushed deadlines for work, the way he'd risked failing his assessments—that side of him that had been an adrenaline junkie, carefree and daredevilish.

His mischievous, confident grin had pulled her in like a fish to a lure and she'd been hooked. His attitude had been so different from anyone she already knew—so different from that of any of the men in her own family. He'd been that breath of fresh air, that beam of light in the dark, that sparkling, tempting palace in a land of dark and shadow.

He'd shaken her hand then and introduced himself, and instantly she'd heard his soft, lilting Scottish burr and been charmed by it. The very way he'd said her name had been as if he was caressing her. He'd made her feel special.

She'd not wanted to be dazzled by a charming man. Not at the start of her career. But family, love and marriage were high on her agenda and she'd desired what her parents had. A good, steady partner, with a love so deep it was immeasurable. Beau had had no doubt that she would find it one day.

She just hadn't expected to find it so soon.

Gray had stuck to her side and they'd worked together, played together, studied together and then, after one particularly wild party, slept together. It had seemed such a natural step for them to take. He'd filled her heart with joy. He'd made her feel as if she was ten feet tall. Every moment with him had been as precious as a lifetime. She'd wanted to be with him. She'd wanted to give him everything—because that was what love was. The gift of oneself.

And he hadn't disappointed her.

Afterwards, as she'd lain in his arms, she'd dreamed about their future. Wondering about whether they would get married, where they might live—not too far from her parents, not too far from his, so their children would have a close relationship with each set of grandparents—and what it would be like to wake up next to him every day for the rest of their lives together.

She'd liked the way he acted differently with her—calmer, more satisfied, considerate. *Relaxed.* He'd been a hyperactive buzzing student when they'd met, full of beans and so much energy. He'd exhausted her just watching him. But when he was with her, he wasn't like that. As if he didn't need to be. And she had found the side of him that she could fall in love with...

Gray smiled now. 'I hear you. Cooperation and peace. Seems like a good start to me.'

Beau chose not to disagree with him. It was already looking as if it was going to be one very long week ahead, and this adventure was going to be uncomfortable enough as it was.

I'm letting go of the stress.

So she smiled back and nodded.

Mack suggested that they all get going again, if they were to get to the first scenario and have enough extra time to pitch their tents for the evening.

They walked through scrub brush, conifers and thick deep grass. The overhead sun powered down upon them and Beau stopped often to drink and stay hydrated. At one of her stops Gray came alongside and waited with her.

'How are your parents?'

Beau fastened the lid on her water bottle. It was getting low. Hopefully there'd be a place to refill soon. 'Not that they're any of your business any more, but they're good, thanks.' She answered in a clipped manner. 'Yours?'

No need for her to go into detail. What could she say? That they hadn't changed in over a decade? That they still went to church every Sunday? That they still asked after him?

'They're fine.'

'Great.' These personal topics were awkward. Perhaps it would be best if they steered away from them? Gray's parents had always been an awkward subject anyway. She could recall meeting them only a couple of times, and one of those occasions had been at the wedding! They'd been a bit hard to talk to. Gruff. Abrupt. Not that keen on smiling. She'd babbled on *their* behalf! Chattering away like a radio DJ, musing on life, asking and answering her own questions. She'd been relieved to leave them and go and talk to others, and had just hoped that they'd liked her.

They'd turned up to the wedding anyway. Mr McGregor in his wheelchair, his face all red and broken-veined.

They trekked a bit further. Beau snapped pictures of columbines and hellebores and a herd of moose they saw in the distance. Then Mack brought them into a large clearing that had a stone circle in the centre.

'Base Camp Number One, people! I'll teach you later how to safely contain your campfire, but first we're going to get working on our first medical scenario—soft tissue injuries. As I said before, these are some of the most common injuries we get here in the park, and they can be minor or major. A soft tissue injury is damage to the ligaments, muscles or tendons throughout the body, so we're looking at sprains, strains and contusions. This sort of damage to the body can result in pain, bruising or localised swelling—even, if severe, loss of function or blood volume.' He looked at each of them with determination. 'You do *not* want to lose either. So what can we do out here with our limited kit? Gray? Care to enlighten us?'

'Normally you'd follow the PRICE protocol—protection, rest, ice, compression and elevation.'

'Perfect—did you all hear that?'

The group all murmured agreement.

'Now, unless you're in the North or South Pole, you aren't going to have any ice, so you might have to skip that step, but can anyone think of an alternative?'

Beau raised her hand. 'If you have a sealable bag, you could fill it with water from a stream and rest that over the injury.'

'You could. What else might happen with a soft tissue injury? Someone without a medical degree care to hazard an answer?'

No one answered.

'You'll need to stop any blood loss. And you have minimum bandages in your first aid kit. So, I want you all to get into your pairs and have one of you be the patient, with a lower leg injury that is open down to the bone from knee to ankle. The other partner needs to use whatever they have to hand to protect the open wound. *Go!*'

Beau looked up at Gray. 'Doctor or patient?'

He shrugged. 'Ladies' choice. You choose.'

She smiled. 'Then I think I'll have to be the doctor.'

Gray nodded and plonked himself down on the ground, then looked up at her, squinting in the sun. 'Can you help me, Doctor? I've got a boo-boo.'

CHAPTER THREE

SHE WATCHED AS he reached forward to raise his trouser leg and tried not to stare.

His leg was thick with muscle and covered in fine dark hair, and she swallowed hard, knowing she would have to touch his skin.

Distracted, Beau opened her first aid kit and tried to concentrate. For an open wound she'd have to use the gloves, the saline wash to clean away any dirt in it, two gauze pads, the triangular arm bandage, tape and maybe even the safety pin. Almost all of the equipment in her first aid kit.

She looked up at Mack, who was wandering through the group, watching people's ministrations. 'If we use all of this on one wound, Mack, that only leaves us plasters, antiseptic wipes and scissors for the rest of the week.'

Mack grinned back at her, mischief in his eyes.

'So what do you want *me* to do? You're out in the field—technically I'm not here. You two need to survive. You need to bandage his wound.'

'Because of blood loss and the risk of infection?'

'So what are you going to do?'

'Use it.'

Mack grinned again.

'But that doesn't leave us much if there's going to be another injury.'

'Well, if you didn't clean the wound properly or stop the bleeding, what would happen to your patient?'

'He could lose consciousness. Or it could become septic.'

'So you have your answer.' He walked on, pointing things out to others, showing some of the less well-trained how best to use the triangular arm bandage.

Beau squatted beside Gray and considered his leg. 'Okay, I'll flush the wound with saline first.' She put on the gloves and cracked the end of the small container, allowed the saline to run down

Gray's leg, watching as the rivulets separated and dribbled along his skin.

'You could use drinking water, too.'

'Yes, but keeping you hydrated would be a strong reason to save as much water as possible, in case I can't light a fire to boil some more.'

He nodded and watched her.

'Gauze pads next, along the shin line.'

'Should I yell? How much acting do they want us to do?'

Beau gave a small smile. 'Whatever you feel comfortable with, I guess.' She looked around her and picked up a short thick stick, proffered it towards his mouth. 'Do you want to scream?' She grabbed hold of his shin and calf muscle and deliberately pushed her thumbs into his pretend open wound.

He grimaced. 'I might have to dock you points for being a sadist.'

She grinned as she pulled open the packing around the triangular arm bandage, then gently and delicately draped it over his shin and tied it as neatly as she could behind the leg, creating some constriction to prevent blood loss, but not making it too tight to restrict blood flow.

'How's that, Mr Patient?'

'Feels great. I can sense survival already.'

'Good.'

'You *do* have a gentle touch.'

'You see? There's a lot you don't know about me.'

She sat back on her haunches and looked around the rest of the group to see what everyone else had done. Justin and Claire hadn't used their gauze pads, but everyone had used the arm bandage.

Mack was nodding his head in approval as he walked amongst them. 'Good. Good. You've successfully treated the wound—but what do you need to be aware of whilst you wait for recovery or help?'

Beau raised her hand. 'Whether the patient can still move his toes—and look for signs of infection, too.'

'And how would we know there are signs of infection without undressing the wound?'

Again, Beau answered. 'Signs of fever, pallor, increase of pain in the affected limb, loss of function, numbness, unconsciousness, rapid breathing.'

Mack nodded.

Gray leaned in and whispered, 'Still the teacher's pet?'

She glanced at him. 'I like to learn. I like to know that I'm right.'

'Still, you're a doctor. You need to give the others a chance to answer a few questions. Perhaps they'd like to learn, too?'

She almost bit back at him. *Almost.* The temptation to answer him sharply was strong. To tell him to mind his own business, let him know that he couldn't tell her what to do. But she was also mindful that she'd agreed to a truce and, not wanting more confrontation, she nodded assent.

Mack continued to walk amongst the group. 'What would you do if blood began seeping through the bandage?'

Beau almost answered, then bit her lip as she felt Gray shift beside her. *Let someone else answer.*

'Would we replace the bandage?'

Rick answered, 'No. We could tear strips of clothing and add it on top of the bandage.'

Mack nodded, smiling. 'Good. Okay. You all did quite well there. Now, let's think about setting up camp—and then we're going to tackle recovery position and CPR.'

Gray began to remove the bandage and then rolled his trouser leg down.

Beau watched him, then gathered up the bits and pieces they'd used. 'What shall we do with these, Mack? There aren't clinical waste bins out here, either.'

'We'll burn them on the fire once we get it going.'

Right. She supposed that seemed sensible. All the others were starting to get out their tents and equipment, so Beau turned to her own backpack. This was the part she'd been dreading. Putting up a tent. She'd never done that before.

All part of the learning experience.

'Look at you. Reading the instructions like a real Boy Scout.' Gray appeared at her side.

'I like to be prepared. Proper planning prevents poor performance. I'm not like you. Spontaneous. Off the cuff. I like to know what's happening. The order of things. I don't like surprises. You should know that.'

He shook his head. 'I disagree. I think you take risks, too.'

'Me?' She almost laughed at his ridiculous suggestion. 'I don't take risks!'

'No? Who chose to come on the Extreme Wilderness Medical Survival Course on an active supervolcano?'

Beau opened her mouth to speak but couldn't think of anything to say.

'And the Beau I know wouldn't do any of this if it wasn't part of some bigger plan—am I right?'

She closed her mouth, frustrated.

It was so maddening that he could still see right through her.

Gray hadn't brought a tent like everyone else. He had a tarpaulin that he'd propped up with a couple of walking poles, spread over a hammock that he'd attached to two sturdy tree trunks. It took him a matter of a few minutes to get his pitch all set up, and once he was done, he was eager to get his boots off and relax.

But he couldn't concentrate.

Beau was opposite him, on the other side of the campfire, trying—and failing—to put up her tent. She was *inside* the tent now, and he could hear her muttered cursing.

After one particularly loud expletive he chuckled and went over. 'Er…knock-knock?'

There was a pause in the muttering and angry swearing and eventually her head popped out of the tent. Her face was almost as red as her mussed-up, statically charged hair. *'What?'*

Gray knelt down beside the tent entrance so that he was level with Beau's face. 'Do you want a hand?'

She looked at him, her brow creased with frustrated lines. 'From *you*?'

'Tent erection at your service.'

He watched as she blushed deeply before looking at everyone else around the camp, who all seemed to be managing at a reasonable rate compared to her.

'You know, I could have just let you get on with

it. I'm being kind here. Offering a branch with pretty little olives on it.'

She bit her lip. 'Okay. But this is the only kind of erection I want from you.'

He smiled. 'Okay.'

She nodded and crawled out, huffing and puffing, standing tall and then letting out a big sigh as the tent collapsed onto the ground beside her like a deflated balloon. 'It was meant to do that.'

He managed not to laugh. 'Of course. Have you…erm…ever put a tent up before?'

She pursed her lips before answering and he tried his hardest not to focus on the fact that she looked as if she was awaiting a kiss.

'No. I've never camped before. But I read the instructions and it looked quite simple.'

He held out his hand. 'Give me the instructions.'

Beau pulled them from her back pocket and handed them over. They were folded up and creased.

Gray thanked her, pretended to look at them briefly and then threw them onto the campfire.

'*Gray!*' She stared after the instructions open-mouthed as they were eaten up by the orange flames. She turned back to him.

'You don't need the instructions. Tents are easy.'

'Oh, *really*? Easy, huh?'

'Absolutely.'

'Well, be my guest.' She looked around for a seat but after finding none just sat on the ground with her arms and legs crossed. She looked smug, almost as if she expected him to fail and become as frustrated as she'd been when she'd tried.

Gray grabbed the poles he needed, from where Beau had laid them out on the ground in logical order and size, and instantly began threading them through fabric tubes and forming the outer shell of the tent.

He heard her curse and tried not to smile at his own smugness when he saw the look on her face. He picked up the pegs and pinned the tent to the ground. Within minutes he had it ready.

Wiping his hands on his trousers, he turned to her with a happy smile. 'There you go. The best erection in camp.'

'How did you…? Where did you…?' She sighed. 'How…?'

Gray shrugged. 'A gentleman never tells.'

She cocked her head to one side and smiled. 'I'm not asking a *gentleman*.'

'Ouch!'

'Come on…how did you do that so fast?'

He considered the tent briefly before he replied. 'I've got one of these.'

She looked at his tarp. 'But not on this trip?'

'I prefer the bivvy and tarp during the summer months.'

'Okay. Well, thank you very much. I appreciate it.'

He could tell that it had taken her a lot to thank him. He simply smiled and let her get her equipment into the tent, even helped her roll out her sleeping bag. Once they were done, they both stood there awkwardly, staring at each other.

Gray felt so tempted to tell her everything there and then, but something inside told him that now was not the right time. Beau was still suspicious of him. Trying to show that she was indifferent to his presence. Which obviously meant she was still angry. Perhaps he would talk to her in a few days. Give the shock of them both being here a chance to pass away. Give her time to cool down and be receptive to what he had to say.

Perhaps if he showed her during this course that he was a good guy—reliable, dependable, someone she could trust with her life—then maybe by the end of the week she'd be much more amenable to hearing what he had to say. And they could put the past to rest.

Mack made his way over. 'Hey, Gray, you're rostered for cooking duties tonight. Feel like running up a culinary masterpiece with some beans?'

Cooking? He didn't feel confident about that. And not for other people! Not if they wanted to stay alive. He could perform heart transplants or bypass grafts or even transmyocardial laser revascularisation—but cook up something tasty? That was edible? That didn't require its film to be pierced and to be shoved in a microwave?

'Er...sure, Mack.'

Beau stood watching him now, her arms

crossed, one hip thrust to the side and a grin on her face.

'Problem, Gray?'

Of course she would remember his fear of the kitchen. When they'd been together, Beau had done all the cooking after his one disastrous attempt at a beef stroganoff had resulted in a weird brown splodge on their plates that had tasted, somehow, of nothing.

He'd never learnt from his mother. The kitchen had been her domain—the one place she'd been able to escape from the men in her family and know they wouldn't disturb her. The mysteries of the kitchen and its processes had always eluded Gray, but that had always been fine with him. The hospital had a canteen, and when he wasn't there, he ate out.

'Maybe.'

'I thought you'd camped before? Whatever did you eat?'

'I brought army ration packs. They were self-heating. I didn't have to do anything.'

'Okay…what ingredients do you have to work with?'

Beau headed over to the bags Mack had pointed out and rummaged through the ingredients. There were butter beans, tomatoes, potatoes and a small can of sardines.

'That's not a lot for thirteen people,' she said.

Mack grinned. 'Well, this *is* a survival course. Be thankful I'm not making you forage for in-gredients. Yet.'

Beau's face lit up. 'Of *course*!' She disap-peared into her tent and came back out holding her guidebook on Yellowstone. 'This will tell you what we can eat. We could get some of the others to forage for foodstuffs and add them to the pan. You stay here and chop up the potatoes. Leave the skin on, Gray—the most nutritious part of the vegetable is just under the skin.'

'Is that right?' He was amused to see her so en-ergised. It reminded him of the sweet Beau he'd used to know so well. 'Are you chaining me to the kitchen sink?'

She shrugged. 'Stops you running away.'

Then she headed off to clear her plan with Mack and gather some of the others to help find food.

He watched her. Asking Mack for advice on

foraging and safety. Organising people. Arranging them into teams. Showing them what they might be able to find. One pair was dispatched to gather more firewood. Another pair to collect water for purifying.

She was in her element.

Gray sighed, sat down by the potatoes and grabbed a small, short knife, ready to start chopping.

Considering she hadn't even been able to bring herself to even look at him earlier today, they had already taken huge steps towards bringing about a ceasefire. Maybe soon they could have those peace talks they so desperately needed.

While everyone waited for dinner to cook, Mack began teaching the recovery position.

'If you come across a casualty who is unconscious and breathing, then you'll need to put them into the recovery position. Anyone tell me why?'

Beau's hand shot into the air and Gray smiled.

Mack looked for someone else to answer, but when everyone looked blank, he allowed her to. 'Yes, Beau?'

'Rolling a patient onto their side stops the tongue from blocking the airway and also helps prevent choking in case of vomiting.'

'That's right. Beau, perhaps you'd like to be our pretend patient?'

She nodded and went over to the ranger and lay flat on her back on the pine-needle-covered ground.

'Before we put the patient into the recovery position, what should we check for?'

'Check breathing again?' suggested Conrad.

'You could. But let's assume she's still breathing. You'll need to check to make sure there's nothing in her pockets that will jab into her when we roll her over. So, things like car keys, pens, pencils, sticks—things like that. We should also remove the patient's glasses and turn any jewelled rings towards the palm.'

He demonstrated by sliding a ring round on Beau's hand.

'There's also a little poem you can remember to remind yourself of what you need to do here. *"Say hello and raise my knee, then take my hand and roll to me."'*

He placed Beau's hand palm-up by her face, as if she was saying hi, and then grabbed her trouser leg and raised the knee of the opposite leg, so that her foot was downwards on the forest floor. Then he grabbed her other hand, put it by her face and, using the trouser leg of the raised knee, rolled Beau over onto her side, adjusting the hand under her face to open the airway.

'Simple. Okay, tell me the poem.'

'"*Say hello and raise my knee, then take my hand and roll to me.*"'

'Good. You need to keep repeating that to yourself. It'll stand you in good stead. Always remember to position yourself on the side you want the patient to roll onto. Now, what if your patient is pregnant?'

'You'd need to roll them onto their left side,' said Gray.

Mack nodded. 'Absolutely. Why?'

'Less pressure on the inferior vena cava.'

'Thank you, Gray. Now, I'd like you all to get into your buddy pairs and practise this. Take turns at being the patient. Off you go.'

Gray stood over Beau and smiled. 'Want to stay there?'

'If I must.'

He knelt beside her and awkwardly patted her pockets. He hadn't expected to be *touching* Beau. Not like this. Not holding her hand in his and laying it by her face. It was too much, too soon.

Talking to her he could handle. Joking with her and keeping the mood light he could handle. But this enforced closeness…? It reminded him too much of the past, when touching her had been easy and pleasurable and had made her eyes light up.

Not now, though. Now she lay stiffened on the floor, uncomfortable and gritting her teeth. Was it that awful for her? Him being this close? Was she hating every second of it?

Once she was in the recovery position, she leapt up and brushed herself down. 'My turn.'

Disarmed, he lay down and closed his eyes, not wanting to see the discomfort in *her* eyes, not wanting to make this any more difficult for her than it plainly already was.

Beau got him into the recovery position quickly. 'You're all done.'

He got up and brushed off the pine needles and they stood there awkwardly, staring at each other, not knowing what to say.

Clearly the activity had been difficult for both of them and Gray couldn't stand it.

'I'll just check on the food.' He went over to the cooking pot and gave it a stir. It didn't look great, but it did smell nice. Mack had shown Beau and the others where to find some small bulbs of wild garlic, and they'd added that to Gray's dish.

He glanced through the simmering steam at Beau and began to wonder just how the hell he was going to get through this week.

Mack got everyone up. 'Okay, folks, that's it for today. The rest of the evening is your own. Gray is our chef this evening, so let's all keep an ear out for him ringing the dinner bell.'

Gray had no idea when it would be ready. Claire came over and asked, and when he shrugged, she stuck the small paring knife into the potatoes to check.

'Seems good to me.'

'Yeah? I'd better dish up, then.'

Gray served them all a portion that was quite meagre, even with the additions. It actually tasted nice, which was a surprise. The others made satisfactory noises whilst eating it anyway, so he could only hope they weren't just being polite.

Afterwards Gray was ready for bed. His foot was starting to trouble him and he ached in places he hadn't been expecting. Not to mention that his nerves were still on edge from the recovery scenario.

He had to get around the way it felt when he touched her. He had to forget the softness of her skin, the smooth creaminess of it and the knowledge that he knew exactly how the rest of her felt.

It would feel so good to caress her again.

He sneaked a glance at her whilst she was talking to Dean and Toby. He saw the twinkle in her eyes, her joyous smile. Heard her infectious laughter. She looked relaxed, as if she was enjoying herself.

I want her to be that way with me.

* * *

Later, Gray and Beau carried the pile of tin dishes down to the creek and laid them beside the shallow running water, trying to rinse them in the darkening light. Beau was struggling for the right thing to say. How could she start a conversation with the man she'd once thought she'd known inside out…?

But he started it instead. 'I'm glad we're both making the effort to try and get along.' He paused to glance at her. 'It's good.'

'It's easier than trying to ignore you.'

He smirked. 'I'm in joyous rapture about that.'

The dishes rinsed well in the stream, and Beau figured the small particles of food that were getting rinsed off would hopefully feed some of the fish or wildlife further downstream.

'Your cooking has improved.'

A smile crept across his face. 'A compliment? I'll take it.'

'No, really. It was a nice dinner. Considering.'

'Considering it was cooked by me?'

She nodded and laughed.

He smiled at her, as if pleased to hear her laugh again. 'Thank you. I'm just glad everyone was able to eat it without choking. No one's been taught the Heimlich manoeuvre yet.'

She laughed again, her gaze meeting his, and then suddenly she wasn't laughing any more. She was caught by the deep mossy stare of his eyes, the longing she saw within them, and by her own fear as old feelings came bubbling to the surface.

She stood up abruptly. 'We ought to head back. It's dark. Who knows what's out here with us?'

He stood, too. 'Yeah, you're right.'

The deepening shadows around them just served to make his eyes more intense as he looked at her. She could feel old urges reasserting themselves, and memories of how easy it had once been to be with this man—how she'd loved him so much she hadn't thought there was anything left of her own soul that was just her.

Beau bent to gather the dishes. Gray helped, and both of them were careful not to touch each other before they headed back to camp. Walking a good metre apart.

CHAPTER FOUR

SHE'D COME A long way since her arrival at the ranger station that morning. If anyone had told her that by the end of the day she'd be sharing a meal with her ex-fiancé and washing dishes by a stream with him—whilst *smiling*—she would have told them that they were crazy. No chance.

But she had. And now she sat across from him, with the campfire crackling away between them as night fell, catching glimpses of his face in the firelight.

He was still the same old Gray. Slightly more grizzled, slightly heavier set than before, but still with the same cheek, the same nerve. The other hikers all seemed to like him. But he'd always had that effect on people. Dean and Rick, the brothers from Seattle, were currently seated on either side of him, and beyond them everyone seemed to be listening to the story Gray was weaving.

He was a born storyteller, enamoured of holding everyone's attention. It was probably why he'd chosen cardiology, she thought. Heart surgeons always seemed to act as if they were the best. Because without the heart the body wouldn't work at all.

Well, Gray, without a brain the heart doesn't stand a chance, either.

That was the difference between them. She could see that now. Beau had always been the steady influence—the thinker. The planner. Everything meticulously detailed. Whereas Gray had always been the rash one, the passionate one, the spontaneous, carefree daredevil.

Initially she'd been excited by those qualities in him. His indifference to planning the future, his studies, his life. She'd loved the way he could get excited about one thing and then develop a passion for something else entirely further down the line. How he could be thrilled by new technologies, new inventions, new medicines. Whereas *she* had always been cautious—researching new methods, new techniques, checking the statistics on their success, talking to the people involved about their experiences, making sure everything was *safe* before she considered using anything in her work.

Beau did not like surprises. Especially unpleasant ones. And Gray had caused her the most unpleasant surprise in her life so far by not turning up to their wedding. A wedding could be planned in advance, carefully thought-out, with alternatives arranged, waiting in the wings, to prevent any last-minute hitches. You planned the day meticulously so that you didn't have to worry about it running smoothly, so that it *just did*. And on the day itself you were meant to just turn up and go with the flow. Put on your dress, do your hair, do your make-up, smile for the camera and *enjoy*.

And because she'd planned her wedding so well, she'd not expected anything to go wrong at all. She'd been naïvely blissful, secure about her feelings for her husband-to-be, anticipating the joy that their marriage would bring, knowing the happiness they already had was growing and growing with every day.

So when he hadn't shown up, it had felt as if she'd been punched in the gut! A blow that had come out of nowhere. And her heart…? It had been totally broken.

And then the questions had flooded her mind. Why had he abandoned her? Had she been wrong? Had it all been one-sided?

Looking at him now, adored by his fellow hikers, she still found it hard to tell herself that he had actually just left her there. Without a word. Without a hint of concern.

Had there been signs in the days *before* the wedding that he'd planned to run out on her? She couldn't recall. He had seemed a little distant occasionally, when she'd gone on about the arrangements, but weren't all grooms-to-be like that? Surely it was the bride's prerogative to go overboard when planning her perfect day?

The pain had been incredible. It had made her doubt their love. Made her doubt *herself.* She'd spent weeks worrying that there was something wrong with *her.* That she was lacking something—that there was something Gray needed and couldn't get it from her.

But what? She was a nice person. Clever. Kind. Friendly. Loving. She'd never been shy in showing him her affection. Their sex life had been great! *Hadn't it?* Of course it had been. No man could make a woman feel like that and then say things were lacking in that department.

He hadn't said much in the days leading up to the wedding, she supposed. He hadn't said much in regard to their marriage, or his hopes and dreams, so she'd talked about hers, hoping to draw him out. But he'd never said anything. Just smiled and looked...nervous.

Beau poked at the campfire with a long stick and watched as the embers collapsed and spat heat upwards and outwards, tiny flecks of flame bursting forth and disappearing into the night sky above. The dark blue of the night revealed the sparkle of stars that she could never have hoped to see from her home town of Oxford. Even from the hospital roof you couldn't see a sky such as this.

The vast openness of Yellowstone made her realise that there was so much she wasn't used to seeing. Or noticing. It made her aware that she wouldn't know if something else was out there until she made the time to look for it.

Was there something about Gray that she'd not known about?

She glanced up at him once more and caught his gaze upon her through the heat of the orange flames. He looked pensive, and he rubbed at his jaw before he turned to answer Rick, who'd asked him a question.

He looks weary.

She wasn't used to seeing him look worn down. He'd always looked sprightly. Ready for anything. Raring to go.

Had today done that to him? Had *she*? She didn't like how that made her feel, how uncomfortable she suddenly was, and her stomach squirmed at the notion.

Perhaps there was more to this situation between them? Something she'd not been aware of because she'd never thought to look for it. Was it something obvious? Was it staring her in the face? Like the stars—always there, but not always seen?

Was I so wrapped up in the wedding that I forgot to focus on us?

Beau threw her stick into the fire and watched as it got swallowed up by the flames. She knew with certainty now that this week was going to be one hell of a learning experience.

And not the kind that she'd been expecting.

Beau had spent an uncomfortable night in her tent. Before the trip she'd bought a decent one, and a groundsheet, a sleeping mat and a sleeping bag, and had thought that would be enough for her to get a decent night's sleep. But the ground had been hard and unforgiving and she'd tossed and turned, worrying about being away from her patients, being here with Gray—not to mention the possibilities of insect invasion—before she'd finally fallen into a broken sleep at about five o'clock in the morning.

Unfortunately Mack had woken them all up around seven by banging a tin bowl with a rock right by the entrance to her shelter, and she'd woken blearily, feeling as if her body was bruised all over.

'Okay, okay…I'm awake,' she'd moaned, rubbing her eyes and blinking thoroughly until they seemed to operate correctly.

Now she sat up, stretching out her back muscles and rolling her stiff shoulders and noting, with some small satisfaction, that her tent had not filled with ants overnight. *Perhaps it's safe to sleep on the ground after all?* Then she pulled herself from her sleeping bag, put on a fresh set of underwear, the clothes she'd worn yesterday, and put her hair up into a ponytail and unzipped her tent.

'Morning, Beau.'

Gray was already up, looking freshly groomed, his eyes bright and sparkly.

She groaned. Used to her normal schedule, Beau was not a morning person. She needed a good-sized mug of coffee, a Danish pastry and a blast of loud music in her car to wake her properly before she got to the hospital, and she guessed she wouldn't get that here.

She peered gloomily at the pot that Barb was in charge of. 'What's for breakfast?'

'Oatmeal.'

'Porridge? Great,' she replied without enthu-
siasm.

It wasn't exactly a buttery, flaky pastry delight,
but never mind. It would have to do. She warmed
her hands over the fire and then ducked back into
her tent to grab her toothbrush and toothpaste.
She stood and cleaned her teeth and rinsed her
toothbrush with the last of her bottled water.

'I've got a pot of boiled water cooling down already,' Barb said when she returned. 'Have you
got your purifying tablets?'

'I've got a filter.'

'Brilliant.'

Beau was quite pleased with her state-of-the-
art filter. It meant that she could collect water
from any source, pour it through, and all protozoa
and bacteria would be removed, including giardia
and cryptosporidium, the two biggest causes of
infection in water. It saved having to boil water
and wait for it to cool before it could be put into
containers. It had been one of her new purchases,
thoroughly researched and tested, and she'd even
looked up reviews from previous customers to
make sure it was the best for the job.

After she'd put her toiletries away, she stretched her back once again and took in the view. Now that she was more awake, she could appreciate where they were. High up on a mountainside, on a grassy plateau, surrounded by nature, with not a building, a towering spire nor a frantic cyclist in sight. Just clear blue skies, promising the heat of another day, the sun, a gentle warm breeze and the bright, cheery sounds of birdsong lighting up the morning.

'It's gorgeous, isn't it?'

'It certainly is.'

Gray smiled down at her, making her jump. She sat up.

'What are we doing today?'

'Mack said we need to cover CPR, as we missed it last night, and then we're heading higher up to cover altitude sickness.'

She nodded. 'Right. How far up do you think we already are?'

'Four or five thousand feet?'

'And altitude sickness sets in at…what? Eight thousand or more?'

'Depends on the climber. Could be now.'

'Mack won't want to take us up that far, will he?' she asked, feeling the pain in her calf muscles from yesterday's climb.

'No, I won't,' Mack answered as he came out of his tent. 'It's a survival course, not a medical experiment.'

She smiled at him. 'Glad to hear it.'

Barb gave the oatmeal a stir. 'This is done. Everyone hungry?'

Everyone nodded and grabbed their metal dishes to receive a small helping of breakfast before sitting down around the fire to eat quietly.

Porridge wasn't her thing, but Beau ate it anyway, and Justin and Claire offered to get everything washed up before they packed up camp.

They soon covered the CPR training—how to do it effectively without defibrillators. Two breaths to thirty compressions in two rounds, before checking for signs of life—breathing, pulse rate, chest rise and fall. Mack showed them all how to find the right spot on the chest for compressions. How to place their hands. What sort of rhythm they needed and how fast. Showed them that even if they did it properly they might hear ribs break—which made everyone cringe at the thought!

Then there was a short break before Mack showed them how to put out the fire safely, and once they'd packed up their tents and equipment, they all set off once again on the next hike.

Gray fell into step beside Beau and she noticed that he was limping.

'Blisters?'

He didn't quite meet her gaze. 'Er…no. Not really.'

'How did you sleep?'

'Well, thanks. The hammock was great.'

'Lucky you. I barely got forty winks before Mack's alarm. The ground mat I bought felt as thin as tissue paper.'

He smiled. 'That's why I brought a hammock. Off the ground is better. Even the most comfortable bed is on legs.'

'The voice of experience?'

'Most definitely.'

Mack led them up a stony trail. Like a line of ants they began their ascent, and in the early-morning warmth they were all soon puffing and panting, stripping off layers as they got higher and higher. Beau focused on one point—the shirt of the person in front. Her mind was blank of everything as she simply concentrated on putting one foot in front of the other. Plodding on, climbing bit by bit, until they reached a lookout high on the side of the mountain.

Mack indicated a rest stop by dropping his backpack to the floor. 'Let's take an hour here. Get fluids on board, and then we'll start our next lesson from this beautiful viewpoint.'

Beau slipped off her backpack and used it as a seat as she took a drink of water from her bottle. She was hot and sweaty, totally out of breath, and the muscles in her legs *burned*. She stretched her legs out in front of her and counted her blessings.

This was what she had come here for. To find nature. To escape the confines of the hospital. When had she last climbed anything? She didn't even climb stairs any more—she changed floors at the hospital by using the lift, and the same at home. Her flat was on the sixth floor and the lift worked perfectly every time she needed it. She *needed* this sort of workout. Blowing away the cobwebs on muscle groups that she ought to have been using. Using her body and not just her brain. Breathing in this fresh, crisp mountain air and feeling alive!

She watched a large bird, far out above the canyon, circle effortlessly in the air. 'Now, *that's* the way to climb to new heights.'

Gray squinted up at the sky. 'I wonder if birds get altitude sickness.'

'Or have a fear of heights. Can you imagine?'

'We humans think too much. We worry and fret, build our anxieties on imagined threats. If you think about it, animals have it easier.'

She took another drink of water. 'What worries *you*, Gray? You never struck me as a worrier.'

He stretched out his legs. 'I worry about lots of things. I just choose not to show it.'

Leo came over and rested against the rocks next to them. 'You're a surgeon, though, aren't you? You can't show your patients that you're worried. They'd have no confidence in your abilities if you did.'

Gray nodded. 'That's right. It's a strength not

to wear your heart on your sleeve. Patients need to see that you're confident and sure.'

But Beau was thinking about their past. 'And what if you're *not* sure about something?' she asked, her face curious. 'Do you talk to them about your concerns? Do you ever share your doubts so they know the full picture?'

It was obvious he knew she wasn't just referring to his work. 'I always let my patients know the full picture. They always understand the risks. Letting them know about dangers and possibilities doesn't stop you from being confident.'

'But what if you're *not* confident in an outcome? What then?'

He stared at her, long and hard. 'Then I don't proceed.'

She nodded, her face stony. 'You don't move forward?'

'No.'

Leo looked between the two of them, clearly puzzled at the tone of the conversation and at the way they were looking at each other. He took a bite from his trail bar. 'Looks like Mack's about to start the next lesson.'

He was right.

Mack gathered them all round. 'Okay, I'm sure that as we made the climb up here we all noticed we were getting a little out of breath. Now, imagine being like that all the time…not being able to breathe, feeling like there isn't enough air, struggling to take in enough oxygen. How do you think that's going to affect you on a day-to-day basis?'

Rick put up his hand. 'You'd struggle.'

Mack nodded. 'Too long in too high an altitude, without a period of adjustment, can affect thinking skills and judgement calls, and it leads to hikers and climbers taking risks. Luckily here in Yellowstone we don't have the extreme elevations that provoke serious cases of altitude sickness, but we do have heights over eight thousand feet, and as soon as you go beyond this number, you'll start to see symptoms. Now, can anyone tell me what those symptoms are?'

Beau was itching to answer, but she thrust her hands in her pockets and bit her lip to stop herself from speaking.

Conrad suggested an answer. 'Dizziness?'

'That's one. Can you give me another?'

'Nausea?'

Mack nodded. 'Most people complain of a headache first. They get nauseous, feel exhausted. Then they might be short of breath, might get nosebleeds, muscle weakness. So what do we do to alleviate the condition?'

Beau gritted her teeth, let Mack continue.

'We descend. Height creates the problem, so going back down to where it's easier to breathe solves it. People *can* adjust, though. This is why on mountain climbs—and specifically when tackling Everest and those sorts of places—climbers ascend and then come down for a bit. Then they go up again—then down. It's a back and forth dance. Two steps forward, one step back. It acclimatises them to the new altitude. It allows their bodies to get used to the thinner air.'

Everyone nodded.

'The air itself still has oxygen at about twenty-one per cent. That doesn't change as you go higher. What *does* change is the air pressure, and that's what causes altitude sickness. Unfortunately we can't tell who will succumb. Some of you may even be feeling it now.'

He looked around at them and Claire raised her hand and mentioned that she had a headache.

He nodded once. 'So we start to head down. Let's go!'

They all got to their feet and slung on their backpacks wearily. The air did seem thinner. Everything seemed so much sharper up high. But the trail Mack led them down quickly led them into a beautiful green valley where they had to wait for a herd of moose to pass by.

Beau got out her camera. They were magnificent animals! As tall as she was, heavyset, with brown-black coats and long, horse-like faces. There was one with huge cupped antlers, and he stood there proudly as his herd passed the hikers, heading for a crop of willow trees, where they stopped to graze.

She took shot after shot, excited by getting her first close-up with an animal she hadn't a chance of seeing in the wild in the UK, and when she finally put her camera away, Gray smiled at her.

'What?'

He laughed. 'You're still the same.'

She shook her head, disagreeing with him. 'I'm older. Wiser, I hope.'

'I grant you that…but you still have that joy in you that I saw all those years ago. You always saw the joy and goodness in everything.'

'That's my problem. I *thought* I saw it in you once, but…I was wrong.'

He stopped walking and sighed. 'You weren't wrong.'

'Then why did you hurt me so badly?' She stopped to look at him directly. The others were ahead. They couldn't hear.

Gray looked down at the ground. 'That wasn't my intention. I was trying to stop you from being hurt further down the line.'

He passed her and began to walk to catch up with the rest of the group.

Beau watched his retreating form and felt the old hurt and anger begin to rise. She pushed it down, refusing to show him that he could still press her buttons.

She hurried to catch up, too, and as she passed

him, she muttered, 'Just for your information…
it didn't work.'

Gray stopped and stared after her.

They walked for a few more hours. They passed
through rocky canyons, small copses and grassy
open plains. They followed the Gallatin River,
passing a few men who stood in it in waders, fly-
fishing, and giving them a wave.

Gray could feel the weariness in his legs—
particularly his left leg—and ached to stop and
stretch out, but he said nothing, preferring to
soldier on.

They were all alert and on the lookout for bears,
knowing that these mammals were keen on fishing themselves, but they saw none, and Mack
soon led them off the popular trail and deeper
into wilder country.

Just as Gray was feeling the familiar pinching
pain in his left calf that told him a cramp was
about to set in, he heard crying and groaning.
His ears pricked up at the sound and his doctor
radar kicked in. Someone was afraid and in pain.
And then suddenly, there before them, in a clear-

ing, were three people lying on the ground with blood everywhere.

Adrenaline shot through his system. The cramp was forgotten as he raced past the others in his group with Beau to attend the casualties before them.

There were two men and a woman. First he needed to assess them all, find out who was in the most medical danger, and he knelt by the first patient—the woman—who lay on her back, clutching at a bleed in her thigh, hopefully not her femoral artery. Out here, a bleed like that could be fatal.

'Lie back! Can you tell me what happened?'

He went to check the leg, already pulling off his belt so that he could create a tourniquet, and then he noticed that there was no wound. No tear in the fabric. And the blood was fake. He looked up at the others, to see Beau looking confused, too.

Mack knelt down beside him, grinning. 'Pretend patients! The wounds aren't real, but you might come across people on your travels with serious injuries. I want you to work in groups of four. Each group take a patient. Assess the injury, ascertain what happened, and then I want you to tend to that patient. We'll feed back to the group what we did and why. Gray, you work with Beau, Conrad and Barb. Jack and Leo—you're with Dean and Rick. The rest of you, tend the third patient.'

Gray had already got fake blood all over his hands and he let out a huge breath. *Thank goodness it's not real!* It had really got his own blood pumping, though.

Beau knelt beside him and Conrad and Barb gathered round.

'Barb and I will let you two take the lead, Doc,' said Conrad. 'We're sure you know more than us.'

'Maybe, but you need to learn. Let's see what our "patient" can tell us.' He looked down at the woman on the ground. 'Can you tell me what happened to you today?'

'We were camping when we were attacked.'

'By animals?'

'No, some lads came into our camp. They were drunk and waving knives around.'

Gray nodded. He'd actually been in a similar

situation once before, hiking in the Peak District. A group of rowdy teenagers had wandered into his campsite, drunk and disorderly, and had become very threatening. Luckily he'd managed to talk them down and send them on their way— but not before one of them had tripped over his guy rope and broken his nose.

'Was your leg injured with a knife or something else?'

'I'm not sure.'

He nodded, then looked up at Conrad and Barb. 'What do you think we should be thinking about doing here?'

'Stopping the bleeding?' Barb suggested.

'Good. How?'

'We could apply some pressure? Raise the injured limb?'

He nodded. *Good. They knew some basics.* 'What else? What if it was an arterial bleed?'

'Pressure and a tourniquet?'

'Good—but you'd have to be quick. Arterial bleeds spurt, and with force. The area around the wound will get messy quickly and the patient can lose a large amount of blood in a short time. What else do we need to do?'

Conrad and Barb looked blankly at each other. 'We're not sure, Doc.'

Beau smiled at them. 'Once you've dealt with an arterial bleed, and it appears to be under control, you need to do two things. Find a way of getting more help, but also look for further injuries. Too many people assume that if a patient has one major injury that's all they have to look for. But patients can quite often have more possibly fatal injuries, so you need to assess your patient properly once the bleeding is stemmed and under control.'

'What if the bleeding doesn't get under control?'

'Then your patient could go into hypovolaemic shock. If they don't get help, they'll die.'

Barb paled slightly and Conrad put a comforting arm around his wife's shoulders. 'That's terrible.'

Gray showed the couple how to check for further injury, and how they could assess their patient's level of consciousness, then Mack gathered them all together.

The three 'patients' stood and had a bit of a stretch, grinning.

'Okay, so what did we all learn?'

Gray gave a brief rundown on what they'd covered with Conrad and Barb. One group had dealt with a venous bleed to an arm; the other had dealt with what had looked like a simple contusion— or bruising—to the abdomen.

Mack focused on this last one. 'Who else thinks that this was just a simple case of bruising?'

Beau put up her hand.

'Yes, Beau?'

'There could be internal bleeding. A bruise is the definition of an internal bleed, in fact.'

'So what could happen to our patient if this is ignored as a minor injury?'

'He could die. There are multiple major organs in the abdomen, all at risk—the liver, the spleen, the pancreas...'

'Dangers of internal bleeding, please?'

'Exsanguination—possibly a tamponade on the heart.'

'Which is…?'

'A closure or blockage. Fluid collects around the heart, between the organ and the pericardial sac, and surrounds it, applying pressure and preventing it from beating.'

Mack looked at the group. 'Do we all see how different injuries—even ones that *seem* minor—can have devastating effects on a patient?'

The group nodded and agreed.

'And can we all agree that when you've been hiking for a long time—when you're exhausted, maybe sleep-deprived, hungry or starved of air, perhaps in a dangerous situation—how easy it might be to miss something important when assessing a patient or to make a mistake?'

Again there were murmurs of assent from them all.

'Out in the wilds you need to be on your game. You need to see the present danger, but you also need to be looking three steps ahead. Keeping your wits about you. Not making avoidable mistakes. Now…the likelihood of getting help immediately can be small. You might find yourself on your own, needing to get help and having to over-

come obstacles to find it. Everyone get ready—
I'm about to show you how to cross a river safely.
Without a bridge.'

Gray raised his eyebrows. Surely everyone was
exhausted? They'd hiked miles today and barely
eaten. Though he guessed this was all part of
the package. Trying to replicate the environment
people might find themselves in and show them
how easy it was to make a mistake.

He knew all about mistakes.

He'd made plenty.

He fell into step beside Beau and found himself drawing into himself. As always, when he
focused on medicine he could exclude every
other worry or emotion in his head—but when
he wasn't, and real life had an opportunity to
take residence, there was nothing to distract him.

Beau's presence had shaken him. With her
here, he couldn't ignore what he'd done any more.
Every time he looked at her it was a reminder of
the pain he'd caused, even though at the time he'd
told himself he was doing it to save her greater
pain in the long run.

Beau had had aspirations for their future. It

wasn't just going to be marriage for them—it was going to be a whole life together. Children. Grandchildren. *Great*-grandchildren. That was what she'd seen for them when she'd said yes to his spur-of-the-moment proposal.

She hadn't just said yes to him, but yes to all that, too. She'd seen years ahead of them, spent happily in each other's company as they went on holidays or had romantic weekends away, had picnics in the park, ice creams on the beach. She'd seen cosy chats, the pair of them snuggled under a quilt, holding hands, kissing, enjoying being with each other. Snatched kisses in the hospital as they passed each other on their way to work.

She'd only ever seen joy…

How could he ever tell her that he'd seen something different? How could he tell her that if he'd married her it might have been okay to start with, but then there would have been little differences of opinion? Silences and resentment and screaming arguments. How could he say he had known how their fallouts would turn into sleeping in separate rooms? That they would go without talking for days or, if they did talk, would only snipe at each other and resent the other person for making them feel so bad? How could he tell her that he saw slamming doors and broken plates as well as broken hearts? How could he begin to tell her that he wouldn't have—*couldn't* have—brought a child into all of that?

Marriage had meant something different to them both and she'd had no idea. There'd not been any way for him to tell her that marriage for him meant torture and ruination. How could you show that sort of vision to someone who viewed everything as though the world was only full of good things? Of hope and promise and happily-ever-afters.

Beau had been the light to his dark. The sun to his shadow. She had always been better than him. She'd had such a pure outlook and he hadn't wanted to spoil her beliefs. Dilute her sunshine and make clouds cover her world.

He'd walked away that day, knowing he couldn't face marriage. That he just didn't have it in him to stay and say those vows when he didn't believe they could be true. To love and to cherish?

Maybe to start with. For better, for worse? Definitely too much of the latter! Until death do us part? Why would he want to put either of them through *that*?

Marriage to Beau should have been the greatest thing, but he'd been unable to see past his dread. He'd been a child of a loveless marriage. He knew what it was like to be forgotten. Unwanted. Not loved as a child should be loved, but *used*.

He could almost feel another wound ripping across his heart at the thought of it. His love for Beau had meant he'd tried to do the decent thing. He'd wanted her to be married. Happily. To someone who could give that to her and who stood an equal chance of believing in the same possibility of happiness. There had to be a man out there who thought the same as Beau. Who wanted the same things.

And yet… And yet Beau was still single. Alone. Her career was her shining light. Her joy.

They were both in their thirties now, and Beau still hadn't any children. What was that doing to her? It had been her dream to have kids…

Gray closed his eyes wearily and rested against

a tree for a moment to catch his breath. His leg—his *foot*—hurt physically. Trying to ignore it, trying to gather his mental strength, he opened his eyes to carry on—but stopped as he noticed that Beau had come to stand by him.

'Are you okay?' she asked.

He tried to gauge if she really was concerned. But the look in her beautiful eyes was enough to convince him that she was truly worried. Her brow was lined with worry. She'd even reached out her hand to lay it on his upper arm.

He nodded. ''Course. Just trying to ignore something that's not there.'

Beau looked puzzled. 'Are you in pain?'

He shrugged. 'A little.'

She tried to make him hold her gaze. 'Anything I can help you with?'

Gray let out an angry sigh. He was angry with himself. Angry at having got everything so wrong. Angry at hurting Beau. For still hurting her even now. And she was being *nice* to him. Showing care and concern when she had every right in the world to be ignoring him still.

But when he looked into her eyes, he got caught.

He was trapped and ensnared by her gaze. Her concern and worry for him was pushing past his defences, sneaking around his walls of pretence and bravado, reaching around his heart and taking hold.

Hesitantly he reached up and stroked her face. 'You're so perfect, Beau.'

She stiffened slightly at his touch. Was she afraid? Shocked? But then she began to breathe again. He saw the way her shoulders dropped, her jaw softened.

She gazed right back at him. 'Just not for you.'

'But we were so close, weren't we?'

She nodded, a gentle smile curling her mouth. 'We were.'

He took a moment just to look at her. At the way the sunshine reflected off her hair, at the way the tip of her nose was beginning to catch the sun. The way the smile on her face warmed his heart...

Gray looked away. He had no right to enjoy those feelings any more. He tried to cast them aside, to stand straighter, to concentrate on the task ahead—the walking, the hiking. He couldn't start to feel that way for Beau any more. He'd only ended up hurting her in the past. He'd not been able to offer her what she'd needed then— and now...? Now he had even less. He wasn't even a whole man. He was broken. His mistake had been to think he had been whole in the first place.

He stepped past her, feeling her hand on his arm drop away as he moved out of reach. His heart sank. He had to be firm with himself. It was at moments like these when he might all too easily slip into thinking about another chance with Beau.

What would be the point? Where would it lead? To a relationship again?

No. We'd just end up in the same place.

Gray almost let out a growl of frustration. Instead he gritted his teeth and pushed through the pain he was feeling.

CHAPTER FIVE

THE RIVER GENTLY flowed from east to west and was about twelve feet wide, with gentle ripples across its surface. On the other side their campsite waited for them, taunting them with its closeness.

They were all tired. It had been a long day—first hiking up the mountain and then their rapid descent, with the medical scenario on the way down. Beau was beginning to see how people might make mistakes with their decision-making when they were tired, hungry and sleep-deprived. It would be easy to do when you just wanted to be able to settle down and rest but knew you couldn't.

Now Mack stood in front of them, before the river, giving his safety lecture.

'Whenever you need to cross water, my advice

is to always travel downstream until you come to a bridge. *That's* the safest way. But sometimes there may be an occasion where you need to cross without one, and you need to know how to do this safely. I would never advocate that you do this alone. It's always best to do this with someone else, and if possible with ropes.'

He pulled some ropes from his backpack and lay them out on the forest floor.

'Basic instructions are these—when you cross, you cross the river by facing *upstream* and slightly sideways. You lean *into* the current, because this will help you maintain your balance. You do *not* want to be swept off your feet.'

Beau glanced at the water. How deep was it? It looked pretty tame, but she guessed that there might be hidden currents, rocks beneath the innocent-looking water or even a drop in the riverbed's level.

'You shuffle your feet across the bottom. You do *not* take big steps and lift your feet out of the water. You do *not* cross your feet over, and your downstream foot should always be in the lead.' He demonstrated what he meant before turning around and staring intently at them. 'Do you all understand? Okay—practise that step on dry land.'

Beau imitated what he'd shown them. It seemed simple enough, but she could imagine that in the water it would feel different. She glanced at Gray and could see a worried look on his face. Why was he so concerned? Surely this was a thrill for him? The kind of thing he found a challenge?

'If there is a long stick available—a tree branch, a walking pole, something like that—you can use it for extra balance and to feel beneath the water for obstacles. If you find an obstacle, you'll need to put your feet upstream of it, where the water will be less powerful.'

She was getting nervous now. This was a lot more complicated than she'd thought.

'With a stick or pole, you can place that upstream, too. You move the pole first—then your feet. If the water gets higher than your thighs, and there is more than one of you crossing, you'll need to link arms and lock your hands together. This is called chain crossing. The biggest team member should be upstream, the smallest member downstream. You'll then move through the water using the same principles, parallel to the direction of the current.'

'What if it's too deep for that?'

'Then we use ropes, if available.' He began to lay out the instructions for using rope to cross water. He showed them how to anchor it, how to use a hand line, how to use a second rope as a belay and all the safety concerns involved.

It all got quite serious, quite quickly, and they were soon forging into the water to test its depth.

Considering the warmth of the day, the water felt cold, and Beau gasped as it came to just above her knees, soaking through her brand-new boots and socks and quickly chilling her to the bone. It was an odd sensation, being so cold below the knee but quite warm up top, and the sensation made her shiver and shake a little.

The water's current was deceptively strong, and she could feel it pushing and shoving hard against her legs like a persistent angry child. She was now shaking so much it was hard to tell where her feet were in the water, and feeling a rock beneath the water, she instinctively lifted up her foot to step over it, forgetting Mack's warning.

In an instant the current took her—unbalancing her, sweeping her off her feet.

She was down, with the water closing over her head in a frightening wave, filling her mouth, and she felt the cold suck at her clothes and body as the current tried to push her downstream. Gasping and spluttering, she tried to rise upwards, to find her feet and grab hold of something—anything—so that she could regain control and stand up. But the sheer coldness of the water, the disorientation she was feeling from being hungry, exhausted and sleep-deprived, meant she didn't know which way was up.

She opened her mouth to breathe, but it just filled with water. Beginning to panic, she splashed and opened her mouth even more to call for help—only to feel two strong arms grab her around the waist and pull her upwards.

'I've got you!'

She blinked and spluttered, gasping for air, wiping her wet hair from her face, and saw that Gray had her in his arms. She was pressed against him, soaking him through, but the joy of feeling her feet against the solid riverbed floor once again, and being upright and out of the cold, stopped her from feeling awkward.

She coughed to clear the water from her throat and clung tightly to him. 'Thanks.'

'You okay?'

She pulled a piece of river grass from her mouth and looked at it for a moment, disgusted, before throwing it away. The other hikers were looking at her with concern, still making their way across the river. It was then that she realised just how up close and personal she was with Gray.

Pushing herself away from him, she felt heat colour her cheeks—before she shivered slightly and recoiled at the feel of her wet clothes clinging to her body.

'I'm fine.' Why was he looking at her like that? There was far more than just concern in his eyes and it made her feel uneasy.

Anxious to get out of the water and to the campsite to dry off, she made her way across the river and clambered onto dry land with some difficulty. Her boots were full of water and her backpack had got soaked in the water, too. It would take her ages to dry everything off! Though she supposed the hot June weather might help, if she laid her things out on some rocks...

Once the others were all safely across, Gray insisted on putting her tent up for her quickly so she could get changed. As she'd suspected, everything in her pack was wet, but Claire kindly lent her some spare clothes to wear whilst her own were drying.

Mack was stern, giving her what felt like a lecture, and feeling like a naughty child, she sat by the river alone, her chin against her knees as she looked out across the innocent-looking water and thought about what might have happened.

She didn't have too long to think about it before Gray came to sit alongside her.

'How are you feeling?'

She shrugged, not willing to answer right away. Her fall in the river had disconcerted her. She *never* got things wrong. She always got things right—picked up new things quickly, learnt easily. Fording the river had shown her that control of things could all too easily be taken away from her when she wasn't expecting it. She'd thought she could handle the river—she'd been wrong.

And she'd thought she could convince herself that her feelings for Gray were those of uninterest and anger. She'd told herself that she didn't care about him any more. She'd been wrong on that count, too.

The way he'd rescued her in the river...the way she'd felt talking to him again...it was confusing. This was a man she should be *hating*! A man she should be furious with. Not even *talking* to. But being around him was stirring up feelings that she'd told herself she would *never* feel for a man again.

Gray jilted me! Rejected me!

And yet it had felt much too good to be in his arms again. Much too comfortable to be pressed up against him...much too familiar and safe and...and *right* to be that close to him again.

He'd felt solid. Sturdy. Strong. A safe haven. A certainty. And for a long time she'd tried to tell herself that Gray was an *un*certainty. An unstable individual who had always been a risk to her security and happiness.

How could she be getting this so wrong? Why was she so confused about him?

Even now, as he sat next to her on the rocks, she could feel her body reacting to him. To his presence. It was almost as if it were craving his touch again, and to be honest it was making her feel uncomfortable. It wasn't just the discomfort of being in someone else's clothes, or the knowledge that she'd made a mistake in the river and might have drowned, but also the discomfort of knowing that the chapter in her life which concerned Gray was not as closed as she'd once thought it was.

Somehow he was breaking back in and opening that door again.

'I was really worried about you.'

She didn't want to hear that from him. 'Don't be.'

'I saw you go under. I… My heart almost stopped beating. You just disappeared under the water like you'd been swallowed up by a beast.'

She could hear the pain in his voice. The fear. It was tangible. Real. She had no doubt he meant every word he said.

But I can't allow myself to react to him. Gray's no good for me.

'But you caught me, so everything was all right in the end.'

She refused to turn and face him. She couldn't. If she did turn—if she did see the look in his eyes that she knew to be there—she would be lost. She needed to fight it. Fight *him*. And her reaction to him. Her desire to feel him against her again. It had to go.

She stared out at the water, cursing its calm surface, knowing of the torrent below.

'If you had been swept away—'

'But I wasn't! I'm okay.'

She glanced at him. Just briefly. Just to em-phasise her words—she *was* here, she *was* safe. Then she turned back to the river, her stomach in turmoil, her whole body fighting the desire to turn and fling herself into his arms again.

He didn't speak for some time and she could sense him looking out at the river, too.

'Are you cold? Would you like my jacket?' he asked eventually.

His jacket? The one that would carry his scent?

What was he trying to do? Drown her in *him* instead? How would she even be able to *think*, wrapped in its vast depths, with the echo of his warmth within them?

'No, I'm good, thanks,' she lied.

'You're still shivering.'

'I'm not cold. It's just…just shock. That's all.'

'Well, shock isn't minor, either. We need to keep you warm, hydrated. Come and sit by the fire—we can get some hot tea into you.'

'Honestly, Gray, I'm fine.'

It was killing her that he was trying to take care of her. It would be easier if he left her alone for a while. Allowed her to gather her thoughts. To regroup and rebuild those walls she'd built for the past eleven years. Because somehow, in the last few hours, they'd come crumbling down and she felt vulnerable again. Vulnerable to *him*. And that was something that she couldn't afford.

'Come and sit by the fire, Beau. I insist.'

He grabbed her by the arm and gently hauled her to her feet. His arm around her shoulders, he walked her over to the fire and sat her down on a log next to Barb. Then he disappeared.

Just as she thought she could relax again, he came back. She tensed as he wrapped a blanket around her shoulders.

'How's that?' He rubbed her upper arms and knelt before her, staring into her eyes.

He was close enough to kiss.

She tried not to think about it—tried not to look down at his mouth, at those lips that she knew were capable of making her shiver with desire. She tried not to notice the way he was looking at her, the way the lines had increased around his green eyes, the way his beard emphasised his mouth—his perfect mouth—the way his lips were parted as he stared back at her, waiting for her response.

I could just lean forward...

She closed her eyes and snuggled down into the blanket. *No.* She couldn't allow herself to do that. It was wrong. *He* was wrong. What the *hell* was she doing, even *contemplating* kissing him?

Beau scrunched up her face and gritted her teeth together before she opened her eyes again and looked directly back at him. She nodded to indicate that she was fine, but she wasn't.

She was fighting a battle within herself.

And she really wasn't sure, at this moment in time, which side would win.

Rick was next on the rota to make a meal, and Mack provided him with a small amount of rice and some tins of tuna. It wasn't great, but it was protein and carbohydrates—both of which they all badly needed—and despite its blandness, despite the lack of salt and pepper, they all wolfed their meal down, hungry from restricted rations and exhausted from the long, tiring day.

Except for Beau.

She toyed with her food, pretending to eat, but in reality she was just pushing it round her dish, trying to make it look as if she was eating.

Gray sat next to her, put down his dish. 'You need to eat.'

'I'm not hungry.'

'You've had a shock. You need to eat for strength. You're too thin as it is.'

She could hear in his voice that he was concerned about her. Could hear that he had good intentions. But she didn't want to hear them from him. She didn't want to be reminded that he cared, because if she acknowledged that, then she would need to accept that *she* still cared about *him*, too.

'I'm fine.'

'No, you're not. You're hardly eating and you're as thin as a stick of rock.'

She sucked in a breath, trying to not get pulled into an argument. 'Honestly, Gray—just leave it, will you?'

'Beau, I care about—'

She stood up and cast off the blanket and walked away from the campfire, aware that everyone would be wondering what the hell was going on, but not having the energy or the inclination to explain. Irritated, she stamped over to the riverbank and checked to see if her clothes had dried on the rocks.

Luckily for her they were almost dry, the heat of the sun having done its work, and she scooped them up and headed to her tent to get changed. Clambering in, she turned and zipped up the tent beside her, shutting out the outside world before she collapsed on the ground, trying her hardest not to cry.

How dare he show me that he still cares? Does he not understand what that is doing to me?

Just a couple of days ago, safe in her work environment, if one of her colleagues had asked her how she felt about Gray McGregor, she would have been able to answer calmly and easily that he meant nothing to her any more. That she hardly ever thought of him, and that if she did, it was only because of a vague curiosity as to what he might be doing now.

That would have been true. But *now*?

Now she felt all over the place. Confused, upset, *disturbed*.

I wanted to be in his arms! I wanted to kiss *him!*

She'd only been with him for two days. Two days into a week together! What on earth would she be like at the end of it? Beau had thought she was strong. She'd thought—she'd assumed—that she was resolute in her feelings towards the man. That those feelings wouldn't change…that she'd be able to carry on with her life and every day would be the same as the one before it. Just the way she liked it.

Only, Gray being here had changed everything.

She pulled off the clothing that Claire had let her borrow, and as she sat there in her underwear, she heard Gray clear his throat outside her tent.

'Ahem…knock-knock?'

Just hearing that lilting Scottish accent, purring away so close to her, sent shivers of awareness down her spine.

Gritting her teeth, she pulled her tee shirt over her head and retightened her ponytail. 'Yes?'

'I've come to see if you're okay.'

Growling inwardly, she lay flat to pull herself into her khaki cargo pants and zipped them and buttoned them up before she yanked open the zip to her tent and stuck her head out.

'I'm fantastic.'

His head tilted to one side and he raised a questioning eyebrow. 'You sound it.'

'Good. Then maybe you'll leave me alone.'

'So you're angry with *me*?'

She scuttled out from within her tent and stood up, straightening her clothes. 'Yes—and don't say that I don't have good reason.' She knew she sounded petulant, but she didn't care.

'I'm sorry. I didn't realise that asking if you were all right was a capital offence.'

She didn't answer him, just knelt down to gather up Claire's clothes so she could return them.

'Only if *you* do it,' she said eventually.

He shrugged and squinted into the bright sun. 'My apologies, then. I was just trying to show that I care.'

'Well, you can't.'

'Why not?'

She turned to him, exasperated, but kept her voice low so as not to share their argument with the whole camp. 'Because it's *you*, Gray. You. I put my life in your hands once before. I gave you everything and you abandoned me. And...' she raised a hand to stop him from interrupting '...just when I thought I knew where to place you on the evolutionary scale—which, for your information, was somewhere below pond scum level—you turn up here and you're nice! You're *annoyingly* nice and pleasant and charming, and then you have the nerve to save my life and make me feel *grateful*! Do you know what happened to me the last time I was grateful to you, Gray? Hmm…?'

All through her rant, all through her rage and exasperation, he'd stood there, staring calmly back at her, not saying anything. Just listening. Just being *gracious* about the whole thing, for crying out loud!

'I was just worried that you weren't eating enough.'

'That's for *me* to worry about, Gray. Not you. *I* get to worry about me. You don't get that opportunity any more—do you understand?'

He nodded once. 'Okay. If that's what you want.'

She let out a pent-up breath. 'That's what I want.'

'Okay. Well, I figured you might want this. I sneaked it into my backpack and I was saving it for a special occasion, but…but I think you might need it more than me.'

He reached into his pocket and pulled out a

chocolate bar. Not just *any* chocolate bar, but her *favourite*.

She blinked uncomprehendingly. Then she reached out and picked it up, almost not believing it was really there until she held it. Her anger—which had been simmering quietly ever since she'd stepped foot into that ranger station and seen him there—disappeared.

'I love these.'

'I know.'

'But…but you didn't know I was going to be on this course.'

'No, I didn't. But I've always bought them. Ever since…' He stopped talking and looked down at the ground. 'Anyway, you can have it. Seeing as you skipped dinner.'

He walked back to the campfire and joined the others, his back towards her.

She stared at the chocolate bar, which was slightly crumpled and soft from where it had been tightly packed into his bag, and felt her heart melt just a little bit more.

He still bought them. Even after all this time.

And I've just said all those horrible things...

Beau swallowed hard. Now she felt guilty. Guilty for being so harsh towards him just because *she'd* been feeling confused. Was it *his* fault that she felt that way? No. She should be in greater control of her feelings. Hadn't she always been before? Since he'd left her, she'd kept a rigid control over everything. Even down to making sure there were no unexpected surprises during her day. Her life had been timetabled to within an inch of its life. Knowing what would happen and when had kept her safe for so long. Had kept her from being hurt again.

But maybe...maybe surprises could be a good thing? Maybe a little uncertainty, a little risk, was okay? Didn't babies learn to walk by falling over? They didn't expect the fall, but they learnt from their mistakes.

Perhaps I need to let myself make a few mistakes? Take a few risks? Maybe there might be a little something out there for me, too.

She peeled open the chocolate bar and took a small bite.

* * *

The next morning Mack woke them early again and began teaching them another lesson. The topic this time was fractures.

'You have to know, even as a layman, how to evaluate an injury—either for someone else in your group or yourself.'

Beau could appreciate that. She was having a hard time assessing herself right now.

'You need to consider three things—the scene, a primary survey and a secondary survey if you're to come to the most accurate conclusion and assist yourself or another hiker out in the wild.'

'What's a primary and secondary survey?' asked Leo. 'I always get confused about those things.'

'Good question. A primary survey means looking at your patient and checking for life-threatening injuries or situations. So ABC. *Airway.* Is it clear? If not, why not? Can you clear it? *Breathing.* Is your patient breathing? Is it regular? Are there at least two breaths every ten seconds? And last of all *circulation.* Is there a major bleed? What can you do to stop it? That's your primary survey.'

'And if there aren't any of those signs?'

'Then you do your secondary survey. This also consists of three things. Remember with first aid and CPR there's generally a rule of three—ABC is one set of three. Scene survey, primary survey, secondary survey is another. If you remember to check three, you can always feel secure in knowing that you've checked everything. The secondary survey includes checking vital signs, taking the patient's history into account and a full head-to-toe body exam.'

'I'll never remember it all!' declared Barb.

'You'd be surprised,' Gray said.

'Once you've checked their vitals are okay, you can ask if they have pain or an injury. Find out how that injury occurred. Does it sound like there was enough force to create a fracture? Then you check the body, feeling firmly for any pain or deformities. But remember—even if the patient seems okay, their condition could change at any moment. You need to be alert. You may miss an injury because the patient is focusing on the pain from a bigger injury. And then what? Beau?'

'Then you swap hats,' said Beau, happy to answer. 'You take off the hat that states you're treating a fracture and put on the hat that says you're treating someone who's unconscious—you put them into the recovery position. If it gets worse again, you put on the CPR hat.'

Mack nodded. 'So, now let's focus on the fractures themselves. You look for the signs and symptoms of a fracture. Gray, can you tell us what they are?'

'Inability to bear weight on a limb, disabled body part, obvious deformity, pain, tenderness or swelling, angulation or bone protruding through the skin or stretching it. The patient might also mention hearing a crack.'

'Good. Did you all get that? You need to treat all possible skeletal injuries as if they are fractures. Even if you suspect a sprain or a dislocation, treat as a fracture until proved otherwise.'

'Okay, so how do we do that with no splints available?' asked Rick.

'There's always something you can use,' Gray

continued. 'You've just got to think outside the box. Splinting is correct. It stabilises the break and helps prevent movement on the splintered ends—which, believe you me, can be excruciatingly painful.'

He rubbed at his leg, as if remembering an old injury.

'If you don't splint an injury, it can lead to further damage—not just to the bone, but to muscle, tissue and nerves, causing more bleeding and swelling, which you do *not* want.'

'So what do we do?' asked Rick.

'You need to get the bones back into the correct anatomical position. Which means traction—which means causing yourself or your patient *more* pain. But you must do it—particularly if you're hours or even days from medical help.'

Claire grimaced. 'I'm not sure I could do that.'

'You'd have to. It can be upsetting, but it's best for the patient. Causing pain in the short-term will help in the long-term.'

Claire nodded quickly, her face grim.

Mack took over. 'Let's imagine a break on the lower left leg, near the ankle. This will be the most common injury you'll come across. People hiking and trekking across strange open country, falling down between rocks, not putting their feet securely down—all that contributes to this kind of injury. Claire, why don't you be my pretend patient?'

She got into position before him.

'You need to grasp the proximal part of the limb—that means the part of the limb closest to the body—and hold it in the position it was found. Then, with your other hand, you need to apply steady and firm traction to the distal part of the limb—this is the furthest point—like so.'

He demonstrated by gripping above and below Claire's 'fractured' lower leg.

'You do this by applying a downwards pull, and even though your patient may cry out, or try to pull away, you *must* slowly and gently pull it back into position. This will help relieve the patient's pain levels. Okay?'

Everyone nodded, even if they were looking a bit uncertain about their ability to do it in a real-life situation.

'Before you apply a splint, there's a rule of

three again. You need to check CSM—their *circulation*, their *sensation* and their *movement*. Can you feel a pulse below the injury? In the case of this one, can you find a pulse in the foot?' He demonstrated where to find it. 'Is the skin a good colour? Or is it pale and waxen, indicating that the positioning may still be off? Does the patient feel everything below the injury? Can they wiggle their toes? If there's anything restrictive, like a tight boot or socks, you can remove it to help reposition the limb properly.'

'What if the break is inside the boot?' asked Rick.

'You leave the boot on. The boot itself can act as a splint around the ankle sometimes—it's for you to judge what needs to be done.'

'What if we do something wrong?'

'You might never know. Or the patient might get worse, in which case you'll assess and treat accordingly. You can use sticks for splints, or walking poles, backpacks, snowshoes, the straps off your packs—anything that will provide a steady and supportive purpose.'

Rick nodded. 'Okay, but when we put a splint

alongside the injury, how exactly do we attach it? In the middle? Where the injury is?'

'No. Fasten the splint above and below the suspected fracture.'

'Right. And what about an open fracture? Do we bind it? Compress it?'

'No. Leave it uncovered before you splint, and if you can find enough splints to go around the injury on all sides, that's even better. Use padding, if you need to, to prevent discomfort—torn clothing…whatever you can find. But remember to keep checking it afterwards, because the wound may cause swelling and the splinting may then be too tight. You need to assess frequently and often. Have you all got that?'

They nodded.

'Right. Now the practical. With your buddy, I want you to practise assessing for and splinting a left ankle break. Remember to do a scene survey, and a primary and secondary survey. Remember your rules of three and use the environment around you to find and locate splints. Patients— give your doctor a few surprises. I'll come round and assess when you're done.'

Beau looked to Gray. It was his turn to be the patient. But for some reason he looked extremely uncomfortable, and she wondered briefly what it was that was worrying him. He'd seemed fine just a moment ago.

Was he thinking of a way to surprise her? As Mack had suggested? If he was, then she was determined to be ready for him.

CHAPTER SIX

'MAYBE I SHOULD be the doctor for this one,' Gray suggested.

'No. You've already rescued me. It's your turn to be the patient.'

'I was the patient for the leg wound. It's your turn.'

She looked at him, feeling exasperated. Why was he getting antsy all of a sudden? Why didn't he want to be the patient? He'd get to sit down and have a rest!

Beau decided to give him 'the look'—the one that told him, *Sit down right now. I don't have time for this!*

Gray cursed silently, his lips forming expletives she couldn't hear, before he shook his head in defeat and sank down to the floor.

'Do my right ankle.'

'Mack said the left.'

'Well, I'm surprising you. I broke my right one.'

'Gray, what's the matter with you? Now, first of all the scene survey. It's safe for me to approach you…there are no hazards.' She knelt down beside him and smiled broadly. 'What seems to be the problem?'

Gray tried his best glare, but when he could see that it wasn't having any effect on her, he resigned himself to what was about to happen. 'My ankle hurts. I think I've broken it. I heard something snap.'

'Uh-huh. Which one?' She smiled at him sympathetically and saw his face soften under her onslaught of sweetness.

He let out a breath. 'My left.'

She nodded, glad he was finally playing ball. Though why on earth he'd wanted to swap ankles was beyond her. She *had* noticed that he had been limping slightly. Perhaps she was about to find out that he really did have blisters and hadn't been looking after them properly.

'Okay. So, primary survey—your airway is clear, you're breathing normally and there don't

appear to be any bleeds. Do you feel pain anywhere else?'

'Only in my pride.'

She laughed, puzzled by the strange discomfort
he seemed to be displaying. 'Okay…so, secondary survey. Lie back—be a good patient.'

Gray lay back on the ground, but she could see
he wasn't relaxed at all. He looked tense. Apprehensive. It was odd. This was a simple scenario—
he should be fine about all of this.

'Okay, and on a scale of one to ten, with zero
being no pain and ten being excruciating pain,
how would you rate it?'

'Definitely a ten.'

'And how did you damage your ankle?'

'I slipped. I wasn't concentrating.'

'Uh-huh. Okay, I'm going to check the rest of
you and make sure there are no other injuries.
Just relax for me, if you can.'

She felt around the back of his neck and pressed
either side of his neck vertebrae. No reaction.
Then she felt his shoulders, checked his clavicle,
then ribcage.

There was plenty of reaction. In her own body!

Touching him like this, enveloping the muscle groups as she checked both his arms, patted down his hips and applied a small amount of pressure on the hip bones, aware of how close her hands were to his skin, was almost unbearable. Her hands encompassed the thick, strong muscles of his thighs, moved past his knees down to his...

Huh? What was that?

She sat back and frowned, staring at his lower leg, then glancing up at his face in question. Waiting for him to answer. To explain.

'What is that, Gray? A brace?'

Had he hurt his leg? Had he been hiding an injury all this time? What had he done to himself?

Gray sat upright and his cheeks coloured slightly. His brows bunched heavily over his eyes and the muscle in his jaw clenched and unclenched before he answered her, without meeting her gaze. 'It's a prosthetic.'

She felt a physical shift in her chest, as if her heart had plummeted to the dirty ground below, and her stomach rolled and churned at the thought that he'd been so hurt somehow. That Gray—her once beloved, powerful and strong Gray—had been hurt to such an extent that he had physically lost a part of him.

'A what?' she asked in an awed whisper, not wanting to believe him.

The word 'prosthetic' literally meant an addition. An attachment. An artificial piece that replaced a missing body part. Something lost from disease, or a congenital condition, or trauma.

She could feel herself going numb. Withdrawing, almost. If she heard his answer, it would make it even more real.

Gray sighed and lifted up his left trouser leg, looked at her directly this time. 'I lost my foot, and some of my leg below the knee.'

She stared at it. Watched as he peeled off his boot and then his sock and revealed it to her in its full glory. The shiny plastic exterior…the solid metal bar from mid-shin down to the ankle, where the fake foot began.

'Gray…'

'Please don't, Beau. Don't tell me you're sorry. There's no need to be. I can still do what anyone else does. People have climbed Everest with a prosthetic.'

'I know, but…'

'You always told me—always warned me—that I took too many risks and, well…here you are. You were proved right. I did something stupid.'

She reached out to touch it, then stopped. She had no right to touch him there. Or anywhere, really. Her hand dropped back to her lap. 'Are you okay?'

'Apart from missing half a limb?'

'How did it happen?'

He pulled his trouser leg back down. 'It's a long story.'

'I want to hear it.'

'Why? We're not together any more—you don't have to prove you care.'

'Gray—'

'Please, Beau, leave it. Just splint the ankle.'

'Are you sure? I could just—'

'Just…splint it.'

She looked at his downcast face, the anger in his eyes, and her heart physically ached for him. To see him like this—bared and open…wounded. Not the strong Gray he'd always shown the world, but having to—being forced to—reveal a weakness… Beau knew how that must be making him feel.

But it didn't matter. His prosthesis didn't make him any *less*. He was still Gray. And he was right. People today could do anything with a prosthesis. Look at all those athletes. Or any ordinary person, carrying on with life. He was still a top cardiologist. It didn't stop him from operating. It didn't stop him from saving people's lives. But how to say that to him without sounding preachy? He knew it already. Surely?

He's still the same Gray. Life tries to strike you down, and though it feels, at the time, like it's the worst thing you'll ever have to get through, like you'll never survive...well, you do get through it. You do *survive. You're changed. You're different. But you survive.*

She knew Gray must have gone through a period of grieving for his lower leg and foot. A part of him truly *was* missing. But he was strong. Resilient. She had to believe in that. He was *here*, wasn't he? Hiking across Yellowstone for a week.

You didn't do *that* on a prosthetic unless you were determined and believed in yourself.

Beau began to look around her for something to use for splints. There was plenty of wood, but she needed to find something sturdy enough to support a joint. There were some thick pieces of wood over at the treeline and she gathered them and came back to Gray. She silently began attaching them, using the bungee cords from her backpack. She fastened them, checked to make sure they weren't too tight, then knelt back and waited for him to look at her.

'Please tell me how it happened.'

For a moment she didn't think he was going to speak at all, but then he began.

'There's a place called St John's Head on the Isle of Hoy, in the Orkneys. Have you heard of it?'

She shook her head. 'No.'

'It's considered the world's hardest sea cliff climb and I wanted to give it a try.'

She nodded. Of course he had. That was what he'd always been like. Pushing the envelope. Pushing boundaries. Seeing how far he could go.

'You're not just fighting the heights and the rock there, but the gale-force winds, the rain, the birds dropping…' He paused for a moment to think about his choice of words. 'Dropping *stuff* on you. It's a sheer rock face, with almost no fingerholds. There's a route called the Long Hope. It's amazing. You have to see it to believe it.'

'It sounds…exposed.'

He gave a laugh. 'You have no idea. When you're up there, you feel like you're the only person in the world.'

'You went alone, didn't you?'

He nodded. 'I was trying to free climb it. No ropes, no equipment. This other guy managed it a few years ago. I'm an experienced climber—I'd done free climbing before—I thought I'd be okay.'

'But something went wrong?'

Gray nodded. 'Before I knew what was happening, I was falling. I hit the rocks below, broke my leg in three places, fractured my pelvis, had an open fracture of the ankle. Luckily I had my phone. More importantly, I had a *signal*. Mountain Rescue and the coastguard joined forces and got me to a hospital.'

'Did they try and save your leg?'

'They tried. I had three surgeries. But an infection set in and they had to amputate. It wasn't the fall that lost me my foot—it was bacteria.'

She felt sick. It was awful. Yet he'd got himself back up, carried on with his demanding work, come on this course...

'Is that why you're here? To prove to yourself that you can still achieve things?'

Gray shifted on the ground and fidgeted with the splint she'd assembled on his lower leg. 'Maybe.'

'You're still *you*, you know? Just because there's a physical piece missing, it doesn't mean you're any less than who you were.'

She was a little shocked that she hadn't realised he was injured in this way. She'd noticed the limping, but it hadn't occurred to her that it might be something so significant. What else had she missed about Gray?

'I know that. I was mad at myself for making a mistake on the cliff. Even now I can't pinpoint what went wrong, and that irks me. But I knew if I got one of the more expensive prosthetics I could still do things like this. Still have my adventures.'

She smiled at him. That was better. The fighting spirit she knew and...

She glanced at the ground, feeling her cheeks colour. 'Go on, then—tell me. I know you're dying to. What are the specs on this thing?'

He gave a sheepish grin. 'It's got a tibial rotator, which allows the leg to rotate even when the foot is placed firmly on the ground. It also helps prevent skin irritation in the socket, where there's an extra gel padding cuff for hiking trips. The foot itself is multiaxial, so it can tilt and rotate over uneven ground.'

'Sounds top of the line.'

'It is.'

'I'm glad you're out here.'

Gray looked surprised, then reached out and laid his hand on hers, curling his fingers around her palm and squeezing back when he felt her hand squeeze his. 'Thank you, Beau. I don't deserve you. I never did.'

She didn't know what to say. He was wrong! He *did* deserve her! Even now she could feel...

Beau swallowed hard, trying to find an anchor in this sea of swirling emotions she was reeling under. She wanted to wrap her arms around him and hold him. She wanted to press him close. To feel him safe in her arms. But another part... a much smaller part...told her to keep holding back. Told her that this was *Gray* and she was crazy even to be thinking of giving this man comfort.

Instead she concentrated on the feel of his hand in hers. Its steady strength. Its warmth. The solidity of him near her. His presence—all too real and all too confusing.

Why couldn't she have been there to help him during his time of need?

Would I have gone if he'd called me and asked? Yes. I would have.

They sat quietly, holding hands, until Mack came alongside them to assess Beau's splinting skills and medical surveys. They dropped each other's hand like a hot coal at the ranger's approach. Only once Mack had given Beau a big thumbs-up and suggested that they swap roles did they manage to look at each other again.

Something had changed between them.

Something weird and almost intangible. Whatever it was, it had strength and influence, and Beau lay on the ground and tried to ignore the feelings raging through her body as Gray assessed her for injury and applied a splint to her left ankle. Her cheeks kept flushing, she felt hot, her stomach was turning and spinning like a roulette wheel, and she tried to tamp down the physical awareness she felt with every touch of his hands.

When Mack called for a break, and told them all to make camp and put up their tents, she hurried over to her backpack and put her tent up quickly, eager to get inside and just *hide* for a while. Gather her thoughts. Regroup her emotions. Wipe away the solitary tear that rolled down her cheek at the thought of Gray broken and alone at the base of a sea cliff.

What does all this mean?

Am I in trouble?

* * *

It was Leo's turn at the cooking pot, and he had rustled up a spicy potato dish. Gray had no idea what had gone into it, just knew that it tasted good and he wanted more. But, as always, Mack had limited the rations so that they were always just the empty side of full, burning more calories in the day than they were able to take in, so they could see how hunger might affect their choices.

Tomorrow would see the start of the paired orienteering—sending the buddied couples out into the wild on their own, to see if they could navigate to a particular spot, make it safely and deal with any issues on the way. It had been the part of the week that he'd been looking forward to the most—surviving on his own wits with just one other person. But now...now he wasn't sure.

Now Beau knew about his leg. He'd tried his hardest to hide it from her, feeling a little foolish about it at first, but now he'd come clean and she wasn't fazed at all.

But I still feel incomplete. Is it just my leg? Or is something else bothering me?

If he'd ever felt he might stand another chance

with her, that feeling had died when he'd fallen from that cliff and lost that part of his leg. It had been a physical manifestation of the fact that he wasn't whole. That he wasn't the complete package. That he couldn't offer her what she wanted from life. And that realisation still hurt like hell. He might have a new bionic foot and ankle, capable of coping with any terrain thrown at it, but what about *him*? What could *he* cope with?

Beau had meant everything to him. She'd made his heart sing and he'd been able to forget all the drama and misery of his own home when he'd been with her. She had brought him comfort and repose. A soft place to fall. *She* had been his home.

But he'd ruined it. That tiny slip, that tiny lapse of concentration, and he'd blurted out the one question he'd never thought he'd ask... *Will you marry me?*

It had changed everything. Turned his happiness upside down, put a deadline on his joy. No, not a deadline—*a death sentence*. Marriage would have killed who they were. Their happiness at being in each other's presence would slowly have been eroded and familiarity would have bred contempt. Living in each other's pockets would have caused them to seek time apart, space from one another, just so they could breathe again. They would have grown to dread being in each other's company, started to hate the way they ate their food, the way they fought about who wanted to go out and who wanted to stay in, whether they squeezed the toothpaste tube right... *Every tiny thing* would have been used as a stone to throw at the other.

He'd lived it. He'd seen it. Been stuck in the middle of two warring factions—both sides of which he loved for different reasons, both sides of which he stayed away from for the same reasons...

It was a fact that children imitated their parents. Gray might try not to be like them, but he was sure little things would sneak through. Sure, he might just have little quirks that at first Beau would find amusing, and then irritating, and then soon she'd be so opposed to them she would threaten to leave him unless he changed his ways...

Marriage was only possible for people who knew what they were doing. Who were emotionally available. Who had the strength to get through it. But for him and Beau...? *No.* He was damaged goods. He'd been broken before they'd even got started.

He knew he should have spoken to her earlier, but she'd seemed so happy, so confident in their happiness. Had he been wrong to try to let her be happy for as long as she could? Not to decimate her dreams? She'd even started talking about how after the wedding she would come off birth control so they could try for a child straight away...

That had been terrifying. Being responsible for bringing another child into another potential battleground? No. He couldn't do it. He'd *been* that child and look at what it had done to him.

The problem was whether Beau would understand all this. Her world was perfect, and her parents—the strangest couple in the world, who actually seemed still to *love* each other after many years—had been a different example entirely. There were no broken marriages, as far as he knew, on her side of the family, so *some* people got it right, but...

Beau was in the dark regarding his experience. She couldn't possibly know how he felt about marriage. The fear it engendered in him. That pressure to get it right when he had no idea how.

When everyone had finished eating, he volunteered to wash the dishes in the river and noticed after a few minutes that Beau had joined him.

'Hi,' she ventured.

He glanced at her—at the way her beautiful wavy hair tumbled around her shoulders, at the way her eyes glinted in the evening sunshine. She was still the most beautiful woman he had ever met. And then some.

'Hi.'

'Want a hand?'

'I've got two of those, thanks. Do you have a foot handy?' He laughed gruffly at his own joke and carried on swirling the dishes in the crystal-clear running water.

'Only my own. I don't think you'd want one of them—they've got sparkly pink nail varnish on the toenails. But I'd give it to you if you needed it.'

She took the dishes from him as he finished and began wiping them with a towel.

'You never know. My prosthetic has got all the latest tricks and flicks, but it doesn't have sparkly pink nail polish. I think that may be the latest upgrade it needs.'

She smiled at him. 'You know, I've been thinking about your accident…'

He paused briefly from his washing. 'Oh?'

'Just wondering who…who supported you through all that.'

'I got myself through it.'

'What about your family?'

He shrugged. He'd refused to lean on them for any kind of support. 'Well…'

'Did you tell them?'

'Not at first…'

'But they *do* know?'

'They do now. I told them after it was all over. Once I'd healed.'

'Why didn't you tell them?'

He shifted his stance, switching his weight from one foot to the other. 'We aren't that close. Never were. And my mother had enough to do, looking after my dad, so…' He trailed off, not wanting to say more. He'd always protected her from the reality of his family and it was a hard habit to break.

'You know, one day you're going to have to tell me. I'm not going to let this rest.'

He nodded. 'I know. When I'm ready.'

Beau gazed at him and smiled. 'I can wait.'

Perhaps she was nearly ready to listen? He let his fingers squeeze hers, acknowledging her support. For a moment he couldn't speak. He was so taken aback that she was saying these nice things. They'd both certainly come a long way in the last few days.

'And, you know…apart from the fact that you've got a body part that will *never* wear out… you'll make a cracking pirate if you choose to put a wooden peg in its place!'

He smiled. 'Of *course*! Stupid me for not seeing the best of my situation.'

'Well, you've always been guilty of *that*, Gray.'

His smile dropped. 'What do you mean?'

She looked up at him, startled by his reaction,

realising she'd said more than she should. She'd answered too quickly. Without thinking.

'Erm…I don't know… Forget it.'

'No. You meant something when you said that—what did you mean?'

Beau looked uneasy, shifting her eyes away from his. 'Just that…back then…well…you had *me*, Gray.'

Her gaze came back to his, slamming into him with a force that almost knocked him off his feet.

'I thought we were happy together. That we had something special. That our love was stronger than anything else!'

The tears beginning to run from her eyes were real. Knowing that he was still causing her pain almost ripped him in two.

He cradled her hands against his chest. 'It *was*!'

She shook her head. 'No, it wasn't. You didn't love me enough—you let your doubt, or whatever it was, tell you to abandon me. Leave me. Without a word. Not a *single* word!'

'Beau—'

'I wasn't enough for you. Our *love* wasn't enough. You focused on something else. Something that tore you away from me. And do you know how that made me feel? *Worthless!*'

He pulled her towards him, into his arms, pressing her against his chest, hoping to dry her tears, hoping to show her that she could never be worthless to him. But feeling her against him, feeling her cry, woke something in him that he'd buried deeply. Buried so far down he'd thought it could never be found again. He'd found it now, though, and it had him in its grip.

He pulled back to look at her, to make her look him in the eyes, so that he could tell her that she was the most important person who had *ever* been in his life...

But as soon as his eyes locked with hers, he was mesmerised. Her shimmering sapphire eyes were staring back at him with such pain in them that he felt compelled to take that pain away, and before he knew what he was doing—before he had a chance to think twice—he lowered his lips to hers and kissed her.

It was like dropping a lit taper into a fireworks factory. There was a moment of shock, of disbelief and wonder at what he was doing, and then—

boom! He lost control. All those years of being without her, all those years of never allowing himself to *feel*, came crashing down and his body sprang to life. It was as if she was a life-giving force and this was the kiss of life.

His arms enveloped her and pressed her to him. He couldn't get enough of her. He *had* to feel her. All of her—against him. Her softness, her delicate frame was protected by him. Her lips were against his, and the way she gasped for air and breathed his name was like oxygen feeding his fire.

It could have become something else, something...*more*, but just as he thought he couldn't resist her, couldn't resist the desire to feel her flesh against his own, the others in the group started catcalling.

'Get a room, you two!'

They broke apart and stared at each other, shock in their eyes, both of them not quite sure how that had happened.

Then Beau walked away, pulling open the flap to her tent and darting out of sight.

Gray gathered the dishes and took them back

to camp, where he received many pats on the back from the other men and some raised eyebrows from Barb and Claire, whom he glanced at sheepishly.

'Well, that explains a few things,' Barb said. 'I *knew* there was something going on between you two. Feel better now?'

He didn't answer. He wasn't sure. The kiss had been amazing. More than amazing. But what was Beau thinking? She'd said some things… Had he made things worse? Had he made things better? Surely she wouldn't be in her tent if he'd helped in any way. He wondered if he should go and talk to her.

He glanced over at her tent, but Barb shook her head. 'I'd leave her a while, if I were you. It looks like you woke something up between the pair of you and she needs time to get used to it.'

'But shouldn't I—'

'Give her space, Gray. You'll have more than enough time on the orienteering hike, alone together, to talk out any last wrinkles. For now, give her time to absorb what's happened.'

'Shouldn't I at least go over and apologise?'

She cocked her head at him. 'You're *sorry* about kissing a girl like that?'

He thought for a moment. 'No.'

Barb grinned. 'Good! The world would be a lot better if husbands kissed their wives like that a bit more, I can tell you. Con? You listening to this?'

'Sure, honey.' Conrad, who was tending the campfire, turned and grinned at them both.

'Pah! You old romantic! Anyway, if you ever kissed *me* like that, I think I'd drop dead from the shock—and I ain't ready to go yet.' She laughed. 'But, Gray, listen to me—and listen good. You and Beau look like you have something special going on. Something deep that comes from *here*...' She pointed at her heart. 'You don't let that go. Not ever. That kind of love is the stuff that gets you out of hot water.'

He frowned. 'How do you mean?'

'You don't need no old lady telling you how to live your life, but if I had one piece of advice to give you, it'd be to tell yourself every day just *why* you love that other person. What you're grateful for. What they do to make you feel loved and special. Because if you're busy focusing on the good stuff all the time, the bad times, well… they can seem a lot easier to get through.'

He nodded to Conrad by the fire. 'Is that what you do?'

'Sure is!' Barb leaned in, speaking in a mock whisper. 'Or I'd have killed him already! The man could snore for America!'

Gray glanced over at Beau's tent. *Was* it as simple as that? Just thinking of the good things? Reminding yourself every day why you loved that person? Reliving moments like that kiss they'd just shared? *Could* it be that easy?

He didn't know. He wasn't sure he wanted to admit that it could, because if he did, then the pain he'd put them both through had been for nothing. If he believed that, then everything could have been avoided if only he'd had enough faith in his love for Beau being stronger than any day-to-day drudgery trying to ruin it all.

Did I ruin our lives because I didn't think I was strong enough? No. I thought I was protecting her. Protecting me. I couldn't bear the idea that she could ever hate me.

But hadn't that happened anyway?

Gray rubbed his hands over his face and groaned. Why couldn't this be easy? A case of two plus two equalling four? Why did life have to have so many twists and turns, dead ends and multi-car pile-ups?

He stared at the entrance to Beau's tent, willing her to come out.

CHAPTER SEVEN

THERE WAS ANOTHER breakfast of porridge the next morning. Beau had suffered a long, uncomfortable night, having stayed in her tent for most of the previous evening, only coming out when Claire and Barb had called for her. She'd grabbed her toiletries bag and hurried away with them, her head downcast, ensuring she didn't make eye contact with Gray.

They'd kissed!

And she'd forgotten how wonderful kissing Gray had been. Her feelings had been all topsy-turvy, her heart hammering, her pulse pounding and her brain bamboozled and as fragile as a snowflake above a firepit as she'd fought to decide whether she should continue with it or fight him off. But it had been too delicious to stop.

I certainly didn't fight him off!

No. She'd breathed his name, gasped it, making those little noises in her throat that now made her feel so embarrassed as she thought of them. Had he heard her? *Of course he had!* He would have had to be deaf not to, and there was nothing wrong with his hearing. Or any of his other body parts...

She tried not to recall the sensation of him pressed hard against her.

And now I'm sitting here, around a campfire, eating porridge that's as difficult to swallow as week-old wallpaper paste, trying not to look up and catch his eye. What am I...? A mouse?

She gritted her teeth and looked up. He was opposite, talking to Mack in a low whisper, and by the way Gray was pointing at his leg, she assumed they were discussing his prosthetic. Or maybe the accident that had caused it? She supposed Mack must have known about the prosthetic beforehand. Health and safety—these were the all-important buzzwords everywhere these days. Surely Gray had *had* to declare it beforehand? He might not have been allowed on the course otherwise.

Gray glanced over and caught her gaze, smiled.

Quickly she looked away. This was going to be awkward. Today they would be splitting up into their pairs for the orienteering challenge, after one final lesson around the campfire with Mack. She and Gray would be alone together. Just the two of them. Hiking through Yellowstone to a pre-approved grid reference, where apparently there would be a checkpoint to collect supplies before they headed to another grid reference, where they would find the ranger station. They would have to talk. There would be no escape for either of them.

And we're hardly going to be able to get through it in silence, are we?

Silence would be nice after that kiss. Preferable, actually.

No, forget that. Not coming on this trip would have been preferable.

But she had. So had he. And they'd kissed. And it hadn't been one of those polite kisses you gave at family gatherings, either. That polite peck on the cheek for a family member you hadn't seen for a few months.

It had been hot. Passionate, searing, breathtaking, goosebump-causing...

He had to have felt something, too. A reawakening. A refiring of something that had once burned so hot. That *unfinished* feeling between them... That entwining of souls—the kind of feeling that was so intimate it touched your heart.

Beau knew she had to get a grip. Take control. Let Gray know that, yes, she acknowledged something had happened between them, but that was all it could be—*something*. An undefined moment. And there was no need to explore it further. She had to make it very clear that they should leave it alone and get on with finding their way back to civilisation, thank you very much.

The situation they were in was so intense. It was risky. People got close to each other in this kind of situation because that was what happened in a high-pressure moment. It created a false reality. And when life returned to normal afterwards, the feelings just weren't there...

He *had* to know that this didn't mean anything for them. She'd come on this course alone and, damn it, she was going to leave it alone, too.

There would be no need for further contact. She wouldn't be exchanging telephone numbers or email addresses with him. He would go back to Edinburgh and she would return to Oxford and life would continue. Everything in its neat little box, the way it always had been. In *her* control.

The reason the kiss had happened in the first place was because the whole thing had got *out* of her control. This wasn't reality.

But something *had* changed between them, and she'd learnt more about him in the last few days than she'd ever known before. She knew that there was so much more to understand about her enigmatic ex-fiancé. And that wasn't all. Though she hated to admit it, her lips still tingled from his kiss.

Her senses had gone into overdrive since, and though she'd been huddled in her tent, preferring to believe that she'd caught some sort of strange disease and was suffering from a weird kind of fever, she'd been aware of exactly where Gray was outside her tent. Whenever he'd come close or walked by, she'd known. Whenever he'd spoken during that evening, she'd frozen, just so she

could listen to what he said. Her body had ached
for him.

Ached!

She hadn't wanted someone this badly since…

Since Gray.

If she could have, she would have groaned out
loud, but instead she shoved in another spoon-
ful of the dreadful porridge. She filled her mouth
with the soft mush just to stop herself from crying out.

Are you kidding me?

She sat there, miserable in her silence, staring at Gray, all rumpled and tousled opposite
her, wanting both to kiss him and beat her fists
against his chest in equal measure.

'Okay, everyone. Last-minute stuff before I send
you off in your pairs out into the big, wide world.
You remember what I said about the big animals
in the park, yes?'

They all nodded.

'Well, now you need to know about the smaller
beasts. They may be lighter than a two-thousand-

pound bison, but they can still knock you off your feet if you're not careful.'

'Such as...?' asked Claire.

'Snakes, for one. There have only been two recorded snakebites in this area, and your main culprit is the prairie rattlesnake. You'll find her in dry grasslands and the warmer river areas. You all know what a rattlesnake looks like? Sounds like?'

Again, they nodded sagely.

'You hear that rattle—you head in the other direction. You give her a wide berth. Usually they rattle to warn you, before you get too close, but not always—so be on your lookout when you walk.'

'Are they always on the ground?' asked Gray.

'Mostly. But they have been known to climb trees, or rest in crevices between rocks, so always check your surroundings. There may be the rare occurrence of a snakebite, and a rattler bite will inject you with plenty of nasty stuff—hemotoxins that cause the destruction of tissue. If you don't have a reverse syringe handy—which you don't—you need to keep your patient calm and still, and wrap the affected limb tightly. Apply a splint and get yourselves some medical help as soon as possible.'

'Shouldn't we attempt to suck out the poison with our mouths?'

'Technically, it should be safe to suck out the venom if the person doing the sucking doesn't have an open wound in their mouth. Poisons only affect you if you swallow them. But we're not dealing with poison here—we're talking *venom*. Venom is toxic only when it's injected into the lovely soft tissues of the human body and its rich bloodstream. So if you suck out venom from a snakebite, you *should* be okay—but we don't advise it any more. My advice? *Don't do it.* The human mouth isn't that clean, either, and you're just as likely to introduce bacteria into the wound and do as much damage as the snake did.'

He looked at their sombre faces.

'Walk with a stick when you're out in the wilds alone. You can tap the ground before you, and if there is something you've missed, the stick is more likely to get attacked before you.'

'And that stick will come in handy for a river crossing—let's not forget!' said Conrad.

Everyone smiled and the sombre mood was lifted.

'The next thing is stating the obvious—you need to keep an eye on your buddy. Heat exhaustion and dehydration can set in quickly. This time of year it's hot—you're sweating constantly and you'll need to keep up your fluid intake and stay out of the midday sun for as long as is possible. Beau, do you want to let people know the signs?'

She coloured, feeling Gray's eyes upon her, and her answer, when it came, was not given in her usually confident voice. 'Erm…you might feel weak, thirsty. When you go to the loo, your urine might be only a little amount, deep in colour, or it might even hurt to try and pass water… Erm…'

Gray helped her out. 'You might feel drowsy, tired, dizzy, disorientated. Faint when you try to stand. These are all signs of it getting worse. You must keep putting the fluids in, even if it means stopping to purify water. Water should be your top priority.'

Mack nodded. 'Then there are the mosquitoes,

the leeches, the spiders, the ticks. These could all just be minor irritants, but long-term might lead to other problems. Tick bites, especially, could lead to Lyme disease.'

'Ooh, that's *nasty*. My cousin has that,' Barb said.

'I know you've all got bug spray, and some of you have citronella. These are all good repellents, but you need to check each other at every stop for ticks. If you get one, don't just try to pull it out. You need to remove them by twisting them out with tweezers or proper tick removers.'

He smiled and stood up.

'Right! Let's pack up camp, douse the fire, and then I'll hand out your coordinates and maps. You'll each be given a different route to follow, but we should all arrive at the ranger station by Heart Lake sometime tomorrow afternoon. When we do, you can all tell me how wonderful I've been whilst you sip real drinks and eat a proper meal. Sound good?'

They all cheered, and he nodded and headed over to his own tent, started to take down the guy ropes.

Beau helped Barb wash the breakfast dishes. 'Are you nervous about heading into the wild with just you and Con?' she asked.

'No. I know he'll look after me and I'll look after him.' She looked up at Beau. 'You nervous?'

'A bit.'

'About the wildlife problem or the cute doctor problem?'

Beau blushed. 'One more than the other.'

'Oh, don't you worry, honey. That man has got your back. And maybe some time alone together is just what you two need. A romantic walk together... A campfire beneath the stars all on your own...'

'But what if it *isn't* what we need? What if we find ourselves alone and it all turns bad? What if we really hate each other?'

Barb tilted her head as she gazed at Beau. 'I don't think that's going to happen. Do you?'

Beau wasn't sure. Having the others around had provided a security she hadn't realised she'd been relying upon. Now they were all about to go their separate ways and she'd be on her own with Gray… Well, there were enough butterflies in her stomach to restock a zoo.

When the dishes were done and packed away, she headed over to collapse her tent—only to find that most of it had been done already and Gray was kneeling on the pine-needle-littered ground, putting her rolled-up tent back into its bag.

'Oh! Erm…thank you.'

'No problem. I saw you were busy, so…'

She nodded. 'I can take over now.'

She held out her hands for her things and took the tent from him, started to rearrange her pack. Keeping her back to him, she breathed in and out slowly, trying to keep her heart rate down. But it was difficult. He was so close! So near. Watching and waiting for her…ready to say goodness only knew what when they were alone.

Perhaps she could pre-empt him. Let him know there wasn't going to be a continuation of what happened yesterday. Because if there was… Well, she wasn't sure her senses and her heart would survive the onslaught. Gray was like a drug to her. She could feel that. The effect he had on her was as if she *had* been bitten by a rattlesnake!

With her body turning to mush and her ability to think shot to pieces...

She had to let him know where she stood. Where *they* stood.

Beau turned and faced him, squaring her shoulders and standing her ground as if she were about to go into battle. 'Gray? You need to know that after...after last night...what happened...I... It won't be happening again. We can't let it happen. We can't.'

Try to look him in the eyes!

'But we do need to work together to get back to the ranger station, so can you promise me that you won't do anything? You know...won't provoke something of a similar nature?'

The corner of Gray's mouth turned up in a cheeky way. '*Provoke* something? What do you mean?'

Beau looked about them. Was anyone listening? She leaned into him, closer, so that she could whisper. 'I mean the kissing! Please don't try to do anything like that again!'

Gray stared deeply into her blue eyes, searching for an answer he obviously couldn't see. But he must have heeded her words, because he stepped back and nodded. 'I won't start anything. You have my word.'

'Thank you.' She felt her cheeks flush with heat again at the relief.

'But only if...'

'Only if what?'

'Only if *you* can keep *your* hands to *yourself.*'

He turned away from her to haul on his backpack, and when he turned back to face her, he was grinning widely. He really was maddening!

'I'm sure I'll try to restrain myself.'

A few hours later they had been given their co-ordinates and were walking to their first checkpoint. Or so Beau hoped. Gray was the one reading the map and leading the way and she was putting her trust in him totally.

Feels familiar. And look where it got me before!

'Er... Gray? Could I just glance at the map?'

'Well, that depends...'

'On...?'

'On how often you've used a map to navigate across country.'

She let out a tense breath and glared at him. 'I made it from Oxford to Heathrow in one piece.'

'By GPS?'

'It can't be that hard! Could I just have a look?'

He handed her the map with a smile on his face. 'There you go. You're in charge.'

She nodded with satisfaction and glanced at the map. She'd expected a few place names, splodges of green for woodlands and trees, maybe patches of blue to mark out lakes and blue lines for rivers. This map *had* all of those things—but it also had other lines that went all over the place. And where were the grid references…? 1…2…3… It was all numbers!

She bit her lip, her eyes scanning the map, looking for some sort of point of reference that was familiar with their surroundings. 'Is this even the right map?'

'You have to know our longitude and latitude to start with.'

'Which is where again?'

She wouldn't look him in the eye. So he stood by her side and pointed at a small spot on the map. 'Just there.'

'And we're heading to…?'

'Over there.' He pointed again. 'Our first check-point.'

'Right.'

It wasn't getting any clearer. What were all those other lines? Elevation? That seemed about right…

'So we need to take this trail ahead of us until we reach this…' There were a lot of lines all tightly together. 'This high spot?'

He nodded and smiled. 'Looks like it. We should make it there by nightfall. Camp overnight and then tomorrow we need to cross another river.'

Now she looked at him, feeling the cold memory of her previous accident shiver through her body. She wasn't looking forward to that. What if it was deeper and more dangerous than the last one?

'Oh…'

'But we should be able to get to the ranger station by lunchtime. Just imagine—tomorrow we can be drinking real tea and tucking in to a restaurant meal with all of this behind us.'

'Sounds simple.'

'Should be.'

She passed him the map. 'Maybe you *should* have this.'

They'd parted company from the rest of the group—everyone with nerves and butterflies in their stomachs, everyone hugging each other, whispering words of encouragement into each other's ears before setting off—turning around occasionally until the others were out of sight.

Each pairing had been given a different checkpoint to reach, and then from that checkpoint they all had to navigate their way back to the ranger station. Nothing too arduous, but enough of a toe in the water to prove to themselves that they *could* do it, that they'd survive and, if need be, could cope with any injuries on the way.

Beau had learnt a few things on this trip so far. She'd learnt that she could cope with being around Gray. With talking to him. Being civil. They'd even got...*close*...and she'd discovered her feelings for him were still very much up in the air. He was maddening and gorgeous and frustrating and sexy and... Had she mentioned gorgeous?

He still bought her favourite chocolate bars. He'd been incredibly hurt and had survived alone. The idea of him lying there, broken and hurting, at the bottom of that remote sea cliff had been nauseating. Heartbreaking. What had he thought of as he'd lain there? Had he thought he was going to die? Had he had regrets?

Was I one of them?

Beau had never rested. Since the day he'd left, she'd pushed herself. Striving, challenging herself, working harder and harder, until the hospital had become the only thing in her life worth a damn.

But there was always a part of me missing... and that part was Gray.

She'd never had any closure. She'd never found out the reason for his disappearance.

There were a few clues now. Maybe it was something to do with his family? Had someone warned him *not* to marry her? It certainly couldn't have been anyone from *her* family.

They'd all been so pleased for her when she'd announced their engagement.

Beau glanced at him as they walked, admiring the cut of his jaw, the stubbornness there in the line of his mouth, his tightly closed lips, his low-ered brow as he slowly led them up an incline.

And he was doing all this with a prosthetic leg! He was amazing. He was still the man she'd known all those years ago, still challenging him-self, pushing the boundaries, taking risks.

I'd be a fool to get involved with him again.

Gray held out his arm in front of her chest and Beau walked straight into it, frowning.

'Hey!'

'Shush!' He held his finger to his lips and pointed ahead through the treeline. 'Look...a herd of bison.'

Bison?

She stared hard, feeling the hairs rise on the back of her neck as the huge beasts passed them.

It was a large herd. Easily a hundred or so an-imals, maybe more. It was made up of mainly adults, as tall as her and Gray, with a few youngsters trotting alongside. They were thick, broad animals, with shaggy fur, some of it clumped, accentuating their humped backs as they ambled along, in no hurry at all. Several of them nibbled at the ground, others were snorting and looking around, keeping watch.

Instinctively Beau and Gray knelt out of sight by a large rock at the side of the trail. Beau's legs felt like jelly, but she drew on the reserves inside her that she always drew from. The reserves that had got her through sixteen-hour surgeries, nights on call and the all too numerous occasions when she'd had to sit at a family's bedside and deliver bad news, trying her hardest not to cry alongside her patients' relatives.

She'd had to stay strong. She'd made a profession out of it. Forcing herself to stay dry-eyed, forcing herself to stay on her feet, to answer one more patient call, to do one more consultation, perform one more surgery.

Shifting her feet, she glanced at Gray, excited at having seen these amazing animals up close. 'Should I take a picture?' she whispered.

'Does your camera have a flash?'

'I can switch it off.'

He nodded and she struggled to get her camera out of her fleece pocket. Once she'd deactivated the flash, she pushed herself up onto her knees and peered over the top of the rock. Breathing heavily, she used the zoom to focus in on one particular specimen that was snorting, using its tail to bat away flies as it scanned the horizon, alert for any danger.

'Wow...'

Back down behind the rock, she showed the digital picture to Gray and he smiled and whispered, 'It's good. But no more. We don't want them to know we're here.'

'Surely they can smell us?'

'Maybe. But I think we're upwind, so I'm going to go with no. Let's stay out of sight until they've passed.'

They sat with their backs to the rock and got some fluids on board.

Beau glanced at Gray. 'I don't suppose you've got another chocolate bar stashed away in those pockets?'

He smiled. 'No. Sorry.'

'Trail mix it is, then.' She rummaged in her pack for the small resealable bag and pulled it out, offering him some.

'No, thanks.'

She shrugged. 'More for me.' She ate a mouthful. Then another, savouring the taste of rich nuts and dried fruit, regretting that none of them was covered in chocolate. 'You know...you surprised me a lot the other day.'

He turned to her, an eyebrow raised in amusement. 'On which occasion?'

'The chocolate. That was my favourite bar. The kind you always used to buy me whenever you passed the shops on the way home from a shift. You said you still buy them. Why?'

Gray shifted on the hard ground, as if it had suddenly got a lot more uncomfortable in the last few seconds. 'Because...' He let out a heavy sigh. 'Every time I pass a store, every time I have to shop, I buy them. Eat them. They remind me...'

'Of me?'

He gave a smile. 'Of some happier times. I have this image in my head of you curled up in the corner of the sofa, your head buried in a pile of medical texts, nibbling away at a bar, one piece at a time, savouring each block before you ate the next. I don't know…it probably sounds stupid… but having them, eating them, makes me feel… closer to you.'

Beau stared at him, her heart thudding away in her chest. That was so sweet. That he still bought those bars. And for him to openly admit… She wondered if he would talk to her about his family, open up more if she asked.

But she didn't. This moment wasn't the right time. Now was the time for being honest—but not in that way. It was not the moment to bring up painful stuff that could turn all this on its head. And she didn't want this going wrong. They were heading in a good direction. Communicating. Opening up about little things. It was a start. And she liked it. Liked talking to him. Right now they were building bridges. They were forging new pathways ahead of them and they were doing it together. That was what was important.

So instead she smiled at him. 'We're close now.'

She reached out and took his hand, squeezing it, looking up into his eyes and feeling warmth spread within her, as if her heart was opening up and letting him in again. It was scary, but strangely, suddenly, it felt so right.

Their kiss now seemed like a dream, and she began to wonder how it would feel to kiss again—but this time when she was ready for it. Prepared. Able to appreciate it properly. Even instigate it?

Perhaps she ought to take a leaf out of Gray's book? Be daring. Take a risk. Put herself out there on the ledge. Make that leap of faith.

To where, though? Where do I want us to end up? If I kiss him, what message will that send?

Gray smiled at her, then laid his head back against the stone and closed his eyes.

I could kiss him now, but...

Something held her back. She stared at him for a moment longer and then let out a breath, the tension leaving her chest, her shoulders relaxing. Now was not the time.

They continued to wait for the herd to pass. Gray with his eyes closed, resting. Beau just watching him, taking in all the details of his face, questioning her heart's desire.

After the last of the bison had gone, they forged

onwards until they reached their checkpoint—a tree marked with a wooden first aid box. Upon opening it, as instructed, they found the extra 'luxuries' that Mack had promised them would be in there. They'd daydreamed about what they might be. Food? Chocolate, maybe? Perhaps even a small bottle of wine to celebrate?

But no. Upon opening the box they found a standard first aid kit, a roll of toilet paper and a tick remover.

'Great...maybe we can eat those?' Beau suggested wryly. 'What *is* the correct way to cook loo roll? You're meant to boil it, right?'

Gray smiled, then they got to work setting up camp for the night. He successfully lit a small fire that they edged with rocks and they ate a rather tasteless lentil broth, their thoughts drifting to dreams of the next day, when they would be back at their luxury hotels. Though even that dream was tempered by the sour note that by then they would have parted ways, and there was still so much they hadn't said...

Beau gazed through the flames to look at Gray. He was looking straight back at her, but this time she didn't look away. She held his gaze, thinking of how they'd once been with each other. The way he'd made her feel. How happy he'd made her. Before their wedding day anyway. She'd loved him so much.

She swallowed hard, determined not to cry over something she'd shed enough tears over. That had been then. This was now. They'd both changed and here they were, in the heart of Yellowstone Park, beneath the stars, sitting around a campfire, with just the sounds of crackling wood and distant insects, the air scented with woodsmoke and pine.

'At any other time I would say this is quite romantic.' She smiled.

He smiled back. 'But not this time?'

Now she felt awkward. She didn't know how she should reply. She wanted to keep the good mood. Keep the good feeling they had. She'd missed it. The *ease* of being with him. And she didn't want to let it go. She wished they were sitting closer. Not separated by the flames.

'Well.' She shrugged and grinned, feeling her cheeks flush with an inner heat. 'It's kind of awkward. Don't you think? If we were still together, we'd take full advantage of this moment… The stars, the campfire beneath the moon, just the two of us…'

He nodded, agreeing. 'But let's not forget that I promised to keep my hands to myself.'

She matched his nod. 'Yes, there's that, too.'

They stared at each other across the fire. Smiling. Breathing. Keeping eye contact.

Beau felt a strange awareness inside her. She could feel the weight of her clothes against her body. The tightness of the tops of her socks, her waistband digging into her stomach. She felt uncomfortable. Keen to move.

She stood up and nodded some more. 'I think I ought to go to bed.'

Gray stood, too. 'If that's what you think is best.'

'I do.'

There was a tense silence. The air was charged with a heat that did not come from the flames below.

Beau kept remembering the way he'd kissed her the other day. How it had felt to be back in his arms. That ease of being with him that she'd never felt with anyone else. He was so close now! So available. But was she brave enough to start something?

'Right, I'm going, then.'

'All right. Goodnight.' He slipped his hands into the pockets of his jacket, his jaw clenching and unclenching in the moonlight.

'Goodnight.' She stared at him, unwilling to walk away. Not really wanting to go to bed. Not alone. Anyway. 'Gray, I—'

She didn't get to finish her sentence.

Gray stepped forward, and for a brief moment she thought he was going to take her in his arms—but, disappointingly, he didn't. Instead he began to speak.

'We need to talk.'

Beau sucked in a breath. *Okay.* This was going to be one of those moments, wasn't it? One of those life-changing moments when your path in life forked and you could choose to go left or right.

'All right.'

He reached out and took her hand, enveloping it in both of his, gazing down at them as he stroked her skin, inhaling deeply, searching for the right words to begin.

'I need to be honest with you. If anything is to...happen...between us, then we need to be honest with each other. That's what destroyed us in the past. Secrets. I *did* want to marry you, Beau. I need to say that. Right at the start. Because you *must* believe it. I did. I wanted you to be mine for ever. I wanted to know that you'd be there for me every single day of the rest of my life. I loved you. Deeply. Do you believe me when I say that?'

She searched his face, saw the intensity in his eyes, felt the way he squeezed her hand whilst he waited for her answer. Yes. She believed him.

'I do.'

'Good. That's good. The wedding...the actual day itself...that would have been easy for me. That wasn't why I left—the pressure of the day. That wasn't the bit that worried me. It was the next part I was worried about.'

'The honeymoon?'

She didn't understand. How could he have been

worried about that part? She'd spent many a night with Gray McGregor and he certainly knew what he was doing. This man had made her body *sing*. He had made her cry out in ecstasy and shiver with delight. She'd used to lie in his arms and fall asleep, feeling secure, loved and cherished. He had been her other half. The part that had made her whole. She'd never found that since. With anyone. Connections she had made had seemed… wanting. Unreal. There'd always been something missing.

'No, not that. The *marriage* part.'

Oh. Beau frowned. She didn't understand. 'Why?'

'You were right when you said that there was something about my family you didn't know. There was something…*is* something. Even now.'

She remained silent, waiting for him to explain, but she stroked the back of his hand absentmindedly, being supportive, as much as she could be, whilst he told her his story. She was apprehensive, too. For years she'd wanted to hear his explanation, and now that it was here, well…she wasn't sure if she could bear to hear it. What if it was terrible? What if it was something sad? What if all these years he'd been hurting, too?

'When my parents first met, they were madly in love. They were like us. Young. Hopelessly enchanted with each other. All they could see was a bright future ahead of them. They thought that no matter what happened they would face it together and they would be *strong*. That's what they believed.'

She smiled at the mental image, picturing it perfectly. But her smile faltered when she remembered that something had then changed.

'But…?'

'But that didn't happen. They got married, yes, but they were poor. Jobs were scarce. My mother got a job in a factory, part-time, just as she learnt she was pregnant with me. My father was working as a mechanic in a garage, fixing and tending buses for the council. He worked incredibly long hours. She hardly saw him. But he had to work to bring in the money. Especially when she stopped working to have me.'

She nodded, understanding their financial struggle. Even though it wasn't anything she'd experienced herself, she had seen it in others. 'It must have been difficult for them.'

This was all new information for Beau. She'd known almost nothing about Gray's family. Just that his father was in a wheelchair, paralysed from the waist down, and that his mother hardly spoke, her face for ever shut in a pinched, tight-lipped, sour way. Their early years together sounded like a tough time.

'It was. And I was a difficult bairn. Mum found it hard to cope. Dad couldn't help—he was always at work. When he got home late each evening, he was exhausted, barely having enough energy to eat before collapsing into bed each night.'

She squeezed his hand.

'Mum begged him to help more at home, but he had no time. He was afraid that if he took time off work he'd lose his job, and they couldn't afford that. She started taking in sewing and ironing to earn a few extra pennies, and they simply began living separate lives. I had colic. I barely slept, apparently. Crying all the time and nothing would soothe me. My mother felt like a single parent. They became true ships that passed only in the night.'

She felt his pain but wondered what this had to do with *their* relationship. 'What happened?'

'I don't know... My mum would bad-mouth him to me all the time. Say that he was useless, that he was a waste of space. He wound her up. The way he was never there. The way he irritated her when he *was*. The way he never lifted a finger to help her at the weekends. She even suspected there might be something with another woman. The receptionist at the garage. I didn't know if he was having an affair, but my dad would go on at me the same way. Say that my mother was a harridan, a nag, that she couldn't leave a hard-working man in peace.'

Beau felt uncomfortable. How awful that must have been—to be stuck between two warring parents. The two people you relied on and loved most in the whole world.

'Their verbal battles sometimes got physical. He didn't hit her or anything, but they both threw things. The soundtrack to my childhood was yelling and hearing ceramics hitting the walls. I even ended up at the doctors once, after accidentally treading on something sharp that had been missed in the clear-up afterwards.'

He let out a deep breath and his face brightened just slightly.

'That was where I began to love medicine. It was the only place where I'd been tended with real care and compassion.'

His eyes darkened again.

'My parents hated each other. Despised each other. The slightest thing would set them off. A look. The way the other one chewed their food. Whether they snored. Anything. And I was left as a go-between. Used like some pawn in a battle that I didn't understand. Then one day my mum decided she'd had enough. She packed her bags and waited for him to come home so she could tell him she was leaving.'

Beau was shocked. 'Without you?'

He nodded. 'The time he should have been home came and went. She got furious because she thought he'd gone to the pub with the other woman, spending money we couldn't spare on booze, and said that he was preventing her from giving him the performance of a lifetime. She'd planned on telling him once and for all how he was a good-for-nothing husband and she was leaving, But then the phone rang. He'd had an accident. A bad one.'

Beau felt sick. 'The one that paralysed him?'

He nodded again. 'A bus had come off a raised ramp and rolled over him, crushing his spine and pelvis. I'll never forget the look on my mother's face as she heard the news. Shock...disbelief... and then a deep sadness. Resignation. We went to the hospital, but he was in surgery. The nurses were very good to me—loving, caring. It was there I decided I wanted to be like them. Nothing like my parents. I wanted to become a doctor. We learnt later that Dad was paralysed.'

Beau could picture it all. The shock of the accident. The complete one-eighty that Gray's mother must have had to do...

'And then your mother felt she *couldn't* leave?'

'That's right. She unpacked her things whilst he was in the hospital and I've never seen a sadder woman since. They just get on with things now. She helps him. Cares for him. But they barely talk. They just exist in the same house. Despite what had happened, what they'd gone through together, they've become more separate. Their marriage has become a prison. Each is saddled with the other for eternity. And to think they once loved each other so much...'

He couldn't look at her, his eyes downcast, lost in the painful past.

She was silent for a moment. Taking it all in. What had happened to his parents was awful. The way their relationship had crumbled under tough times. The accident... The paralysis... The way his mother must have felt obligated to stay... The way his father must have felt, stuck with a nursemaid wife he could barely tolerate speaking to...

'That's horrible, Gray. And I can't believe I'm only hearing about it *now*. Why didn't you tell me before?'

He looked at her then, sadness in his eyes. 'I've *never* known them to be happy, Beau! Not *once* can I see, in any part of my memory, either one of them smiling, or laughing, or being happy! I grew up in a dark, stormy world, full of crazed arguments, broken china and tense silences you'd need a machete to cut through! I loved being at school because I was *away* from them. I stayed away from home as much as I could because it was the only way I could be happy—without *them* dragging me down, dragging me into their battles. And when I met *you*...my sweet, beautiful Beau...I couldn't believe that a man and a woman could be so happy together! You were a breath of fresh air to me—the first hint of spring after a lifetime of bitter, endless winter...'

She could hear that he was trying to explain how he'd felt when he'd met her...but he'd *left* her. Surely it couldn't be true that their perfect future had been ruined because of what had happened to his *parents*?

'But, Gray, how could you have left me because of *them*...?'

Beau stared up at him, tears burning her eyes. Her hurt, her humiliation from all those years ago came flooding back again. The pain was fresh once more. All those years she'd thought there'd been something wrong with *her*. Something she'd been lacking. Something missing that had made him walk away. Maybe into the arms of another woman? And she'd racked her brains, trying to think of how she could have been *more* so that he would have stayed. Had pushed herself ever since, trying to prove that he'd been wrong to walk away and give her up.

'Gray, I'm sorry your parents had an awful time, but it hurts to see that you let that impact *us*. So your parents gave you a bad example...? Mine gave me a *great* example of what marriage could be.' She smiled through her tears. 'They still do. After all this time. Are you saying that my experience of *my* parents' marriage is wrong? *Why* couldn't you believe in a happy marriage? With their example?'

He shook his head. 'Because your family was the exception to the rule. Everywhere I looked I saw married couples barely getting along. Couples who had nothing to say to each other after many years. Couples who could only talk about their children. Couples who did things separately. Who took time apart, holidayed on their own. Couples who looked like all joy of life had left them.'

'You thought that would happen to *us*?'

She almost couldn't believe it. His parents' story was tragic, and she felt for him that he had been trapped in it. But that had been his parents' pain. Not *theirs*. She and Gray had been happy. Strong.

'I feared things would end up that way. Because I couldn't be honest with you about this before we got married, so what you saw in me was a lie. I was a lie. *We* were a lie. We wouldn't have survived! I accept the fact that leaving you at the church like that was a cowardly thing to do, and I should have turned up to tell you to your face that I was leaving. But at the time I was so racked with guilt, so broken in two at knowing that I *had* to walk away from you—away from the woman I truly loved so that I didn't take her into a tortured future—that I wasn't thinking clearly. So I'm sorry I left you at the altar, Beau, but if I hadn't, then you would have left *me*. At some point.'

'I would *never* have left you.'

Tears flowed freely down her cheeks now. His pain was so raw. His suffering so real she couldn't imagine how he had managed to keep it so contained. And how had she not known? How had she not noticed?

'I should have pushed for more. I should have made you tell me back then. We could have avoided this.'

'We couldn't. Because we were based on a fantasy. *You* thought we were perfect.' A pained look crossed his face. He didn't want to hurt her. 'We *weren't*. I couldn't tell you because you didn't want to hear it. You didn't ask about *me*. All you could see was the romance and the fun and the laughter.' He stared hard at her. 'You didn't want the reality of me. You were so caught up in the wedding preparations you couldn't see what was right in front of your eyes.'

Her cheeks were wet. She could feel the drips of her tears falling from her jawline. 'What? Are you saying that I…I *failed* you somehow? That I didn't listen? That I didn't give you the chance to tell me what you needed to say?'

It hurt to think he might believe that. *Had* she been at fault?

'I wasn't ready, Beau. I had doubts. A real

fear as to what awaited us in the future.' He sighed heavily, as if worn down by the argument. 'I wanted to love you for ever, Beau. I really did. But I knew it couldn't happen. Unless we were honest. You weren't ready to hear that, so I walked away.'

She looked out across the plateau at the mountains in the distance, now dark with greying shadow as the sun set. The sky was filled with glorious tones of orange and pink. It all looked so pretty. So wonderful. But how could this sunset be so beautiful? So warm? There were blooming flowers in the distance. The crackle and pop of burning wood and the scent of woodsmoke drifting past them. The last of the day's bird chorus slowly fading to nothing.

Was she also to blame for their relationship failing in the way that it had? And if that was the case, didn't she need to take some of the responsibility for everything that had gone wrong? For the fact that what they'd had in the past had all been *fake*?

She pulled her fleece jacket around her. 'I loved you. That part was real...'

She looked away, her bottom lip trembling. She feared that maybe he'd never loved her. That their relationship had never been what she'd thought it was. She tried to pull her hands free of his, tried to separate herself from him, acknowledging that she had somehow always imagined things wrongly. That their past relationship had been some sort of dreamworld she'd been living in. Had she been deluding herself that he loved her?

But Gray wouldn't let her get away. He held on tight, pulling her back and making her look him in the eyes.

'I loved you, too. More than *life*! And I refused to put you through that. I refused to let us go blindly into the future with you thinking that everything was fine when I knew that it wasn't.'

'Our love was real?' Her bottom lip trembled.

He nodded and pressed his lips to her forehead before looking down at her. 'It was. I couldn't lie about that.'

'But—'

'Beau, look at me.'

She looked up at him with eyes glistening from salty tears, with her heart almost torn in two by the heartbreak of knowing that she'd caused him pain and that she'd kept him *silent*. Unable to tell her what he needed. She so badly wanted to put that right. So she would listen to him now. Hear what he had to say.

'Yes?'

He stared deeply into her eyes, as if searching for something. 'We had something special, but it wasn't our time then.'

'Is it our time now?' she asked, with hope in her heart.

Gray swallowed, cupping her face, his hands so tender, warm and soft, and then he took another step towards her, breathing heavily, lowering his head until their hungry lips met.

She sank into his embrace. Against his hard, solid body. Tasting him, enjoying him, her hands up in his hair, grasping him, pulling him towards her, desperate for his touch. Remembering, recalling *this*—how good it had always felt to be with him. How special.

Their past was forgotten in that instant.

She *needed* Gray. Had missed him so much it was painful. But now he was back in her arms and it felt so good. She didn't want to let him go. She wanted to enjoy the moment, and to hell with the consequences, because right now she needed this. *Him.* It didn't matter what he'd said. All that pain he'd shared. Because *this*—this was what was important. Being with him. Reconnecting.

Her fingers fell to the hemline of his top and she began to lift it, to pull it over his head, so that her hands could feel the touch of his skin, his broad shoulders, his taut chest, that flat stomach she remembered so well. His sleeve caught on his chunky wristwatch and she had to give it a yank, but then it was gone, discarded.

For a moment she just looked at him, taking in the beauty of his body, the solidity of his muscles, his powerful frame, and then she was pulling off her own top, kissing him again as he unclipped her bra in a fervour. She wriggled her arms so it would fall to the forest floor. Gasped as his hands cupped her breasts and brought them to his lips. So in need for the feel of his hot lips against her skin.

The touch of his tongue tantalised her, causing her to gasp and bite her lip. She felt as if she was on fire. Her whole body a burning ember. A delicious liquid heat seared from her centre right through her body, inflaming every nerve ending, every sensation, every caress, stroke or lick, driving her insane with need.

'I want you, Gray.' She made him look at her as she spoke, wanting him to know in no uncertain terms what she wanted him to do.

He stared back into her heavy eyes and nodded, then took a step away from her.

She almost cried out, fearing that he was going to stop, leave her in her fevered state, that he was going to humiliate her just as she'd laid herself bare.

But no. He was grabbing a groundsheet, a blanket, and then he took her hand and pulled her towards it.

Hungry for him, hungry for more, she moved to him and felt the core of her burning with need as his fingers began to unbutton her trousers. Hurriedly she kicked off her boots, then her trousers were cast aside, and she hopped from one foot to the other as she removed her socks, before throwing herself back into the safety, security and heat of his embrace.

She wasn't cold. It was a perfect summer's evening. The air on her body felt like a lover's caress in itself, and there was something thrilling about that. As Gray lowered her gently onto the blanket, his hand drifted up the length of her thigh and then delicately began to stroke the thin lace of her underwear before reaching down to feel the heat between her legs.

Yes! Touch me there...

She breathed heavily, her eyes open, gazing upwards at the stars, as she felt his fingertips drift lazily over her body, felt his gaze roaming the expanse of her nakedness, his lips tenderly kissing the underside of her breast, then her waist, her belly button.

And then... Then his mouth drifted downwards, towards the lace, towards the place she wanted him the most.

Beau closed her eyes, her hands gripping his hair, and gasped.

* * *

They slept under the same canvas that night. Naked, entwined, they lay together, his body wrapped around hers, until sleep and exhaustion claimed them.

Gray woke first. He was glad. It gave him a chance to put his prosthetic back on. Beau hadn't really seen him without it yet, and after what they'd shared last night, he didn't want to spoil what had happened with the sight of his stump over breakfast.

He'd grown used to it. Accepted it. But still, sometimes when he saw it, he remembered what his leg had looked like before, what it had felt like to be whole, and he hated the reminder.

He could spare Beau that, at least. Hadn't he shown her enough last night? He'd hurt her with his words. With his confession. He knew it deeply. He'd seen it in her eyes. She'd started to question herself. Look back. He'd hated seeing her pain, but maybe now, after last night, they could move forward?

Their relationship had died a death before because he'd never been honest with her about his family. About his fears of what might happen to them if they married. But last night...last night had been *amazing* and he wanted that to continue. For them to be together again. He and Beau were a good match.

His finger gently swept up the length of her bare arm and he smiled as she groaned slightly and shifted in her sleep, pressing her body against him.

The length of her, naked and warm, was nuzzled into him, and he looked down at her face, soft in repose against his shoulder.

Why had he ever listened to that infernal internal voice? To the voice of logic and reason that had kept niggling away at him? Telling him it would all go wrong, that they would end up behaving exactly like his parents' in a toxic marriage.

Thinking of his parents made him remember his father at his stag party, when he'd said, 'You'll regret it. You mark my words, son, you're about to ruin both your lives...'

He grimaced, refusing to hear those words again. He was not going to let thoughts of his

father's bitterness ruin what he had at this moment. This perfect moment—holding the woman
he had once loved so much in his arms.

Could we start again with a clean slate?

His heart agonised over the possibility.

But he didn't have long to argue with himself.

Beau blinked open her eyes and smiled as she
looked up at him. 'Morning.'

'Good morning. Sleep well?'

'I did. The first time in ages. You?'

He nodded. He *had* slept well. And he was in
no doubt that it was down to being with Beau. He
didn't want to move. Didn't want this moment to
end. Could they possibly lie here for ever?

'Would you like breakfast?'

She smiled and gave him a brief kiss. 'Depends
what's on the menu.'

He laughed and pulled her onto him, feeling his
body spring into life for her once more. 'I think
I could possibly find something a bit more interesting than oatmeal.'

Beau grinned. 'Really? I—' She stopped, tilt-
ing her head at a funny angle. 'Can you hear
that?'

He wasn't sure he wanted to listen to anything. But to humour her he remained silent and tried to listen. He could hear birds singing and… He squinted and sat upright, his hands still holding Beau to him. Was that…*snuffling*?

'Stay here.'

He slid Beau to one side of him and pulled on his trousers and then, hurriedly, his socks and boots. Quietly he slid the zip down on the tent and looked out. There was nothing he could see in front of the tent. He popped his head back in-side.

'I don't think there's anything there, but just to be on the safe side get dressed and we'll go and take a look.'

The snuffling noise was definitely there, and it sounded as if it was *behind* the tent, where they couldn't see without stepping outside.

Gray didn't think it was a mountain lion, and wolves were dawn and dusk creatures. It was now—he glanced at his wristwatch—nearly eight in the morning. When Beau was dressed and had put her boots on, he took her hand and then slowly stepped out, peering over the top of the tent.

And froze.

Behind him Beau was crouched, unable to see what was happening. 'What is it?'

'It's…er…something.'

Beau pushed past the tent flap and came out of the tent to peer past Gray. The second she saw the herd of bison she also froze, feeling her blood run cold.

Mack had warned them. Bison were dangerous. They'd seen that herd last night—they should have *thought*, should have considered that they might still be in the area. But they hadn't. They'd had…*other things* on their minds.

'Gray, what do we do?' she asked in a whisper.

There was nowhere for them to go. The bison herd filled the whole plateau around them. The only place for them to go was the cliff edge.

Where a river ran far below.

About a forty-foot drop.

Gray turned slowly to look at her. 'The tent won't protect us, and these animals can be dangerous.'

'Perhaps they don't even know we're here!'

Gray glanced over and caught the eye of a bull,

which peered at them, snorting through its nose. Was he the leader of the pack?

Gray watched in silent dread as the tail of the bison began to rise.

'It's going to charge!'

'*What?*'

'We need to jump.'

'Please tell me you're joking.'

'Nope.'

He grabbed her hand in his and made a quick run to the cliff edge, where they stopped to look over at the drop.

It was dizzyingly high. Precipitous. And he could feel the pull of gravity as he looked over the edge. He was used to heights. To climbing. To the risk of a fall. But Beau wasn't, and he needed her to jump without hesitating.

A quick glance back at the bison told him it was starting to head their way. Without doubt the animal was going to charge them. Protect its herd. There was nowhere else to go.

'On three...'

'Gray...' She gripped his arm in fright.

'One...two...*three*!'

He held her hand tight and took a leap off the edge, feeling her jump with him, hearing her scream filling the air as they fell, with the water rushing up to meet them.

CHAPTER EIGHT

HER SENSES WENT into overload. Her scream was whipped away by the passing air as she looked down at the terrifying sight of the water rushing up to meet her.

She was falling fast. The air rushed past her mouth before she had time to inhale, her stomach was rising into her chest cavity, and her limbs were flailing madly, trying to find something—anything—to grab on to in mid-air. But of course there was nothing. It was terrifying.

I'm going to die!

The river that had at one point seemed so far away was getting disturbingly close, and then suddenly, *splash*! Her body hit the water, which smacked her in the face as if she'd just been hit by a heavyweight boxer, making her gasp. Water flooded her mouth, her nostrils, her ears, as she struggled against it. Her body stung from the impact, every nerve ending screaming, but somehow there was an even more important agony she had to contend with—the need for oxygen.

It hurt to look about under the water, and all she could see beside her and below were dark shadows, whereas above her there was light. Sparkling sunlight glittering on a surface that didn't seem that far away. She began to swim, her lungs stretched to breaking point.

And just when she thought she wouldn't make it, just when she thought the surface of the water had just been a mirage, she broke the surface, coughing and spluttering as she gasped for air and tried not to swallow more water.

Inhaling deeply and quickly, wiping her wet hair out of her face, she trod water, turning and twisting, trying to get her bearings.

Where was Gray?

He suddenly popped out of the water next to her, his hair plastered over his forehead, looking for her, and he gave a relieved smile when he saw she was right next to him. 'You okay?'

'I'm all right. Are you okay?'

He nodded and looked up. 'Can you believe that? We did it!'

She blew water from her lips and nodded. Yes, they had done it. And now she was treading water in her clothes and the water was colder than it looked.

She could see a bank further downstream, where they'd be able to crawl out and get on dry land, and she pointed at it. 'Over there.'

She tried to swim, trying to remember how to coordinate her limbs for the breaststroke. The current wasn't too strong and she made it easily, clambering from the water like a sodden sheep, the weight of her clothes dragging her down, cold and shivering.

Slumping onto the ground, she turned to wait for Gray, who crawled from the water beside her before flopping onto his back and letting out an exhausted breath.

Beau swallowed hard and lay back against the dirt, exhausted. There was probably mud getting in her hair, but she didn't care.

I jumped off a cliff!

'I can't believe we did that.'

He turned to look at her and grinned. 'Well, we did. You did great.'

Her gaze drifted to the clifftop, where their camp had been. 'All our things are still up there.'

Gray nodded and let out another sigh. 'But the most important thing is down here. With me.'

She met his gaze and smiled, and then she rolled towards him and planted a kiss on his lips. 'Thank you.'

'What for?'

'Saving our lives.'

'I made you jump off a cliff.'

'Yes. But as we are *not* currently a bison's breakfast, I'd still call that a save.'

Gray frowned. 'I don't think bison *eat* people.'

'Maybe not, but they sure as hell can flatten you if they want, and I don't know about you, but I quite like to have my body in full working order.'

Gray looked away and then sat up, running his hand down his left leg towards his prosthetic.

Oh. I shouldn't have said that. I didn't think.

She bit her lip. 'Sorry.'

'It's fine.' Gray got to his feet, testing it out. 'Still works.'

She stood up beside him, looking around them. The river flowed downstream away from them and on either side were gorse bushes and trees and mountains rising high. 'Are we lost?'

He looked at her briefly before turning, scanning their surroundings for himself. 'I don't think so. If I remember correctly, Heart Lake is fed into by this river. If we follow it we should make it back to the ranger station in a few hours.'

She nodded. 'Okay. Should we try and find water, or do you think we can make it without?'

'It's getting warm, but we should be fine if we keep a steady pace.'

She bit her lip and he reached out a hand to grab hers.

'Hey, we'll be fine.'

Beau hoped he was right.

Gray trudged on, leading the way. Apart from being hungry and thirsty, he wasn't sure what to feel. Last night had been bittersweet. He and Beau had become close again last night! And though he'd loved every second of it, he still wasn't sure they'd resolved anything by this morning. Kissing her, then making love to her, had distracted their thoughts, and though he had wanted to lie in her arms for many more hours, enjoying that blissful moment when it had seemed the rest of the world had stopped turning, he'd been well aware that the issues between them were still there.

Jumping off that cliff with her, her hand in his... He remembered with a cold shudder how it had felt to hit the water, to feel his prosthetic weigh him down. He had struggled to swim, to get to the surface. Beau had let go of him and for a moment—a brief, terrifying moment—he'd thought she'd been swept downstream. Until he'd broken the surface and seen her there next to him. Safe.

But only just. How could he look out for Beau when he could barely survive himself?

If he had a magic lamp and he could make a wish, then he'd wish for a long, happy life with Beau. No doubt about that. But...

What could he offer her now? He'd told her the truth at long last, there was that, so they had honesty now—and, yes, there was still that intense heat between them. But relationships had to be more than just sex. There had to be trust, intimacy, love, compassion. There had to be give and take. Compromise. Teamwork. They had to be a unit. A solid couple. He had to feel as if he could protect her and love her in the way she deserved. In the way she wanted. She *needed* that happy-ever-after, but was he the man who could give it to her?

Did he deserve another chance with her?

They didn't live near each other. They each had a career in different parts of the country. They each worked really long hours. Beau had her family in Oxford—his were in Edinburgh. What did he have to give Beau apart from their painful, disappointing past? And although she'd said his leg didn't bother her, it *did* bother him. He wanted to be perfect for her. Whole. If she took him on, she'd be taking on his leg. The phantom pains he still got…the possibility of getting early osteoarthritis in his good knee because of the amputation. She had to accept that he was disabled—like his father.

Did she deserve that? Want that? There were so many men out there who had all four functioning limbs and hadn't hurt her in the way that he had. Men who hadn't let her down.

He didn't want to burden Beau the way his own mother had been burdened—with a disabled man whom she'd grow to resent.

He knew that she wanted him. He'd seen it in her eyes. In the way she'd listened to him reveal his soul and the way she'd looked as they'd made love. She had feelings for him still—he could see it. And he couldn't deny the way he was feeling about her.

The only problem was he wasn't sure if they should pursue it. Because if they gave things another go and it all went wrong, the heartache of losing her again would be too much.

Not worth going through for anything.

Perhaps walking away would be the kindest thing after all?

Around them Yellowstone Park was glorious, dressed in its summer colours: bright blue skies, wispy white clouds drifting past, trees adorned with many greens, from the darkest pine to the lightest willow, blue-white columbines attracting butterflies of every shape and size amongst the yellow cinquefoil flowers like buttercups.

They ambled through the landscape together, breathing heavily under the oppressive heat, until around midday, when Beau had to stop and sit down. Collapsing to the floor, she sucked in oxygen, exhausted. She was as thirsty as anything, her mouth dry as dust.

When had she *ever* felt this spent? She'd been on her feet for only a few hours. She'd had much longer shifts in hospital. But at least then she'd had access to drinks. The river trickling alongside them almost seemed to mock her. All that water...

All that campylobacter. All that giardia. Drink that and you certainly will be in hospital. With sickness and diarrhoea.

She swallowed and tried not to think of a nice cold glass of iced water. Instead she decided to focus on something much better. The fact that she and Gray had grown close again. That they'd overcome the barrier of their past. Gray had shared his concerns and fears. They'd made love under a starry sky and she'd slept in his arms and felt happy again for the first time in an age.

After everything, it seemed things were going *right* for her with Gray, and she'd thought she'd never be able to say that. *Ever.* Yet here they were. Together. Supporting each other, protecting each other, looking out for each other. This was what couples did. They worked as a team. They were strong. United.

Her feelings for him were very strong. She still loved him. She knew it in her heart. She'd been struggling against it ever since she'd walked into the ranger station just a few days ago. Her love for him had never gone away and he was the only man who could make her feel this way.

Last night had been a revelation. A new chapter for them both. She'd been grateful for his honesty. For his making clear that which had been blurry. Explaining the pain. Explaining his reasons for walking away.

It had hurt to feel that she'd been to blame for some of it, but truth sometimes did hurt. She'd listened to it, acknowledged it. Accepted it. *Some of it was my fault.* But then they'd slept together and he'd held her in his arms, and she'd felt so good to be there. She just *knew* she could never let that go again.

'Do you think there's much further to go?'

He ran a hand through his hair. 'Couple of miles, maybe. Not far.'

'We might run into the others soon. They might have water! You know…if they didn't have to jump off a cliff.'

He smiled at her. 'Maybe.'

'I'm glad I'm here with you, Gray. Doing this. It wouldn't have been the same without you. Us meeting again. Getting close again. Opening up. It's been good for us, don't you think?'

Gray nodded and looked about them. 'Ready to go again?'

She stood and slipped her hand into his, surprising him. 'I'm ready.'

He said nothing, just started to walk.

Then, within the hour, they met some familiar faces.

CHAPTER NINE

BARB AND CONRAD waved to them and they hurried over to meet up with the older married couple, who both looked quite fresh and not at all trail-weary.

The two women hugged and the men patted each other on the back—until Barb frowned and looked at them both. 'Where's your gear?'

Beau grinned at Gray. 'A bison took it.'

'Oh! Really?'

'We woke this morning and we were surrounded. One started to charge and we had to jump into a river to escape.'

Barb looked at her husband. 'You weren't hurt? Con, get these people some water.'

But Con was already doing that, and he handed over their flasks to let them both take a long, refreshing drink.

'Oh, wow—that tastes so good!' Beau wiped her mouth and handed it back, but Con waved it away.

'You keep it. We're nearly back to the ranger station. Look over there—through the trees. See that strip of blue? That's Heart Lake.'

Beau squinted and shielded her eyes—and, yes! There it was! They'd made it back, safe and sound, and their friends were okay, too.

Barb threaded her arm into Beau's and walked with her, whilst Gray walked behind them with Con.

'So how did you two get on?' she asked.

Beau smiled and nodded. 'It was good. I think it might just be okay for us.'

'Oh, honey, I'm so pleased to hear that! You two look made for each other.'

It felt good to hear someone else say that. It reinforced everything that Beau had been thinking. She'd made some mistakes in the past. She'd taken Gray's feelings for granted. Had not given him the opportunity to share how he truly felt. She'd been caught up in her romantic tale of love, of how they'd had the romance of the century, but none of it had been true. Well, almost none. They *had* loved each other. But the foundations of their relationship had been shaky.

She'd not known the full truth about her then husband-to-be, but now she did. She'd been so busy trying to have what her parents had that she hadn't realised that he'd been trying to steer them away from what *his* parents had.

But it's settled now. We're nearly back to civilisation. We can make this work. Somehow.

She supposed they'd have to travel to see each other at first. Maybe one of them could try to get a job in the other's hospital. There was always a need for a good neurologist or cardiologist. Then, being close, they could work on just being together again. It was scary—being back with Gray, taking a risk—but it felt *right*. As if she was home.

The brain had two hemispheres and there were connections—neural pathways that connected the two, making the brain a whole so that it worked to perfection. Being separated from Gray had been like having only one hemisphere. She could survive, but there were deficits. She'd known something was missing. That she wasn't whole.

Now they were coming back together and everything was slowly becoming *right*.

The rest of the group began to emerge from different directions as they got closer and closer to the ranger station. Seeing each other's faces brought comfort and joy, and when they were all back together again, they walked into the ranger station with the biggest grins on their faces. Their happiness in their joint achievement filled the room with its glow as they each told their stories—the funny moments, the scary moments. How they'd survived.

Beau listened to it all, her heart full.

As the chatter died down, Mack congratulated them all on getting back safe and sound, and after a quick debrief they all started to decamp. To gather their things and get ready to catch the minibus that would take them back to Gallatin and their own cars. Where they would all part ways.

Seeing as Beau didn't have any gear to sort through, she located Gray and waited for him to end his conversation with Toby and Allan. The guys were promising to keep in touch.

Afterwards, when they'd left, he turned to her and smiled. 'You okay?'

'I'm good! I'm great, actually. Looking forward to getting back to my hotel and changing my clothes. Taking a hot shower. I thought that maybe you'd like to join me?'

It was forward, she knew, but she wanted this good feeling to continue. To make sure he knew they could work on this relationship and make it succeed this time. Now she knew what he had feared, what he'd worried about before, they could move on.

But Gray's face was blank. 'I'll be heading back to my own hotel. I've got a flight to catch tomorrow and I'd like to get some rest.'

Oh.

'Are you sure? I thought that we—'

'This isn't what you deserve, Beau.' He lowered his voice and moved her away from the others. '*I'm* not. I can't love you the way you want me to. I think it's best if we close the door on what we had and just move on.'

Beau stared at him, feeling sick. Was he really saying this? But they'd shared so much!

How could I have read you so wrong?

Gray walked away from her once more, his feet leaden, his heart weary. Every step he took became more and more painful as he increased the distance between them.

It was tempting. So tempting to turn around and go back to her, give her what she wanted, but he couldn't. He needed to get away from her. Create some space. He couldn't think when he was this close to her. He couldn't think when she looked at him like that. With *love* in her eyes.

It was like stepping back in time. Right back to where they started! Surely she could see that he was doing this for both of them?

'Gray!' She grabbed his arm and spun him round. 'What are you *doing*?'

'We're still in the same place. It's eleven years on, and we're in a different country, but we're still stuck in the same place!'

'No. It's different now.'

'Is it? You still see the sweetness and light in

everything. Despite what I've told you. Despite knowing I can't protect you. Can't love you the way that you need. Can't offer you anything but a disabled partner who sure as hell doesn't deserve a second chance.'

'It won't be that way—'

He pulled his arm free. 'Please, Beau! I can't think when you touch me! I can't think with you around. It's too much. Believe me, it's better this way.'

'For who? For *you*? Because it isn't easy for *me*!'

'I just…need some space. Please, Beau, will you let it go? I can't be who you need.'

She looked up at him with sadness. 'Who are *you* to know who I need?'

He couldn't speak then. He couldn't reply. He couldn't *think*. Seeing the tears fall from her eyes was so hard. But what could he do? The feelings that had resurfaced when they'd made love had shaken him. He wasn't prepared for this! He'd expected to apologise, he'd expected her to listen grudgingly, but so much else had happened. Emotions were getting involved again—love and longing, hurt and pain. He couldn't see what he needed to do.

Gray needed her to go.

Gritting his teeth, he turned his back on her and waited for her to walk away.

He hadn't sat next to her on the bus. It had been like a slap in the face. Instead he'd walked past her and gone to sit at the back with Dean and Rick.

So she'd sat there alone, behind the driver, trying her hardest not to turn around and look at him in case everyone else saw the heartbreak on her face.

Where had it gone so wrong?

They'd talked. They'd made love. That night had been exquisite. The sensations he had made her feel had made her…euphoric. He'd been tender, caring, passionate. They'd lain together afterwards, entwined. He'd smiled at her that morning, had kissed her—he'd seemed fine. They'd jumped off that cliff. Survived the fall without injury. Got out of the river without being swept away. They'd both been so happy and exhilarated at what had happened, and then...

He'd gone a little quiet on the trek back—but then again, they both had! They'd been thirsty. Talking had just seemed to make her mouth drier. But whilst she'd allowed herself to think everything was different, had got carried away with imagining the glorious future they could have, he'd been thinking...what?

'I'm not what you deserve. I can't love you the way you want me to.'

How was it *his* choice to decide what she deserved? She deserved *him*! He was her soulmate. Her better half. Her match. In every way. She *needed* him.

She loved him.

Did I do it again? Did I get carried away with a romantic fantasy?

Maybe he was right. Maybe he *could* see right through her. Perhaps he was right not to rush into anything? Could he see that she was falling into old habits?

'I can't love you the way you want me to.'

She just wanted to be loved by *him*. He was the

only man who would do. Who would fulfil the need she felt every day. To be touched by him. Loved by him. Held in his arms. She'd had eleven years to realise she wouldn't be able to find that with anyone else. Not the way she felt when she was with Gray. That sense of completeness.

When he got off the bus, if he left without her, he would be taking her heart with him.

Beau wiped away a tear and looked out of the window.

The minibus trundled along the park's roads, past sights they hadn't seen. Glaciers. Geysers. She saw some elk, and high above some birds circling on the thermals in the blue skies. The raw beauty of the place hurt her eyes. It was too beautiful to look at when she felt so ravaged, so she closed her eyes and laid her head against the window, allowing the motion of the vehicle to rock her to sleep.

She dreamed. She dreamed that she was in the water again, after the jump, and that she'd just exploded to the surface, gasping for air, looking about her for Gray. Eventually his head popped up out of the water, further downstream, and though she called for him, though she waved to show him where she was, he simply got washed downstream, disappearing from sight...

She woke with a jerk, sitting bolt upright, aware that people were getting off the bus. Looking outside, she could see the car park of the Gallatin Ranger Station, and over to her right her rental car. Had it been only five days since she'd parked it there? So much had happened...

Beau stood up, determined to speak to Gray, to not let him get away without a word as he had once before. She turned around to face the back of the bus, where he'd been sitting.

He was gone.

She looked out at the others, still gathering their bags from the bus's storage compartments, but he wasn't there, either.

Beau clambered down the steps and grabbed Barb's sleeve. 'Where's Gray?'

'I think he went into the ranger station, honey. You have a good sleep?'

She didn't answer. She raced for the station, blasting through its doors and scanning the room, then darting past the receptionist into the room in which she'd first seen him. He had to be there! He had to be with Mack or someone.

But the room was empty.

She shot back outside to check the toilets, but they were empty, too. Desperate now, she headed back to the receptionist. 'Has Gray McGregor been in?'

'He collected his car keys just a few minutes ago. I think he's gone.'

No!

She darted outside, aware that the others were looking at her strangely, but not caring. All that mattered was finding Gray. She couldn't see him in the car park and there was no car leaving. Had he already left? Had she missed him?

As Rick passed her, she grabbed his arm. 'What hotel was Gray staying at? Did he mention it?'

'Sorry, Beau, he didn't.'

'But he gave you his number? To keep in touch?'

'Yeah, but it's a UK number.'

'Not his mobile?'

'His cell? No, sorry.'

She almost cried out. How could this be happening? How could he do this to her again?

She stood in the middle of the car park for ages. Con and Barb picked up their car and waved to her as they passed by, as did the others. She stared at nothing. Thought of nothing but her loss as the cars drove past her, some tooting their horns.

She didn't move until her bladder began to scream at her. Only then did she slowly plod over to the bathroom and relieve herself, before going into the station and collecting her car keys and belongings.

The luxury of the car felt wrong. The leather seats, the air conditioning. That new car smell. It all seemed so false. So manufactured. She'd become used to nature in that short week. The fresh, warm air. The smell of pine—*real* pine. Not that stuff that was made in a factory and created from chemicals.

She started the engine and entered the address details for her hotel into the GPS system, began to drive. She drove almost on autopilot, getting back to her hotel, barely remembering the drive at all.

When she'd checked in to her room, she dropped her keys onto the dresser and turned on the shower, shedding clothes in slow motion, feeling as if she was moving through thick treacle, stepping under the warm spray and closing her eyes, trying to feel nothing. Trying not to think.

But it all became too much.

And she sank into the corner of the shower and began to cry.

His hotel room was a world away from the last week's experience. Had it really been just a week? The room, though familiar, looked empty—dry of life. Not real. A false environment. A place that was meant to make him feel as if he were at home, but was so false it almost made him feel sick to be there.

Home was where Beau was.

It always had been. And it had ripped him apart to walk away. Again. But how could he throw himself into their relationship? He loved her. With all his heart and more. But he wasn't *right* for her. If they tried to make it work, one of them would have to give up their career at their current hospital and move. That bit might not be so bad, but what about when the thrill of being back together again wore off? What happened when reality sank in? What if they decided to have children?

He couldn't do it.

All that time, all those eleven years he'd spent away from her, he'd struggled to feel satisfied or happy with anything. And finding Beau again, in Yellowstone, of all places, had made him realise just what he'd been missing.

She had always had his heart. From that very first day when he'd spotted her at medical school—that gorgeous, long-limbed, elegant woman with the flaming red hair—his breath had been taken from him. He'd tried to use his old, familiar chat-up lines and they'd had no effect on her. She'd laughed them off, almost disappointed by his attempt at using them. And so he'd tried a different tactic.

He'd been as genuine as he could. He'd listened to her. Studied with her. Helped her revise. He'd been content with just *being* with her. Basking in her glow. Enjoying the warmth that she'd created in his cold, empty heart. The first time he'd kissed her... Well, that had been something else!

After that he'd been unable to tear himself away from her. Beau had been his bright star, his happiness. His joy. His deep love. He'd never known it was possible to love another person so much. Whenever they'd been apart, he'd thought of her. Whenever he'd been on a day shift and she on a night shift, and they'd met like ships in the dawn of the early morning, their time together had been too short. Bittersweet.

Sometimes they'd meet in the hospital cafeteria and just drink coffee silently together. Happy to be next to each other. They hadn't needed words. They hadn't needed grand gestures to show the other how much they meant to them. They'd just been happy to *be*. Sitting opposite each other, holding hands.

He refused to end up hating her. His heart, his logical brain, told him he wouldn't do that to himself. They'd met again. Cleared the air. Shared a wonderful few days together. And it was best to leave it at that. With good memories. Ending on a high.

So why do I feel like this?

His heart physically ached. He was fighting against the urge to throw caution to the wind and go and find her again. To feel her in his arms just one more time...

But what good would it do? It would hurt them each and every time they had to part ways.

But what if it could work?

The devil's advocate part of his brain kicked in. Presented him with images of them happy together, surrounded by a brood of happy, red-haired, green-eyed children. Mini-versions of him and Beau. Having the kind of marriage people dreamed of.

Some people managed it, didn't they? He'd read about them in the news. Couples celebrating fifty, sixty, seventy years of marriage and giving their advice for a long, happy marriage:

Never go to bed on an argument.

Enjoy each other's company.

Be honest.

Be realistic.

It was that last one he'd held on to. Surely he *was* being realistic? Over fifty per cent of marriages *failed*, and those couples that stayed together he knew were doing it for reasons other than love. They didn't want to be alone. They were staying together for the sake of the kids. It was a habit they couldn't break. It was too expensive to separate...

Which of them were *truly* still in love?

It was hard to admit that he was afraid, but he knew he was. Afraid of hurting Beau. Afraid of having her hate him. Afraid of having her resent him. Afraid of her looking at him the way his mother looked at his father...

He sat on the end of his hotel bed and held his head in his hands.

Trying to convince himself he was doing the right thing.

It didn't help that there was a voice in his head screaming at him that he was doing the *wrong* thing.

He needed some space.

He needed some calm time.

He needed to *think*.

* * *

She'd kept herself busy—reading books, magazines, the newspapers. Watching television. Well...telling herself she was reading. Telling herself she was paying attention to the screen. All so she didn't think about Gray.

It wasn't working.

He was in her thoughts constantly, and her mind was churning with all the possibilities. Perhaps he'd done a good thing for them both by walking away. Because what if he was right? What if they *were* doomed to a future of having one of those relationships where people put up with what they'd got because the alternative was too terrible?

Being alone...

I'm alone now, aren't I? And it sucks!

He was wrong. They were stronger than that. Their love was stronger than that. Because it had lasted for the eleven years they'd been apart— always there, burning away quietly in the background and then roaring back into full flame when they'd met up again.

There was no point in fighting it. When she got

back to the UK, she would go to Edinburgh. She would find his hospital and she would wait in his surgery until there was time for him to see her. He *would* see her. He would do her that honour. And it didn't matter if he listened and then told her he couldn't do it, she had to at least *try*. He had to know that she wanted to be with him. Had to know how much she loved him. Wanted to be his partner, his lover, his soulmate. She was all those things already—it was just that he was refusing to see it!

Could she convince him that there was another kind of future for them? Let him know that there was an alternative? That they could be happy, like her parents? People who had such a deep love for each other were strong enough to get over any day-to-day upsets. Get through the rigours of life. People *succeeded* at marriage! Those couples who were determined to make their vows mean something. Who solved their problems before they became big issues. It was impossible to get through a marriage without there being ups and downs, but it *was* possible to do it without hating each other—and they had a love strong enough to do so.

He needs to know that I won't give up on him this time.

He'd shocked her, and there'd not been a chance for her to say what she needed to say. Well, he'd had *his* chance. And soon, back home, she would have hers.

The plane home was delayed by two hours, so Beau waited in the airport lounge, sipping coffee and finally—*finally!*—able to get her hands on a beautiful, flaky, buttery Danish pastry. She could almost feel herself salivating at the thought of it, but when it arrived, when it came to eating it, she found it difficult. Dry. Cloying. Tasteless.

She left it, pushing her plate away and swallowing the last of the coffee. Just as she was doing so she heard the boarding call for her plane.

She'd got an aisle seat and she settled down, anxious to get her feet back on British soil, where the air would be refreshingly damp and chill and the only animal likely to make her jump out of the way would be her neighbour's overenthusi-astic Red Setter.

She sensed rather than saw Gray arrive. She'd not even been looking at the passengers getting on the plane, but she'd felt someone brush by and suddenly she *knew* who it was. The cologne, her awareness of his proximity—it all pointed to the one man she'd thought she'd never see again.

'Gray...' She almost choked on his name as she stumbled to her feet. It was so unexpected to see him here. On *her* flight.

'Beau. You're looking well.'

He looked washed out. As if he hadn't slept. His eyes were reddened and there was a paleness to his skin, despite their days in the American sun.

'I am. Thank you. You're on *this* flight?'

She winced. What a stupid question! Of course he was!

'Row J.' He pointed to his row, unable to take his eyes off her, then reluctantly moved on. The passengers behind him were getting impatient that he was blocking the aisle.

Beau sank back into her seat, her heart rac-ing, thudding in her chest. She closed her eyes and tried to take a deep, steadying breath. This was it. Her chance. Her opportunity to speak to him. Eight hours' worth of opportunity, before they touched down in the UK. No need to track him down—no need to chase after him. Fate had given her this gift.

She was suddenly afraid. Her stomach felt cold, solid, like a block of ice. Fear was pinning her limbs to her seat.

This is one of those turning points in life, isn't it? Do I want to give us another chance? I really do!

She really wanted a spot of Dutch courage.

Where are those flight attendants when you want them?

Beau blinked and thought of what her life would be like if she didn't go and talk to him. It was too horrible to imagine. She'd be alone again. Driven only by work. Her life empty. Feeling as if she was waiting for something that never came. In limbo. Her life on pause. And though she loved her job, she knew she loved Gray McGregor more. She *needed* him. More than she needed oxygen.

She closed her eyes and tried to breathe.

CHAPTER TEN

THEY'D BEEN IN the air for an hour before she finally got up the nerve to go and talk to him. An hour of letting her stomach churn, of gripping her armrests till her knuckles turned white, before she finally unclipped her seat belt and got up out of her seat. Her legs were like jelly, her mouth drier than a desert.

Instantly his gaze connected with hers, and she saw him suck in a deep breath, too.

Good. He was just as nervous as she was.

If it goes wrong, then fine. I'll just walk away, sit back in my seat, and I'll never have to see him again. But what if it goes right...?

Unsteadily, she walked down the aisle and stopped by his seat. The two chairs next to him were empty.

'Mind if I take a seat?'

'Be my guest.' He got up so she could sidle past him, and waited for her to sit before he sat down himself.

She sat in the window seat, so that there was a gap between them. She didn't want to be too close. She had no idea how this conversation was going to go.

'How have you been?'

He glanced at her, then away, his jaw muscles clenching. 'Okay, I guess. You?'

This was her opportunity. Her chance to tell him how in torment she'd been since he'd left her at the minibus. Since he'd crushed her heart by telling her that he didn't deserve a second chance with her.

'Not bad.' She paused. 'Actually, I've been... thinking.'

He raised an eyebrow. 'Thinking?'

She nodded quickly, her blood zooming through her veins, carried along on a jet stream of adrenaline. 'About you.'

'Oh?'

He wasn't making this easy for her. But maybe he was afraid, too? She saw him swallow. His

Adam's apple bobbing up and down as he thought for a moment. Was he anticipating what she was going to say? She could see fear and doubt playing across his face as he sought to find the best way to remain calm whilst she said whatever she had to.

But she was impatient. Nervous. 'You don't have to say anything. I'll speak first. I think that I should.'

He met her gaze and stared. For just a moment. The intensity in his eyes made her temperature rise and her heart pound. 'Okay.'

How to start?

'I'm sorry, Gray. I'm sorry that I wasn't there for you before. That I didn't make you feel that you could talk to me. I'm sorry for the way I treated you when we met again. I'm sorry that it's taken this long for me to be able to see what was wrong. And where the blame lay.'

'Beau—'

'Let me finish.' She smiled, her mouth trembling with nerves. 'I need to say this. Because if I don't say this right now, then…then I'll never be able to say it, and I think we owe it to each other to be honest.'

It was hard not to cry, too. She'd worked herself up so much that the need to say everything, to get everything out so that he'd hear how she felt, was just overwhelming.

He stared at her, his feelings written across every feature. The concern in his eyes...the tenseness in his mouth...that beautiful mouth. His tight jaw...

'I loved you. I *still* love you. I always have and I always will—whether you allow me to do so or decide you never want to see me ever again. I love you. I think we could work. If you gave us a chance, I think we really *could*. We know who we are. We've put everything out there. Nothing's hidden.'

She reached for his hand and took it in hers, clasping it tightly, hoping he wouldn't be able to tell how much she was shaking.

'I know about your leg and it doesn't bother me. It doesn't stop you from being *you*. I know about your family. What you went through. I know that you think marriage is some sort of prison, but that's not how *I* see it. I see it as a journey.' She laughed nervously and hoped he would laugh, too. 'Yes, I used the J-word!'

He smiled. But he seemed too far away. He still wasn't quite with her. So she got out of her window seat and into the seat directly next to him.

She looked at their entwined hands and felt her barriers breaking down. She wanted this so much! But she was afraid of getting her heart broken again, and now her fear was making her hesitate.

'I want to be with you, Gray. Married or not. I don't need a perfect man. I don't need someone who will never argue with me or grow frustrated with me, because that happens anyway. But what I *do* want is *you*. Gray McGregor. Faults and all. We can do this. We can get it right this time—I know we can—because we both care enough to get it right, and...'

She almost ran out of words. Almost. She looked into his green eyes for inspiration and saw them smiling back at her. She fought back her tears.

'You told me that I deserved someone who

could love me the way I want to be loved. You told me that you didn't deserve a second chance with me. But...but you're the one that I want to have loving me. You're the only one who can love me the way that I want. *I'm* the one who deserves a second chance with *you*! Can't you see that? I love you, Gray McGregor. Can't you love me, too?'

Gray brought her fingers to his lips, closing his eyes as he sucked in a breath and inhaled the aroma of her skin before he began to speak.

'I used to fear that our being together would turn us into different people who couldn't stand to be near each other...but being *away* from you makes me miserable. Sadder than I've ever been in my life. When I fell from that sea cliff and lay on the rocks waiting for help, all I could think of was you. I thought that if I died, then at least it would take me away from the torment of not being with you. But now we have this second chance and...and I *want* to take it. I *do*! I thought...I thought that I didn't deserve another chance and so I walked away again. Just for a moment. I needed to get my head straight. I needed to know that I was thinking clearly about us. That I'd rid myself of all that old clutter, that old pain I used to carry inside. I used to hide behind it. Using it as an excuse. Believing it—allowing it to twist me into this man who was too afraid to be with the woman he loved in case it all went wrong. But...'

He smiled at her and wiped a tear from her soft, soft cheek.

'I know what love is. I know that it's what *we've* got. Something special. We're a team, you and me. We always have been. We've shared our fears, our hopes. Our love. You know everything about me and you still love me anyway. Do you know how amazing I find that?'

She nodded, her tears turning to tears of happiness.

'I got off that bus and I had to drive away. Being around you...I couldn't think straight. But back at the hotel I could. I told you that I was scared of what might happen to us, but that was wrong. I was running away from love because I'd never truly felt it. Not until you came along.

And suddenly everything was moving too fast! Marriage? Talk of having kids?'

He shook his head at the memory.

'My mother didn't want me. My father barely knew me. I was just a messenger boy. A pawn in their horrible game. And whilst I loved you, *wanted* to be with you, I was terrified of doing so in case I got it all wrong. I didn't know how to be loved like that. So strongly. Living apart from you, just dating you, I could hide from that. Disguise it. I thought that if we got married it would expose me for the fraud that I was. It wasn't you. It wasn't us. It was *me*. But now I know I'm stronger. You *make* me stronger. All that we've been through tells me we can do this.'

A stewardess came by with her trolley, offering drinks, but Gray waved her past.

'I accused you of not living in reality, but I was doing the same thing. I was living in a future that hadn't happened. We have no idea of how this will go, but I think—I *know*—the two of us will make it the best it can be. The strongest it can be. And...and I know that I love you, too. That

I'm miserable without you. That my life is *nothing* without you in it.'

'Gray...'

'Fate threw us back together, but even if it hadn't...I would have found you anyway. I can never be apart from you again.' He smiled, his face warming with the strength of it, happiness gleaming from his eyes. 'Beau, you are the most beautiful woman I know. The strongest woman I know and I want you in my life for ever. Will you do me the honour of making me the happiest man in this world and marrying me?'

'*Marrying* you?'

Did I just squeak that? Since when do I squeak?

He nodded. 'I want to marry you, Beau. I want you to be my wife. I want us to be together through good times *and* bad. In sickness and in health. Till death do us part. Dr Beau Judd, my beautiful neurologist...my other half...'

A kiss.

'My soul...'

Another kiss.

'My heart...'

And another.

'Yes!' She nodded, grinning like an idiot and not caring. He loved her! *Loved her!* It was real this time. 'Yes! Yes! *Yes!* I will. Are you going to kiss me properly now, or just keep staring at me?'

'I'd like to kiss you.'

He leant forward and their lips met.

This was it. Their first kiss on the path to true love. His lips were warm and soft, and they caressed hers so expertly that she felt like a molten ball of fire. Her insides were liquid. Her hands scrunched tightly in his hair and she pulled him against her and kissed him back as if her life depended upon it.

And it did.

She knew she was nothing without this man. She had a home, a career and a family. She should have been content with just those things. But having Gray in her life made everything so much better. Brighter. Riskier, yes, but brighter.

She stroked his face, feeling the softness of his fine beard beneath her fingertips. 'I love you so much.'

He reached for her other hand and kissed her

fingertips. 'And I love *you*. We made it off that clifftop—we can make it on solid ground.'

Joy beyond measure was hers. Her happiness scale exploded and blew off its top as she sank into Gray's arms and accepted his love.

But he shifted slightly, reached into his pocket and pulled out a small velvet box. 'I can't believe I had a whole other speech planned for when I tracked you down in the UK. It wasn't very good, but…everything's worked out bonny in the end. You said yes. So…this is for you.'

She took the box and glanced up at him. He looked nervous. It had to be a ring. He'd bought her one before and it had been stored in her jewellery box for too many years. Now she was getting another. But this one *meant* something more.

Beau opened the box. Inside lay a beautiful diamond set in a platinum band. It glittered and caught the light against its velvet nest and she beamed a smile through her happy tears.

'It's gorgeous.'

Gray took it from the box and then took her left hand, sliding it onto her finger. It was a perfect fit.

She kissed him again. As his fiancée. A perfect kiss. A loving kiss.

'I love you, Beau,' he whispered in her ear.

And she whispered back, 'And I love *you*, Gray McGregor.'

EPILOGUE

SHE WAS READY. Her hair was done. Her make-up was done. The dress fitted perfectly. She picked up her small posy of peonies and made her way downstairs, to where her father waited for her, dressed in smart tails and holding a top hat.

'How do I look?' he asked.

'Very handsome.' She smiled.

'You don't think I should have gone with a kilt, like Gray?'

She shook her head. 'No one but Mum needs to see *those* knees, Dad.'

He reached for her hand and let out a steadying breath. 'The car's here. Are you ready?'

There were nerves and excitement in her stomach. Her heart was pounding and her mouth was dry with anticipation. But, yes, she was ready.

'I am.'

Outside, all her neighbours were standing and watching, and there were a few 'oohs' as she came out and they saw her dressed in white.

A silver-grey car, sleek and exclusive, adorned with white ribbons, awaited her, and a chauffeur in a grey suit and cap stood by the open back door, smiling as she approached.

She waved at her neighbours, at the people who'd witnessed her devastation before, knowing they were truly happy for her. That finally she was getting her dream come true. And as they drove to the church, she clutched her father's hand tightly.

'Nervous?'

She nodded. 'A bit.'

'He'll be there, you know.'

'I know he will.'

She wasn't nervous about that at all. She could tell that this time it was different. Gray was a completely different man, a completely different groom-to-be this time. Eager to join in with wedding arrangements, making his own suggestions, telling her how he'd like the day to go. He'd been just as excited for the day as she had. There'd been no doubt. No cold feet. At all.

Just excitement. Just joy at finally getting the day—the *marriage*—they both wanted. Had both dreamed of. The marriage that they knew was now within their reach.

Everyone else was waiting at the church. Her mum had travelled earlier on, with the bridesmaids. All the rest of her family were there, most of them already inside. As she got out of the car, she saw Gray's mother and father go in, too.

The photographer wanted some pictures before she went in and dutifully she posed, her excitement building, her desire to see Gray as she walked down the aisle becoming almost unbearable.

She wanted to see his face. She wanted to hold his hand. Say her vows. Promise to be his for evermore.

The music began and she lowered her veil and took one last deep breath. She'd been here before. She'd just never got this far.

She took her father's arm and nodded.

I'm ready.

And then the doors were open, the congregation stood and she began her walk down the aisle.

She saw Gray at the other end. Beaming with joy as the wedding music soared, almost crying at the sight of her as she walked down the aisle towards him. She could hardly take her eyes off him. He looked so handsome in his red-and-green kilt, his black jacket and brilliant white shirt. Those green eyes were smiling as she drew close, and he reached out to take her hand from her father's.

'You look so beautiful,' he said.

She couldn't speak, she felt so happy. She just took his hand and smiled shyly at him.

As the music died down, the vicar came to stand in front of them and began the service.

Beau and Gray made their vows. Gave each other a ring. And were soon declared husband and wife.

'You may kiss your bride.'

Gray smiled, lifted up her veil and pulled her towards him for their first kiss as a married couple.

After they'd signed the register, they headed

outside for more photos, and when they were standing in the glorious sunshine, waiting for the photographer to organise them into another pose, they kissed some more.

And then they heard an American voice interrupt them. 'Er...guys, I think we told you to get a room!'

Beau laughed and turned to see all their American friends from the Yellowstone trip—Mack, Conrad, Barb and the others. All there. All happy to be sharing their wedding day.

'Don't worry. We will,' said Gray. 'Later.'

'Who'd have guessed it would be the honeymoon suite, though?' asked Mack.

Barb looked at Beau and winked. 'Oh, I think we knew. Deep down, we always knew.'

Beau smiled and then kissed her husband.

* * * * *

If you enjoyed this story, check out these other great reads from Louisa Heaton

ONE LIFE-CHANGING NIGHT
A FATHER THIS CHRISTMAS?
HIS PERFECT BRIDE?
THE BABY THAT CHANGED HER LIFE

All available now!

MILLS & BOON®
Large Print Medical

April

Waking Up to Dr Gorgeous	Emily Forbes
Swept Away by the Seductive Stranger	Amy Andrews
One Kiss in Tokyo...	Scarlet Wilson
The Courage to Love Her Army Doc	Karin Baine
Reawakened by the Surgeon's Touch	Jennifer Taylor
Second Chance with Lord Branscombe	Joanna Neil

May

The Nurse's Christmas Gift	Tina Beckett
The Midwife's Pregnancy Miracle	Kate Hardy
Their First Family Christmas	Alison Roberts
The Nightshift Before Christmas	Annie O'Neil
It Started at Christmas...	Janice Lynn
Unwrapped by the Duke	Amy Ruttan

June

White Christmas for the Single Mum	Susanne Hampton
A Royal Baby for Christmas	Scarlet Wilson
Playboy on Her Christmas List	Carol Marinelli
The Army Doc's Baby Bombshell	Sue MacKay
The Doctor's Sleigh Bell Proposal	Susan Carlisle
Christmas with the Single Dad	Louisa Heaton

MILLS & BOON®
Large Print Medical

July

Falling for Her Wounded Hero	Marion Lennox
The Surgeon's Baby Surprise	Charlotte Hawkes
Santiago's Convenient Fiancée	Annie O'Neil
Alejandro's Sexy Secret	Amy Ruttan
The Doctor's Diamond Proposal	Annie Claydon
Weekend with the Best Man	Leah Martyn

August

Their Meant-to-Be Baby	Caroline Anderson
A Mummy for His Baby	Molly Evans
Rafael's One Night Bombshell	Tina Beckett
Dante's Shock Proposal	Amalie Berlin
A Forever Family for the Army Doc	Meredith Webber
The Nurse and the Single Dad	Dianne Drake

September

Their Secret Royal Baby	Carol Marinelli
Her Hot Highland Doc	Annie O'Neil
His Pregnant Royal Bride	Amy Ruttan
Baby Surprise for the Doctor Prince	Robin Gianna
Resisting Her Army Doc Rival	Sue MacKay
A Month to Marry the Midwife	Fiona McArthur

MILLS & BOON®
Large Print – April 2017

ROMANCE

A Di Sione for the Greek's Pleasure	Kate Hewitt
The Prince's Pregnant Mistress	Maisey Yates
The Greek's Christmas Bride	Lynne Graham
The Guardian's Virgin Ward	Caitlin Crews
A Royal Vow of Convenience	Sharon Kendrick
The Desert King's Secret Heir	Annie West
Married for the Sheikh's Duty	Tara Pammi
Winter Wedding for the Prince	Barbara Wallace
Christmas in the Boss's Castle	Scarlet Wilson
Her Festive Doorstep Baby	Kate Hardy
Holiday with the Mystery Italian	Ellie Darkins

HISTORICAL

Bound by a Scandalous Secret	Diane Gaston
The Governess's Secret Baby	Janice Preston
Married for His Convenience	Eleanor Webster
The Saxon Outlaw's Revenge	Elisabeth Hobbes
In Debt to the Enemy Lord	Nicole Locke

MEDICAL

Waking Up to Dr Gorgeous	Emily Forbes
Swept Away by the Seductive Stranger	Amy Andrews
One Kiss in Tokyo...	Scarlet Wilson
The Courage to Love Her Army Doc	Karin Baine
Reawakened by the Surgeon's Touch	Jennifer Taylor
Second Chance with Lord Branscombe	Joanna Neil

MILLS & BOON®

Why shop at millsandboon.co.uk?

Each year, thousands of romance readers find their perfect read at millsandboon.co.uk. That's because we're passionate about bringing you the very best romantic fiction. Here are some of the advantages of shopping at www.millsandboon.co.uk:

* **Get new books first**—you'll be able to buy your favourite books one month before they hit the shops

* **Get exclusive discounts**—you'll also be able to buy our specially created monthly collections, with up to 50% off the RRP

* **Find your favourite authors**—latest news, interviews and new releases for all your favourite authors and series on our website, plus ideas for what to try next

* **Join in**—once you've bought your favourite books, don't forget to register with us to rate, review and join in the discussions

Visit **www.millsandboon.co.uk**
for all this and more today!

GREAT CONSPIRACIES
AND ELABORATE COVER-UPS

KA 0221897 6

GREAT CONSPIRACIES AND ELABORATE COVER-UPS

Daniel Cohen

The Millbrook Press Inc.
Brookfield, Connecticut

To RAP, who knew. Or did he?
D.C.

Photographs courtesy of Corbis-Bettmann:
pp. 17, 28, 66, 75, 86; Photofest: pp. 23, 95,
107; Author's collection: pp. 40, 48.

Published by The Millbrook Press, Inc.
2 Old New Milford Road
Brookfield, Connecticut 06804

Library of Congress Cataloging-in-Publication Data
Cohen, Daniel, 1936–
Great conspiracies and elaborate cover-ups / by Daniel Cohen.
p. cm.
Includes bibliographical references and index.
Summary: Examines some of the widespread popular theories
about a variety of conspiracies and discusses the people who
promote these theories and the people who believe in them.
ISBN 0-7613-0010-4 (lib. bdg.)
1. Conspiracies—United States—History—Juvenile literature.
[1. Conspiracies.] I. Title.
E179.C625 1997
001.9–dc20   96-36483 CIP AC

Contents

GREAT CONSPIRACIES
AND ELABORATE COVER-UPS

WHAT YOU DON'T KNOW ABOUT BLACK HELICOPTERS, MASONIC SECRETS, AND THE MURDER OF MARILYN MONROE

Did you know that the United States is regularly being crisscrossed by mysterious black helicopters? They have chased motorists, appeared mysteriously in the vicinity of grisly crimes, exchanged gunfire with angry citizens, and sprayed unknown chemicals that have killed pets, plants, and livestock. Government agencies regularly deny that such vehicles exist.

Despite hundreds or thousands of these sightings the major media never report on them. Have the media been silenced about this phenomenon? Is there a conspiracy? Is there a cover-up?

Did you know that the core of Washington, D.C., is laid out according to a "secret Masonic ritual"? By studying street maps of Washington you can find an entire pentagram traced out focusing on the White House, and a satanic horned goat traced around the Capitol. These are symbols that are used to conjure up evil spirits, and open a "spiritual door to the occult, a planned invasion of the powers of darkness," and the nation has "been under siege from the first day our first president walked into the Oval Office."[1]

Did you know that despite the "official" finding that Marilyn Monroe committed suicide by swallowing an overdose of barbiturate pills, no trace of them was found in her body? Did you know that hundreds of hours of secret tape recordings of Marilyn that had been made by the powerful and unscrupulous head of the Federal Bureau of Investigation (FBI), J. Edgar Hoover, have mysteriously disappeared, and Marilyn's diary and other incriminating evidence were removed from the house before police arrived on the scene? And, most shocking of all, did you know that Robert F. Kennedy, attorney general of the United States and brother of President John F. Kennedy, was at Marilyn's house when she died?

Perhaps you didn't know all the details of the invasion of black helicopters, the Masonic secrets of Washington, and the murder of Marilyn Monroe, but I'll bet you've heard rumors. These are the sorts of tales that are hard to avoid, even if you want to. And these tales are so strange, so sinister, and yet so exciting that few of us try to avoid them.

Accounts of the appearance of mysterious unmarked "black helicopters" have been around for several decades now. But in recent years the accounts have increased in frequency and have become an integral part of the lore of many antigovernment groups, who are convinced that there is some sort of federal government or international conspiracy to deprive them of their freedom. The black helicopters are the air force of the conspiracy.

Nation of Islam leader Louis Farrakhan must have surprised and puzzled many of his listeners at the Million Man March in Washington, D.C., in October 1995 when he talked about the strange Masonic origins of Washington. And the description of Washington architecture as downright satanic was contained in material distributed by the Free the Masons Ministries of Washington State.

At least four books and scores of articles have been published describing the "murder" of Marilyn Monroe and pinning the crime on the Kennedys, the Mafia, the Central Intelligence Agency (CIA), the FBI, or all of the above. Someone might tell you the story and then add, with a knowing wink, "Of course it's all been covered up."

Usually you don't hear about these conspiracies on the evening news, or read about them in the leading newspapers and magazines. They don't appear in your history textbooks either. Author Jim Hougan, who wrote a couple of books on conspiracies, said that there are two kinds of history: the safe, sanitized "'Disney version,' so widely available as to be unavoidable. . . and a second one that remains secret, buried and unnamed."[2]

Authors Jonathan Vankin and John Whalen quote Hougan admiringly in their *50 Greatest Conspiracies of All Time*. They add that the second and secret version of history does have a name—it is "conspiracy theory." The "Disney version" they call "the *New York Times* version," "the TV news version," or "the college textbook version." They report, however, that they were "heartened" to discover the "openness" that so many people have to conspiracy theories. Openness is hardly the word for it. In America today large numbers of people positively rush to embrace any one of a huge number of conspiracy theories.

Sometimes it looks as if the nation, indeed the entire world, is awash in conspiracies and cover-ups, and that nothing is as it seems. Often the same set of facts is made to fit half a dozen different, and diametrically opposed, conspiracy theories. Usually the theory a person chooses to believe depends not so much on the available information as on what that person already believes. Most conspiracy theories are flexible enough to fit many different points of view. For those on the political right, President John F. Kennedy was killed by a left-wing political conspiracy. For those on the left, it was a right-wing conspiracy.

One problem in discussing this subject is that there really have been and doubtless still are conspiracies and cover-ups. Groups of individuals, organizations, corporations, and governments have gotten together and tried to do things, usually shameful or unlawful, in secret. Stories have been suppressed, and information burned, shredded, and buried.

The Watergate affair during the presidency of Richard Nixon certainly comes to mind. So does the more recent Iran-Contra affair. Information about the decades-long efforts by tobacco companies to suppress data about the effects of cigarette smoking on health is still being slowly revealed. But the real conspiracies and cover-ups are rarely as grand, all-encompassing, or diabolically clever as those proposed by the conspiracy theorists. President Nixon and his associates conspired to pull some pretty dirty political tricks, and then tried to cover up what had been done. But they didn't plan the assassination of President Kennedy as has sometimes been alleged.

Conspiracy theories really aren't anything new in American history. Fears about the conspiratorial powers of the secretive Freemasons, or Masons, were at their height during the presidency of Andrew Jackson.

Some conspiracy theories, like the one that Elvis Presley faked his own death and is hiding in the FBI witness protection program because his life had been threatened by drug dealers, are harmless and actually quite funny. Others are not. The theory that the world is really controlled by a small cabal of Jewish bankers helped to inspire Hitler and the Nazis, with cataclysmically tragic results.

It's really impossible to say whether belief in conspiracies and cover-ups is more common today than it was in the past. While it seems as if these theories attract more followers than ever before, belief can't be measured accurately. However, what we can say with great certainty is that the belief in conspiracies and cover-ups is still very much with us today.

In order to try to understand some of these beliefs, where they came from and why they are so popular, we will look in detail at some of the more widespread conspiracy theories. And we will start with the most widely discussed conspiracy theory in modern American history, the one in which almost the only people who believe the "official" explanation are the officials themselves.

THE JFK ASSASSINATION CONSPIRACY

Virtually everyone in America who was more than ten years old on November 22, 1963, remembers exactly where he or she was when first hearing the news that President John F. Kennedy had been shot in Dallas, Texas.

I was just returning to the office where I worked on West 57th Street in Manhattan when I saw a group of people gathered around a newsstand listening to the radio. Groups were gathered everywhere around radios or just talking, exchanging the latest bulletins from Dallas.

Pretty soon stores, offices, and theaters began to close down. I went back to the office for a short time, then I went home. No one ever announced the office was closing, we all just left.

The initial reaction was not sadness—that came later. The first reaction was shock or more accurately, surprise. How could the young and vigorous Jack Kennedy be dead, and how could he have been killed—in America!

Other American presidents had been assassinated, most notably Abraham Lincoln. But the last U.S. president to be assassinated before Kennedy was William McKinley, and that was way back in 1901. By 1963 the vast majority of Americans hadn't even been born when McKinley was assassinated. There had been serious assassination attempts on the lives of Presidents Franklin Roosevelt and Harry Truman, but few remembered them. The JFK assassination seemed not only terrible but a singular and utterly improbable event in American history, even though it wasn't.

Over the next few days the feeling of improbability grew stronger as the drama continued. A suspected assassin was arrested within two hours of the killing. He turned out to be an obscure little malcontent named Lee Harvey Oswald—a nobody. And he was supposed to have carried the killing out with a cheap mail-order rifle.

Two days later Oswald himself, surrounded by guards and TV camera crews, was shot while being led by guards through the basement of a Dallas jail. The killing was shown live on national television. The killer was Jack Ruby, owner of a seedy Dallas nightclub—another nobody. There never was a trial for Oswald, and while there were a number of investigations none of them ever seemed very satisfactory. Ruby

This is a photograph of Lee Harvey Oswald as he was being transferred from the city prison to the county jail. Just moments after this picture was taken, Oswald was shot and killed. Photographers and cameramen from across the nation recorded the unbelievable sequence of events.

was tried, found guilty of murder, and sentenced to death. He died before his appeal was heard.

To most of us it seemed not only improbable but downright unnatural that one of the most convulsive events in modern American history could have been created by such unimportant people. And it was in this atmosphere that the most vigorous of all American conspiracy theories grew and still flourishes to this day.

More than two thousand books have been written on the subject of the Kennedy assassination. There have been countless magazine articles and television shows. The assassination has been one of the most popular subjects for discussion on radio talk shows and on the Internet. Groups discussing every conceivable and many inconceivable aspects of the case communicate via e-mail, fax, telephone, letters, and well-attended conventions. As a result, more than four out of five Americans do not believe the official conclusion that Oswald was the lone assassin.[1] The most widely held opinions are that Oswald was framed or that he was part of a much wider conspiracy.

Suspicions and rumors about the Kennedy assassination began to circulate almost as soon as the news broke, and they simply exploded after Oswald was killed. A Gallup Poll taken a week after the assassination showed that only 29 percent of the American public believed that Oswald had acted alone.[2]

The initial suspicion was that the Communists, Soviets, or Cubans were behind the plot. Oswald himself was a highly suspicious character. Though he had enlisted in the U.S. Marine Corps, Oswald was an outspoken Marxist, an ideological Communist though not actually a member of the Communist party. A short time after his discharge from the Marines in 1959 Oswald departed for the Soviet Union. He was reasonably well treated in the Soviet Union, where defectors from the United States were rare. He worked in a Russian factory and married a young Russian woman. Within two years, however, he was ready to come back to the United States with his wife.

The Soviet Union apparently had disappointed Lee Harvey Oswald, but he had not become disillusioned with the theory of communism. After returning to the United States, Oswald was associated with a pro-Castro Cuban group and made inquiries about going to Cuba. All of this information was known almost immediately and naturally led to early suspicions that the assassination was a Communist plot.

The Soviets and the Cubans realized that if they were implicated in the killing of an American president the result could easily be war. Both countries went to extraordinary lengths to deny any association with Oswald and to offer whatever proof they could that there was no conspiracy. At first a lot of people, particularly people in the CIA, didn't believe them. Perhaps some still don't. But in the more than three decades since the assassination not a shred of credible evidence indicating a Communist plot has turned up. And this in spite of an incredibly intensive investigation by members of the intelligence community who were sure the assassination was a Communist plot. With the collapse of communism many of the records of the clandestine activities of the Soviet government have become public. They contain not a hint of a plot.

Strangely, though, it wasn't the idea of a Communist conspiracy that came to grip the American public. The most commonly repeated story was that the president had fallen victim to a right-wing plot.

At the time Kennedy was assassinated his popularity had been rising steadily. But there were plenty of people in America who disliked and even hated JFK. He was a president who stirred deep political passions, pro and con. Kennedy's most vocal foes were on the political right, and Dallas was a conservative city and home to many right-wing groups.

The atmosphere of speculation and rumor had grown so intense and so dangerous that within a week the new president, Lyndon Johnson, appointed a commission headed by Earl Warren, chief justice of the U.S. Supreme Court, to fully investigate the assassination. The Warren Commission had an unlimited mandate and virtually unprecedented powers. It was supposed to answer all of the public's questions about what had happened in Dallas on that fateful day. The final 888-page report was issued on September 27, 1964, some ten months after the assassination.

The Warren Commission conclusion was that Lee Harvey Oswald had fired the shot that killed Kennedy and that he had acted alone—there was no conspiracy. The initial media reaction to the Warren Commission report in the United States was highly favorable. But the public at large was far more suspicious of "official explanations," and soon critics were picking the report to pieces.

In the months following the assassination a whole network of amateur investigators sprang up. They collected and shared information and often misinformation about the assassination, and they passionately believed and argued that all the questions had not been answered. The list of unanswered questions and alternative theories compiled by these "assassination buffs" was formidable and, as far as the general public was concerned, very impressive.

The Warren Commission hurt its own credibility in a variety of ways. The commission was supposed to have had access to all relevant information. As it turned out this was not the case. Both the CIA and the FBI withheld significant material from the commission. For example, the CIA did not disclose to the commission the fact that it had plotted with members of the Mafia to kill Fidel Castro. That would certainly have given Castro a motive to have Kennedy killed. In the end, the information that had been withheld would not have changed the Warren Commission conclusion that Oswald had acted alone. But the fact that such information had been withheld led conspiracy theorists to ask, not unreasonably, what else was being hidden.

The most outrageous, gaudiest, and meanest of the conspiracy theories was the one promoted by New Orleans district attorney Jim Garrison. Oswald had been born in New Orleans, and though he had moved frequently he had returned to the city from time to time, including a visit shortly before the assassination. Oswald's New Orleans connections had been closely investigated by the FBI and the Warren Commission as well as by the assassination buffs.

Garrison was the sort of politician who is most politely described as "controversial." He was known for making sensational charges and then being unable to follow them up with evidence. Garrison had taken an active interest in the assassination from the start. In late 1966 the district attorney shocked the nation and his own staff when he said that he was going to investigate Clay Shaw, a prominent New Orleans civic leader, as a key figure in the plot to assassinate Kennedy. He contended it was a homosexual plot, a sort of "thrill killing." Shaw was known to be a homosexual.[3]

The whole homosexual plot idea grew out of stories told by some unbelievably unreliable witnesses that Oswald was a homosexual. Later Garrison was to assert, without a single shred of credible evidence, that Jack Ruby was also a homosexual.

As soon as Garrison's investigation was announced, he became a media star, not only in New Orleans but throughout the country. And he was a celebrity and major focus for the legion of assassina-

In the film JFK, *the actor Kevin Costner stars as Jim Garrison. When the film was released, many critics charged that it was irresponsible of Oliver Stone to have produced a major motion picture based upon the twisted and sometimes downright untrue allegations of Jim Garrison.*

[23]

tion buffs. As time went on, Garrison expanded his conspiracy. At one point he said it "was a Nazi operation whose sponsors included some of the oil rich millionaires in Texas."[4]

At other times, Garrison targeted the right-wing Minutemen, the CIA, the FBI, White Russians, and anti-Castro Cubans. Anyone who disagreed with him or his investigation automatically became part of the conspiracy and cover-up. This included President Lyndon Johnson, the Warren Commission, and even the murdered president's brother Robert Kennedy. "It is quite apparent to me," Garrison said, "that for one reason or another, he [Robert Kennedy] does not want the truth to be brought out."[5]

For years, Garrison went around floating ever wilder conspiracy tales before a fascinated American public. Finally, early in 1969, Clay Shaw was brought to trial, and Jim Garrison had to present his evidence in court and not on the *Tonight* show. The trial lasted about five weeks. Jury deliberations took forty-five minutes. Shaw was acquitted on the first ballot. Garrison's case was revealed as a complete sham.

But still this wasn't the end. Two days later, Garrison had Shaw rearrested on perjury charges. It was another two years before a federal court issued an injunction against Garrison from prosecuting Shaw. Garrison appealed to the Supreme Court. When he was turned down he said that he was being made a "scapegoat," that the CIA had murdered Kennedy, and that the Supreme Court decision "puts the final nail in John Kennedy's coffin." When Garrison was not reelected as district attorney, he complained that the CIA and FBI had conspired to bring about his defeat.

Clay Shaw was never convicted of anything, but he spent years under a legal cloud and was bankrupted by his legal bills. He filed a multimillion-dollar lawsuit against Garrison and his financial backers. A group of wealthy New Orleans residents had raised money for the Garrison investigation. But Shaw died in 1974, before his case could be brought to trial. He was a broken man, and a completely innocent one. The Garrison investigation was a shameful episode, and it grew out of public fascination with conspiracy theories.

Despite his defeat, Jim Garrison went on to write a book, *On the Trail of the Assassins,* in which he recycled all of his theories. This book itself wasn't very successful, but it became the basis for Oliver Stone's extremely successful 1991 film *JFK.* Kevin Costner played Jim Garrison as a hero, and Garrison himself appeared in a bit part. An entire generation learned much of what it knows about the Kennedy assassination from that film. And the film, which is extremely powerful and persuasive, is also dead wrong.

The more serious conspiracy buffs had become disillusioned with Jim Garrison and his phony prosecution. But they continued to peck away at the Oswald-as-the-lone-assassin explanation. In 1976 a special congressional investigation was launched to look into the assassinations of President Kennedy and Martin Luther King, Jr. The investigation took more than two years and cost over five million dollars. The conclusion was that a conspiracy in the King assassination was likely and that a conspiracy in the Kennedy assassination was a possibility. The most probable conspirators in the Kennedy killing according to this report were members of the Mafia. The reason the Mafia wanted to kill the president was that they hated his brother Robert Kennedy, who as attorney general was waging a campaign against organized crime. Jack Ruby was also supposed to have mob connections, and his killing of Oswald "had all the earmarks of a mob hit."

For a while the Mafia replaced the CIA and the Cubans as chief suspects. A whole flock of alleged hit men have either been accused of the killing or have actually confessed to it. But there is absolutely no solid evidence linking the Mafia to the assassination. Historically the mob has no scruples about killing their rivals or people who owe them money or who have double-crossed them. But they don't assassinate judges, FBI agents, or even reporters. It's just too risky. It is unthinkable that they would even consider killing a president, no matter how much they hated his brother.

Every year about six million people visit Dealey Plaza in Dallas where the assassination took place. Some of them pay seven dollars to visit the Conspiracy Museum, which opened early in 1995. The aim of the museum, according to its director Tom Bowden, is to get people to think. "Maybe that way we can correct the textbooks so that they contain information about the larger conspiracy."[6]

The Kennedy assassination has become an obsession and nearly a religion to many as well as a money-making business for some. Nonetheless, a good number of Americans cling to the assassination conspiracy theory simply because it helps to make sense out of an otherwise senseless event.

This illustration, produced for one of the many illustrated weekly newsmagazines of the mid-1860s, shows the artist's rendition of Booth shooting Lincoln in the box at Ford's Theatre.

THE LINCOLN
ASSASSINATION CONSPIRACY

Before the Kennedy assassination, there was the assassination of Abraham Lincoln. To many Americans there is an almost mystic connection between the two awful events. Both the names Lincoln and Kennedy contain seven letters. The two murdered presidents were succeeded by vice presidents named Johnson. Lincoln was elected (to his second term) in 1860. Kennedy was elected a century later in 1960. However, the Abraham Lincoln assassination really was the result of a conspiracy. The question is, how large a conspiracy and who was really behind it?

First, the known facts: On April 14, 1865, President Abraham Lincoln, newly inaugurated for his second term, attended a performance at Ford's Theatre in Washington, D.C. During the performance John Wilkes Booth, a well-known actor and a member of America's leading theatrical family, walked unquestioned into the president's private box, pointed his derringer behind the president's ear, and shot. He then jumped to the stage in what he must have visualized as a triumphant, dramatic leap. But the spur of Booth's boot caught on some bunting that decorated the president's box and he landed awkwardly, fracturing his shin. In the general confusion he still managed to escape from the theater. Lincoln was carried to a nearby house, where he died a few hours later.

The conspirators had planned a triple assassination. George Atzerodt got drunk and didn't even attempt to kill Vice President Andrew Johnson. Lewis Paine stabbed Secretary of State William H. Seward and seriously wounded him, but Seward recovered.

Booth and an associate, David Herold, managed to flee to Maryland, where a doctor, possibly a member of the conspiratorial group, set his leg. After twelve days Booth and Herold were finally surrounded by soldiers in the barn of Garrett's Farm in Bowling Green, Virginia. Herold surrendered. "I'll shoot it out with the whole damned detachment," Booth cried. The barn was set afire, and Booth was shot by Sergeant Boston Corbett.

A few months later the conspirators who had been arrested went on trial and were convicted. Four were hanged and others given prison sentences.

The version of the Lincoln assassination that has come down to us through most history books is that it was entirely the work of Booth—an egomaniacal, drunken, and fanatical actor. All the others were a motley crew of drunkards and fools under the control of the half-crazed Booth. And there is considerable truth to this version.

Booth was undoubtedly both self-centered and unbalanced. The Maryland-raised actor was a heavy drinker and a fanatic supporter of the Confederate cause—not fanatic enough, however, to abandon his lucrative acting career in the North and join the Confederate army during the Civil War. None of his associates was particularly bright and some, like the loutish Atzerodt, could easily be considered of below average intelligence. The flamboyant actor dominated and controlled them.

But from the moment the news of the president's assassination spread, there were hints, and sometimes shouts, of a wider and more sinister conspiracy. In order to understand this reaction it is necessary to understand the time. Just a week before the assassination, Robert E. Lee had surrendered. The war was essentially over, though some fighting continued. Although Washington was the nation's capital, it was located on the border between the North and South, and was really more of a Southern city. It was loaded with Southern sympathizers and spies. Passage between North and South, even during the height of the war, was quite easy.

At the time it was assumed that the conspiracy to kill Lincoln involved many more individuals than Booth and the handful of nonentities who were ultimately convicted and punished for the crime. In fact,

Jefferson Davis, president of the Confederacy, and a few other high Confederate officials were originally indicted as part of a conspiracy, but these indictments were eventually dropped.

John Surratt, one of the conspirators who managed to escape to Europe, told friends that the plot had been hatched on the orders of Davis. Surratt was captured in Europe two years after the assassination, brought back for trial in the United States, and acquitted on a technicality, although his mother, who had far less to do with the plot, had been hanged.

Booth had met with Confederate agents in Canada before he planned the assassination. A number of the other conspirators were known to be Confederate agents. Confederate codebooks and other incriminating materials were found in the possession of some of the conspirators. It was also said that Booth was a member of a secretive underground group called the Knights of the Golden Circle, who were fanatical Northern supporters of the Confederate cause. But little is known of the group.

If the Lincoln assassination had been a large and well-planned conspiracy, then it is reasonable to assume that Booth and the others would have had a well-planned escape. Clearly this was not supposed to be a suicide mission. Incredibly, Booth was able to escape from the city of Washington and ride south; he did get some help from Confederate supporters and perhaps some co-conspirators along the way. But basically he was on his own.

Perhaps there had been a broader plan once—but after Lee's surrender that would have collapsed. All the evidence indicates that in the end Booth and his followers did not have much organized support

John Surratt, his mother, and several others involved in the assassination conspiracy were Catholic. When Surratt first escaped from the United States, he was hidden by some priests in Canada. In Europe he went to Rome and joined the papal guard under an assumed name. However, after he was identified, the pope's chancellor had him arrested and returned to America. In the mid-nineteenth century, anti-Catholic feeling ran strong in predominantly Protestant America, and there was a widespread belief that the Vatican was somehow responsible for the Lincoln assassination. For some in America it seemed as if the Vatican was responsible for every evil deed in the world. However, a Vatican conspiracy behind the Lincoln assassination was an idea that never really got off the ground.

Booth, incidentally, was an Episcopalian and as a young man had been a member of the virulently anti-Catholic Know Nothing movement.

Most people have assumed, and still assume, that there was a wider Confederate conspiracy behind the assassination. At the very least there is a belief that Confederate higher-ups had some knowledge of what Booth planned, but did nothing to stop it. This may have been covered up by a victorious federal government more anxious to heal the wounds of war than simply to punish the enemy. But this is not a very sensational theory.

What has grabbed the public imagination is the theory that some of Lincoln's own government, his Cabinet members, his friends, and even his family were part of a conspiracy and a cover-up. There are a number of troubling and suspicious elements in the Lincoln assassination. First and foremost is the poor security. Booth was able to walk into the president's box and shoot him.

The outbreak of war hardly improved matters. Death threats arrived almost daily, and there were a couple of serious attempts on Lincoln's life. It was later discovered that one of these attempts was made by John Wilkes Booth, who actually managed to shoot the president's famous top hat off. Yet when Lincoln went to Ford's Theatre that fatal evening, there was only one guard assigned to him, and this guard had wandered off in search of a drink.[1]

The guard was a policeman named John Parker. He had a reputation as an incompetent and a drunk, yet just a week before the assassination he had been recommended for duty at the White House by Mary Todd Lincoln, the president's wife. For some reason Parker's possible role in the assassination, if any, was not investigated, or if it was the results were never made public. Mary Todd Lincoln was not a popular figure in Washington, and there were even rumors that she was a Southern sympathizer—rumors that are totally unfounded.

Shortly before his own death in 1926, Lincoln's son Robert Todd Lincoln burned a large mass of his father's papers. He told a friend that the documents contained evidence of the treason of a member of his cabinet and he thought it was best for everyone that such evidence be destroyed. There has been no way to verify this intriguing statement.

After shooting Lincoln, Booth was able not only to get out of the theater without anyone stopping him, but to get clean out of Washington without being seen. The city was still under wartime conditions and the exit roads were guarded, yet none of the guards reported seeing Booth.

On the night of the assassination the commercial telegraph lines in Washington— controlled by the government in wartime—went dead, delaying news of Booth's escape.

The search for Booth was so badly organized that it reads like a catalog of errors. It's not unreasonable to conclude that if the assassin had not injured his leg jumping from Lincoln's box he might well have gotten clean away.

When the pursuing soldiers finally trapped Booth and his companion, they were under strict orders to take the actor alive if at all possible. The barn was set afire in order to smoke Booth out, but before that could happen the assassin was shot. The man who claimed credit for killing Booth was Sergeant Boston Corbett, the Jack Ruby of the Lincoln assassination. He was a strange man—a genuine religious fanatic who said he killed Booth on orders from God. Despite disobeying orders about taking the assassin alive, Corbett was given a reward and briefly became a well-known and popular lecturer. He got a job as sergeant at arms for the Kansas legislature, but one day he went completely berserk and began shooting up the chamber. He was confined to a mental institution, but then escaped and disappeared.

The best witness to the Lincoln assassination—the assassin himself—was dead, and anything he could have told investigators about the plot was lost.

But Booth was carrying a diary. This was taken to Washington, turned over to the War Department, and then it seems to have been lost for years. When it finally turned up again, it created a storm because eighteen pages—the critical pages covering events leading up to the assassination—had been torn out. The soldiers who found the diary swore that it had been undamaged when they first turned it in.

These are just some of the strange and suspicious events surrounding Lincoln's assassination. They can all be explained away as the result of confusion, coincidence, and incompetence. But true conspiracy theorists do not recognize confusion, coincidence, and incompetence—they see only a massive and smoothly running conspiracy. In 1937, historian Otto Eisenschiml announced that the man behind the plot was Lincoln's secretary of war, Edwin M. Stanton.

There is no doubt Stanton was a powerful man. He was primarily responsible for protecting the president, so the failures in protection may ultimately be laid at his doorstep. He was also in charge of investigation of the assassination and the apprehension of the conspirators. Indeed, in the days and weeks following Lincoln's assassination, Stanton exercised near-dictatorial powers. And he made mistakes—but were they just mistakes? ask the conspiracy theorists.

Why would Stanton have wanted Lincoln killed? The theory is that Stanton, a radical Republican, opposed Lincoln's conciliatory policies toward the defeated Confederacy. He wanted to see the rebels severely punished. But what possible connection could there be between such a man and the fanatic Confederate supporter Booth? Conspiracy theorists generally avoid this fundamental question.

The fallback position is that while Stanton and Booth did not actually conspire together, the secretary of war knew of Booth's plans and allowed the assassination to take place. That is slightly more plausible but still far-fetched. There is, in fact, evidence that Stanton did not want Lincoln to go to Ford's Theatre on the fatal night, but that the president brushed aside his concerns. Lincoln was a fatalist. He believed that if someone really wanted to kill you, then they would probably do so. He was notoriously unconcerned about his personal safety.

One of the most intriguing allegations of the Lincoln assassination conspiracy theory is that John Wilkes Booth was not shot at Garrett's farm—that the dying man dragged from the burning barn was someone else. Booth was said to have escaped. He was placed in locations as diverse as the American Southwest, Mexico, and Europe and most improbably India, where, it was said, he lived to a comfortable old age on a large and secret government pension.

Women claiming to have been Booth's wives, men and women swearing they were Booth's children, and several old men claiming to have been Booth himself surfaced regularly in the late nineteenth and early twentieth centuries. During the 1920s the mummified remains of a derelict painter named John St. Helen were trucked around the carnival circuit as the remains of John Wilkes Booth. This gruesome relic may still be on display somewhere.

In 1996 a lawyer petitioned to have the remains of John Wilkes Booth exhumed and subjected to DNA testing to see if the man buried in the grave was really Booth. This request was rejected, but it did get a lot of press coverage.

The theory that there was a vast conspiracy and a vast cover-up of the Lincoln assassination has become a permanent part of American lore.

THE ILLUMINATI CONSPIRACY

What may be the longest-running conspiracy theory in American history began on Sunday morning May 9, 1798, when the Reverend Jedidah Morse electrified and terrified his parishioners at the Congregationalist First Church of Charlestown, Massachusetts. He warned them that there was a secret group of evil men that were plotting to destroy Christianity and all legitimate governments. Their agents, he said, were already at work in the United States infiltrating schools, political clubs, newspapers, even the U.S. post office. Their aim was to erode religious faith and patriotism.

Who were these evil men? According to the Reverend Morse they were the Order of the Illuminati.

It is not known how many, if any, of those who listened to the sermon on that May morning had ever

*Adam Weishaupt, founder of
the Order of the Illuminati.*

even heard of the Illuminati. But within just a few months nearly everybody in the new United States had heard of them, and a genuine panic developed, particularly in New England.

The group called the Order of the Illuminati (illuminated or enlightened ones) was formed about 1776 by Adam Weishaupt, a professor of canon law at Ingolstadt University in Bavaria, Germany. Inspired by freethinking philosophers like Voltaire, the group's stated aim was to free humanity from "tyranny." For the Illuminati, this meant replacing Bavaria's church-state hierarchy with an egalitarian society based on "reason."

Weishaupt also had a mystical side and was heavily influenced by the Freemasons, or Masons (more about them in Chapter 4). The Order of the Illuminati was a secret society with a strict hierarchy. Weishaupt devised elaborate rituals and secret signs for his group, and he attempted to recruit members from Masonic lodges. Just how large the Order of the Illuminati became is difficult to determine. Deeply committed members may have been limited to Weishaupt and a few friends. There are some estimates that at its height the Illuminati may have had as many as 2,500 members, but the records are so foggy and unreliable that no one really knows.

In 1784 the highly conservative Duke Karl Theodor became Bavaria's chief of state, and he began an investigation of the Illuminati, the Freemasons, and other suspect organizations. Weishaupt lost his position at the university and fled the country. In 1787 the duke came down hard on the Illuminati. The order was banned, and those who were members faced exile or, in some cases, death. At this point the Illuminati simply disappeared from the historical record, probably because the organization disintegrated in the face of the onslaught. Weishaupt himself was ultimately reconciled with the Catholic Church before his death.

Why did this obscure European organization create a conspiracy scare in the United States some eleven years after it ceased to exist? The reason was the French Revolution of 1789, which really did overthrow church and state and traumatized many in Europe and the United States as well. But there were many persons who, rather than trying to understand the vast and complicated interplay of forces that brought about an event as momentous as the French Revolution, found it simpler and more satisfying to blame a conspiracy.

James Robison, a well-known Scottish scientist and mathematician, gathered together all that had ever been said about the Illuminati primarily by its enemies, added his own paranoid notions, and came up with a book called *Proofs of a Conspiracy Against All Religions and Governments of Europe*. It is a masterpiece of conspiracy theory.

Robison said that the Illuminati had not really been crushed in 1787, but had merely gone underground, and the obscure Bavarian professor was the

sinister genius behind the French Revolution and practically everything else that was plaguing Europe. The
book was filled with all sorts of sensational charges.
It said that the Illuminati had developed a detailed
plan for killing all the aristocrats and priests in Europe, and that the order possessed an arsenal of what
would have then been considered high-tech weapons
like exploding boxes and poison gas.

Many Americans, particularly conservative cler-
gymen like the Reverend Morse, blamed the French
Revolution for a rising tide of religious skepticism in
America. For them Robison's book, which first appeared in America in 1789, struck a responsive chord.

Morse's sermon touched off a genuine Illuminati
panic. Soon anti-Illuminati preachings came from pul-
pits throughout New England. The editor of the influential *Porcupine's Gazette* said that every living man
should read *Proofs of a Conspiracy* because "it unrav-
els everything that appears mysterious in the progress
of the French Revolution."[1] The New York *Spectator*
told its readers that they must chose between "INDE-
PENDENCE and SUBMISSION."[2]

Among those who thundered against the evils of
the Illuminati was President Timothy Dwight of Yale.
He said the Illuminati would turn American churches
into Temples of Reason, cast the Bible into the bon-
fire, grind Christian virtues underfoot, and make con-
cubines of Christian women.

The Illuminati excitement had a political side as
well. The conservative Federalist party pointed to Vice

President Thomas Jefferson, a driving force in the liberal Democratic-Republican party, as a possible Illuminati conspirator. Jefferson was an outspoken defender of France, and his religious views were anything but orthodox.

The Quakers, or Society of Friends, who were often persecuted in early America, were singled out as probable members of the conspiracy because of their egalitarian views. The United Society of Irishmen was also viewed with grave suspicion.

Ironically the Freemasons, who were so central to the European ideas of the Illuminati conspiracy, were treated very gingerly at first. The Masons had many powerful members in the new United States. One of America's leading Masons was George Washington himself, a revered, almost godlike figure in that era of American history.

There were no riots or deportations of suspected Illuminati. But those who feared the conspiracy waited anxiously for the plotters to make their move. A year went by and nothing happened. So the Reverend Morse climbed back into his pulpit on April 25, 1799, and said that he now had "complete and indisputable proof" of the Illuminati conspiracy against the United States—and this time the Freemasons were central to the story.

Morse had been given documents indicating that the Grand Orient, France's largest Masonic lodge, controlled a network of some sixteen American lodges plus a seventeenth in Santo Domingo. Most of those in the lodges were recent French immigrants. Only the truly paranoid could find anything sinister in these perfectly routine documents. But Morse and his supporters found conspiracy nonetheless. For example, the new French-dominated lodge in Santo Domingo, which had been the scene of a successful slave revolt, was called Perfect Equality. From that it was—to Morse at least—only a short leap to a belief that there was to be a French-led invasion from Santo Domingo in order to stir up rebellion among American slaves.

Another charge was that Weishaupt had escaped to America, where he had been able to successfully impersonate George Washington, the real Washington having been assassinated by Illuminati agents!

As the Illuminati conspiracy theories became more widely known, they inevitably began to encounter more serious opposition. In Europe, scholars were able to show that Robison's *Proofs of Conspiracy* was not only wrong, it was utter nonsense. Journalists compared Morse's obsession with the Illuminati to the Salem witch trials. By the end of 1799 the Reverend Morse and his supporters either changed their minds or just shut up in the face of critics, and what Jefferson called their "bedlamite ravings" came to an end.

And that should be the end of the Illuminati conspiracy story. But it's not. Once an idea, no matter how ill-founded and downright loony, enters the stream of conspiratorial thinking, it will resurface again and again in one form or another.

[45]

The influential nineteenth-century mythologist Lewis Spence tried to give the Illuminati an ancient history. Instead of beginning in Bavaria in the late eighteenth century, Spence traced their history back to Gnosticism, an early Christian heresy. He said that the ideas really took root in Spain while it was still under Muslim influence, and that later many Illuminati fled to France to escape the Spanish Inquisition. Attempts to trace secret conspiratorial groups back hundreds and sometimes thousands of years are common. Spence's theory is colorful, almost thrilling, but there is not one shred of reliable historical evidence to support it.

Far more sinister than Spence's speculations are the writings of the popular conspiratologist Nesta H. Webster in the early-twentieth-century. In a series of books she attempts to link a number of secretive movements like the Illuminati to all manner of revolutionary upheavals. One was the French Revolution, of course, for she relies heavily on Robison's writings, and another was the Russian Revolution of 1917.

Webster's 1924 book *Secret Societies and Subversive Movements* concludes ringingly:

"For behind the concrete forces of revolution—whether Pan Germanic, Judaic, or Illuminist—beyond the invisible secret circle which perhaps directs them all, is there not yet another force, still more potent, that must be taken into account? In looking back over the centuries at the dark episodes that have marked the history of the human race from its earliest origins—strange and horrible cults, waves of witchcraft, blasphemies, and desecrations—how is it possible to ignore the existence of an occult power at work in the world? Individuals, sects, or races fired with the desire of world-domination have provided the fighting forces of destruction, but behind them are the veritable powers of darkness in eternal conflict with the powers of light."[3]

Webster's books are still in print and still on the recommended reading lists of a variety of conspiracy-minded organizations.

In the 1960s the Illuminati made another and quite bizarre reappearance. In occult circles the rumor spread that an ancient and secretive brotherhood of Illuminati was now "controlling world events." No one seemed to know who the Illuminati were or whether they were supposed to be good or evil.

Two centuries after an obscure professor was chased out of his native Bavaria, and the tiny and short-lived organization he founded dissolved forever, the Illuminati lives on in the world of the conspiracy theorist.

*The Jack the Ripper case was front-page
news for* The Illustrated Police News.
This appeared after the fifth murder.

THE JACK THE RIPPER CONSPIRACY

One of the most bizarre and colorful theories in recent times involves a famous English murderer. What makes the theory so interesting is that the conspirators are supposed to be . . . but no, why spoil the surprise. First let's set the scene.

In the fall of 1888 a serial killer brutally murdered five women in the Whitechapel district of London over a period of three months. The killer, who was never caught, became known to history as Jack the Ripper.

While the crimes were savage there have, unfortunately, been even worse crimes in history. The victims themselves were not famous; they were prostitutes, desperately poor women, and most were alcoholics. They were the sort of people who are murdered all the time—and no one really notices. The fact that the murders remain unsolved gives them a certain fascination, but there are lots of unsolved crimes.

Yet the obsession with the Jack the Ripper case has endured for well over a century. Perhaps it's the time and place, the streets of fog-shrouded late Victorian London, the city of Sherlock Holmes and Dr. Jekyll and Mr. Hyde. Perhaps it's the sinister name given to the killer—Jack the Ripper. Whatever the reason or reasons, these are the most famous murders in modern history. Will people still be discussing the O. J. Simpson case in the middle of the next century? Personally I doubt it. There have been hundreds of books, movies, television dramas, and plays about Jack the Ripper. There is a regular journal of "Ripperology," which examines and reexamines every minute detail of the case. A tour of the Jack the Ripper sites is an increasingly popular tourist attraction in London today.

And it is inevitable that there are those who must believe a case this famous cannot just have happened by accident, it can't be an ordinary murder, it must be something else—something is being covered up—there must be a conspiracy here.

After the first two murders the police were under a great deal of pressure to find the murderer—to "do something." Several different police agencies as well as private groups were literally falling over one another in attempts to catch the murderer and prevent further crimes.

Then on the night of September 30, 1888, there was another Ripper murder—in fact, two of them in a single night. About a five-minute walk from the scene of one of the murders, police found a piece cut from the victim's apron and above it a blurry message chalked on a wall. It read:

> The Juwes are not
> The men that
> Will be
> Blamed for nothing[1]

When Sir Charles Warren, commissioner of the Metropolitan Police, arrived on the scene he declared that the message was "meaningless" and ordered that it be washed away, even before it was photographed. This was the act that first triggered suspicions that the police were covering something up.

There was a lot of graffiti chalked on the walls of Whitechapel, and there is no solid evidence that this message had anything to do with the Ripper murders. The fact that it was said to be "blurry" indicates that it may have been on the wall long before the killings. And the idea that a man who has just committed the second of two brutal murders in an area that he knows is swarming with police would hang around and chalk a message on a wall seems more than a bit far-fetched.

Still, destroying a potential piece of evidence is not good police work, and Warren probably was trying to cover something up—but his motives may not have been sinister in the least.

The area in which the murders were committed was home to large numbers of poor immigrant Jews.

[51]

A chief suspect in the murders was someone known as "leather apron," thought to be a kosher butcher. There was a great deal of tension in the area and Warren believed, with good reason, that if the Ripper murders were linked to the Jews, a riot could easily break out. He may have wanted to avoid inflaming local passions.

The last known murder by Jack the Ripper took place on November 9, 1888. Within a very short time after that, the police essentially closed down their investigation. The special patrols were withdrawn, and the civilian "vigilance" group was disbanded. Some of those involved in the investigation hinted that they knew who the Ripper was, and that he had either committed suicide or had died in an institution. The threat was over.

But very quickly another rumor began to spread: The police knew the Ripper was not some obscure homicidal maniac, but a Very Important Person, whose crimes were being covered up by the authorities. One of those whose name came up in the speculation was Prince Albert Victor, Duke of Clarence. He was a Very, Very Important Person, for Prince Eddy, as he was generally called, was the grandson of Queen Victoria and eldest son of the Prince of Wales. He was therefore in direct line to become king of England. You didn't get much more important than that.

By most accounts Prince Eddy was a rather dim-witted and spiritless young man whose name had been connected with a couple of earlier scandals.

When he died unexpectedly of influenza in January 1892 there doubtless were private sighs of relief mixed with public expressions of sorrow. At least the monarchy would be spared the embarrassment of such an obviously unfit individual becoming king.

It was many decades before Prince Eddy's name really hit the headlines as a Ripper suspect. In 1970, Dr. Thomas Stowell, a retired surgeon, made public the results of research he had made forty years earlier. He had examined the private papers of Sir William Gull, Queen Victoria's physician. Stowell did not actually name a suspect, calling him only "S," but the clues were unmistakable. He said the papers indicated that "S" had not died of influenza as reported, but of syphilis, which had affected his brain and transformed him into an insane murderer.

After the excitement broke, Stowell said that he had not meant to implicate Prince Eddy, but would not say whom he had meant to implicate and refused to explain all the obvious points of comparison between "S" and the heir to the throne. About a week after issuing this denial Stowell died, and his family immediately destroyed all his papers, so his evidence, if there really was any, could not be examined.

The name of Dr. William Gull had come up before in connection with the Ripper murders. Robert Lees, a journalist and psychic at the time of the murders, insisted that he had visions of the murders and that he knew where the murderer lived. He allegedly led police to the home of a prominent physician who lived in an elegant West End house. And Dr. Gull was a prominent physician who lived in an elegant West End house.

It was the next step, however, that elevated the Jack the Ripper story from a simple cover-up to the higher realms of conspiracy theory. In 1973 the British Broadcasting Corporation (BBC) was preparing a television special on the Ripper case. They interviewed an elderly artist named Joseph "Hobo" Sickert who had a very strange tale to tell. Back in the 1880s, Sickert's father, Walter, had been quite a well-known artist who had many aristocratic friends.

According to Joseph, his father said that Prince Eddy had been sent to him for social and artistic tutoring. While visiting the artist's Bohemian studio the prince met and fell in love with a Catholic girl named Anne Elizabeth Crook, who worked in a nearby tobacco shop. The pair were secretly married and had a child, a girl called Alice Margaret.

When Buckingham Palace and the Cabinet got word of this, they were horrified. A secret marriage to a commoner, and a Catholic to boot, might have brought down the monarchy. Royal agents were dispatched to separate the pair. The prince was sent to his family and told in no uncertain terms that he would never see Anne and his child again. Anne apparently was kidnapped and confined to an institution, where she eventually died a pauper and a lunatic.

The child, however, escaped in the company of her nursemaid, an Irish Catholic girl named Marie

Jeanette Kelly. Walter Sickert was able to place the child with some poor relatives. Eventually she became Sickert's ward and ultimately his mistress and the mother of Joseph Sickert. She died in 1950.

Now here's where the Ripper conspiracy comes in. Nursemaid Kelly went back to Whitechapel, where she was reduced to alcoholism and prostitution. With the aid of three of her cronies she decided to blackmail the government. The prime minister, Lord Salisbury, feared that the story not only would topple the monarchy but also that it would curtail the influence that the Freemasons had over the British government. Salisbury was a high-ranking Freemason, and in order to eliminate the blackmailers he turned to some of his brother Masons.[2]

The Masons (or Freemasons) are a secret society that began in England in the seventeenth century. Masonic lore holds that the origins of the order can be traced back to biblical times, but there is no evidence of this. Today the center for the Masons is the United States. The order is generally accepted as a fraternal businessmen's organization. The "secret" rituals and paraphernalia, which are not all that secret, are now regarded by most outsiders as either harmless or silly.

But at some times and in some places the Masons have been viewed with genuine suspicion and real fear.

In Britain some have accused the Masons of having undue political or business influence, but there have been no widespread anti-Masonic panics as have occurred in France, Italy, or Spain.

Chief of the Masons enlisted to get rid of the blackmailing women was a physician, Sir William Gull, and Sir Robert Anderson, one of the police officials in charge of the Ripper investigation. Also involved was a seedy coachman named John Netley.

The three Masons roamed Whitechapel in Netley's coach killing the women one by one. There were supposed to be only four victims, the former nursemaid and her three friends, but one innocent woman was killed because of a confusion of names. The final victim, and the one who was most horribly mutilated, was Mary Jeanette Kelly—the nursemaid herself.

According to Joseph Sickert the killings and mutilations were carried out in accordance with a Masonic ritual. They were to serve as a warning to all who would challenge the power of the Freemasons. There was a suspicion that the killings were more brutal than necessary because Gull had lost his mind. Officially, Gull died in 1890, but there were rumors that he had become a raving madman and was secretly confined to an institution, where he died a few years later.

All of this, of course, was covered up by high-ranking Masons in the police force.

At first glance this story seems to be absolutely absurd. And that is what the BBC program concluded it was. But a young reporter named Stephen Knight was sent by his paper to interview Joseph Sickert.

Knight claims he was very skeptical in the beginning, but the old man was so obviously sincere that he began his own investigation.

Knight was a diligent and resourceful researcher. He was able to obtain Scotland Yard documents on the case that no one had ever seen before, and the result of his researches, *Jack the Ripper: The Final Solution*, is a genuine masterpiece of conspiracy theorizing. It has everything: the royal family, a famous and horrible series of murders, an enormously powerful secret society, a high-level government cover-up. The book was an instant sensation because it read like a piece of thriller fiction.

There is, however, quite an ugly side to Knight's work. He relies heavily on a document called *The Protocols of the Learned Elders of Zion*. This document has a notorious history. It was fabricated by the police in Czarist Russia early in the twentieth century. It was supposed to be the plan of a secret cabal of high-ranking Jews to gain absolute power in the world by treachery and violence. It became a cornerstone of Nazi propaganda and is still central to much anti-Semitic conspiracy theory today.

Knight, however, simply calls the *Protocols* a Masonic document, and says that it shows that at least some Masons would stop at nothing—absolutely nothing—to gain and keep power. He does not discuss the sinister history of the document.

Regarding the notorious *Juwes* graffiti that Police Commissioner Warren ordered washed away, Knight insists the word is not a misspelling of Jews, as everyone else believed. The word, says Knight, comes out of Masonic lore. It stands for *Jubela, Jubelo,* and *Jube*lum, three apprentice masons who were supposed to have murdered the Grand Master Hiram Abiff, the mason in charge of building Solomon's Temple. In Masonic myth the three were tracked down, killed, and mutilated by other Masons as a warning to those who would betray the secret brotherhood. The mutilations, says Knight, were similar to those carried out on the Ripper's victims.

A complicated theory of this kind often has a weak link. In this case the weak link turned out to be Joseph Sickert, the man who had started the whole thing. In June 1978, two years after Knight's book was published, and endorsed by Sickert, the old man gave an interview to the *London Sunday Times* in which he said : "It was a hoax, I made it all up . . . a whopping fib." Sickert stuck to the story about his parentage, but the Ripper story he said was pure fantasy. "As an artist I found it easy to paint Jack the Ripper into the story."[3]

Knight, however, refused to back down. He shot back saying that Sickert was incensed because during his researches he had discovered that the third man in the murderous trio was not Sir Robert Anderson but Walter Sickert. Far from being a protector of some of those threatened by the Masonic killers, Joseph's father was one of the killers himself.

Both Stephen Knight and Joseph Sickert are now dead, and the controversy between them will never be resolved, but the unsupported and wildly unlikely theory of a Masonic conspiracy lives on. New books about the case, and they appear regularly, almost always contain a serious discussion of the theory. Knight's own book is still available, as is a video based on the book.

And if you want to see the case solved, find a copy of the 1979 film *Murder by Decree*. It is quite a gripping film in which Sherlock Holmes uncovers the terrible Masonic conspiracy behind the Jack the Ripper murders. It's all fiction, of course, as it should be.

THE CONSPIRACY KING

In the world of conspiracy theorists there is no one quite like Lyndon LaRouche. It's not that he holds the most bizarre theories—though he does believe that Queen Elizabeth of England is head of the international drug trade—for others have promoted even stranger ideas. It is that LaRouche has turned conspiracy theory into a cult and a business. Lyndon LaRouche is truly the Conspiracy King of the world today.

With his large bald head and thick rimless glasses, LaRouche looks more like a retired insurance salesman than a wild-eyed fanatic. His paid televised political speeches are delivered in such a flat and boring style that a casual viewer could easily miss the absolutely nutty things he says.

LaRouche's odyssey in the world of conspiracy has been a strange one. He came from a Quaker background, and his pacifism led him to become an army medic rather than an active soldier during World War II. After the war he drifted into a variety of left-wing groups. For a time he took the name "Lyn Marcus," after Lenin and Marx. During the upheavals of the 1960s he formed his own group, called the New York Labor Committee.

But LaRouche's left-wing associates began to view him with increasing suspicion. He formed a new group called the National Caucus of Labor Committees, and declared war on his enemies, real and imagined. Some of his followers began beating up members of other left-wing groups. The followers were often arrested for assault, while LaRouche himself remained safely in the background and out of jail.

By the mid-1970s, LaRouche proclaimed that the CIA, along with the Soviet KGB, British Intelligence, the New York City police department, and the Rockefeller family, were out to assassinate him. They were going to kidnap some of his followers, brainwash them, and turn them into robotlike assassins who would be triggered by code words to kill him.

The outside world got a glimpse into the paranoid and violent world of Lyndon LaRouche in January 1974, when a young woman named Alice Weitzman sailed a paper airplane out of the window of her New York City apartment. The plane landed at the feet of a mother and child out for a walk. When the woman unfolded the paper she found it contained a desperate note. Alice Weitzman said she was being held prisoner in her apartment, and that her captors were about to move her to some other secret location. When the mother looked up she saw the young woman waving frantically from her window. She decided it was no joke and contacted the police. Forty minutes later, when the police arrived at the apartment, they found that the note indeed was no joke.

Weitzman had been a member of LaRouche's group, but she had begun to express some skepticism. It was then that the group decided that she had been programmed to kill. She wasn't the first. The group had already tried to "deprogram" several other members. One of them was sent to the hospital when he was found running through the streets screaming, "Decontrol me! Decontrol me!"

When *New York Times* reporter Paul L. Montgomery interviewed members of the group, he found that they "seem incapable of talking about anything but the conspiracy . . . there seems to be anxious expectation about who will be singled out as a brainwashing victim. Mr. Marcus [LaRouche] has told them they are not responsible for their thoughts or actions because of the 'programming.' "

By the early 1970s, LaRouche's view of his own mission had become quite grandiose. "The human race is at stake. Either we win or there is no humanity. That's the way she's cut."

By the mid-1970s, LaRouche had moved from farleft politics to the other end of the political spectrum. He insisted that his earlier alliances with the left had only been "tactical." He formed a close alliance with the Ku Klux Klan and the far-right Liberty Lobby. And he sent his followers to receive militia-like training at a far-right enclave in Georgia.

His conspiracy theories took on a familiar far-right anti-Semitic tone. He announced that Zionism was an evil cult, that a cabal of Jews controlled organized crime, that the Holocaust was mythical, and that the Jewish organization B'nai B'rith "resurrects the tradition of the Jews who demanded the crucifixion of Jesus Christ."[1]

LaRouche has an even more overarching conspiracy theory. He sees all history as a conflict between an evil "oligarchy" and what he has called the force of "neo-Platonic humanism," whose leaders have included Alexander the Great, Charlemagne, and more recently Lyndon LaRouche. The "oligarchy," which includes everything that LaRouche does not like, has committed every imaginable crime.

There is a generous helping of genuine neo-Nazi racism in LaRouche's theories. He says his followers are a sort of superrace of "golden souls," while the enemy, the "Zionist-British organism which must be destroyed so that humanity might live," is really a separate biological species. He wants to see a dictatorship established in the United States and a "total mobilization" in preparation for the "total war" that is sure to come.

But for sheer outrageous goofiness, it is statements like this that have gotten LaRouche the most notoriety: "The entire world's drug traffic has been run by a single family since its inception." Since the statement is taken from a LaRouche publication entitled *Dope Inc.: Britain's Opium War Against the U.S.,* it will come as no surprise to find that he is talking about the British royal family as head of the dope trade.

The royal family can't do it alone, of course. They are aided by a vast collection of secret societies, private policy groups, and intelligence agencies. All the usual suspects are named. But there are also some unusual agents of the conspiracy as well. For example, LaRouche has named the rock group The Grateful Dead as a "British intelligence operation." It was spawned from the CIA's experiments with psychoactive drugs like LSD at Stanford University and similar far-out Bay Area institutions of higher education. "That was an Allen Dulles [a former CIA director] period operation which was run together with the Occult Bureau types in British intelligence, such as Aldous Huxley [a British author who experimented with drugs]." LaRouche continues:

"This is part of this satanism business. Call it counterculture. Call it the Dionysus model of the counterculture.

"Rock is essentially a revival of the ancient Dionysiac, Bacchic ritual. It does have a relationship to the alpha rhythms in the brain. If combined with a little alcohol and more, shall we say, mood-shaping substances with youth, with funny sex, this does produce a personality change of the counter cultural type."[2]

The notion that the "sex, drugs and rock 'n' roll" counterculture of the 1960s was brought about by some sort of conspiracy did not originate with LaRouche; that it is all the fault of the British royal family probably did. More recently LaRouche has suggested that the British government was somehow behind the 1995 Oklahoma City bombing.

In addition to being a dedicated conspiracy theorist, LaRouche is also a dedicated conspirator. There are a variety of LaRouche-sponsored organizations and publications that do not openly disclose their sponsorship. LaRouche followers have attempted to infiltrate and control other organizations—without a great deal of success—and LaRouche followers have often tried to run for public office, again without making their affiliations and their agenda public.

In 1986 a couple of LaRouche followers actually won in Illinois Democratic primaries for lieutenant governor and secretary of state. The reason they won is that they were attractive and articulate individuals, and they never told the voters what they really believed and who had sponsored their campaigns. Since the Democrats were given no chance to win the general election, little attention was paid to the primary election and people voted for the LaRouche followers assuming that they were regular Democrats.

This victory, however, was a mixed blessing for LaRouche. Once it was discovered, the national press

*On April 9, 1986, Lyndon LaRouche addressed
the National Press Club, and this photograph was
taken. While he had been toning down his message
in previous public speeches, at this session he
characterized his political enemies as drug pushers,
homosexuals, pro-Soviet, or insane.*

[66]

suddenly began to examine what the man actually stood for. Lyndon LaRouche, who had up to that time been little more than an eccentric fringe figure, suddenly began to look a lot more menacing.

In his regular runs for president, usually in Democratic party primaries, LaRouche tries to hide his more odious ideas behind code words. For example, in a 1984 prime-time paid political broadcast on CBS, LaRouche did not engage in his usual anti-Semitic diatribes. He just spoke of the influence of "Kissinger and his friends." Former Secretary of State Henry Kissinger is Jewish. The reference might have slipped past a casual listener, but it was not lost on the leader of the Michigan Ku Klux Klan—who saluted LaRouche for "exposing the neo-atheist materialism of Kissinger to the dismay of the Talmudists."[3]

Lyndon LaRouche does not really respond to questions or criticism. Anyone who does criticize him is immediately attacked as a part of the conspiracy against him. For example, at a rare news conference in 1992 when a reporter asked him a question he didn't like LaRouche shot back, "I'm not going to talk to a dope pusher, like you."[4] That reaction is typical.

LaRouche has a devoted, even fanatical following, but not a large one. There are probably not more than a few hundred or so hard-core LaRouchies. Yet he lives in a luxurious and well-guarded estate in Leesburg, Virginia, and his network of organizations seems very well funded. Where does the money come from? Some of it comes from wealthy supporters. His biggest catch to date is Louis Du Pont, a member of one of the richest families in America. In a well-publicized case, Du Pont's parents went into court to prevent Louis from giving everything he had to LaRouche. LaRouche supporters have also sold publications, often with innocuous and misleading titles, in airports and other public places.

But still, that didn't seem to account for the millions of dollars that the LaRouche organization raised. When the U.S. government looked into his finances, it was found that he had fraudulently solicited loans from his supporters, mainly elderly women, and never paid them back. LaRouche was tried, convicted of fraud and tax evasion in 1989, and sentenced to fifteen years in a federal penitentiary. He said that this was all part of the conspiracy against him, and predicted that he would be assassinated in prison. Instead he was paroled in 1994. He walked out of prison uninjured and unrepentant, went back to Leesburg, began grinding out conspiracy theories once again, and filed as a candidate for the Democratic nomination for president in 1996.

LaRouche presents no particular danger to society. Though he has been around for decades, he has never been able to attract more than a small following, and advancing age will not improve his appeal. His theories, awful as they may be, are not original. Most would exist with or without him.

The real danger of Lyndon LaRouche is that he is probably the most active and effective publicist for conspiracy theories in the world today. LaRouche controls a variety of publications and has organizations in several different countries. He also has a dedicated staff of "investigators" and "researchers." These are individuals who collect clippings and rumors about anyone that Lyndon LaRouche doesn't like. That's practically everyone.

LaRouche is not particularly effective in spreading his grand theories. Besides, he is now so well known and notorious that no one with a shred of respectability wants to be associated with him in any way. LaRouche has been more effective working on smaller issues and working behind the scenes. It has often been charged that the LaRouche organizations have been used and even paid to dig up dirt and spread false rumors for others.

An example of this sort of activity surfaced in 1995. The U.S. Senate appeared poised to ratify an international treaty to preserve the Earth's biological resources. It had broad bipartisan support. But suddenly and unexpectedly problems arose. Senator Robert Dole called for a postponement of the vote, and ultimately the vote was never held.

Where did the opposition come from? Much of it crystallized around the idea that "biodiversity" was a new religion and the treaty was a threat to U.S. sovereignty, private property rights, control of natural resources, and individual freedom. And that theory came from an article written by a LaRouche associate and first published in a LaRouche magazine. The article was then widely distributed by a number of completely respectable organizations like the American Sheep Industry Association, which had opposed the treaty from the start but claimed that they had no idea of the origins of the alarmist information they were faxing to their senators.

The October 17, 1996, issue of *The Washington Post* quotes Columbia professor Manning Marable regarding a "budding alliance" between LaRouche and Louis Farrakhan, Nation of Islam leader and sponsor of the Million Man March in 1995.

Said the *Post*, "The LaRouche organization, which frequently advances global conspiracy theories, has worked with the Nation of Islam in the past. But since the march, that connection has grown tighter with former LaRouche vice presidential candidate and civil rights activist James Bevel frequently appearing with Farrakhan."

Lyndon LaRouche has been around a long time. He has dabbled in practically every branch of conspiracy theory. Many of his followers and former associates have gone on to their own careers in the small and murky world of conspiracy theory. His numerous publications have been used as sources for other conspiracy theorists. Lyndon LaRouche is truly the Conspiracy King.

"A CONSPIRACY SO IMMENSE"

For nearly half of the twentieth century a significant percentage of the American public believed that the United States was not merely threatened by the world-wide Communist conspiracy but actually controlled by it. This was the largest, most influential, and most pervasive conspiracy theory in modern American history.

Since the Bolshevik revolution in Russia in 1917, most Americans feared and hated communism. There was also a much smaller but not insignificant number of Americans who were sincerely attracted to the Communist ideology. Of these, some became genuine Soviet agents and spies. But to put matters in perspective, the United States had its own agents and spies within the Soviet Union. And the United States was never in any serious danger of being taken over by the Communist conspiracy. However, you could never convince Joe McCarthy's followers of that. To hear them tell it, the Reds had already taken over, and only one man could save them.

For a few years in the early 1950s, Joseph R. McCarthy, junior senator from Wisconsin, was, if not the most powerful man in America, certainly one of the most feared. McCarthy had been elected to the Senate in 1946, but he didn't make much of an impact in Washington until he discovered the Communist conspiracy.

Most of McCarthy's biographers say that he didn't believe much of what he said, at least not at first. But he said it anyway because it got attention. McCarthy wasn't the first politician to raise the specter of the Red Menace, and he wouldn't be the last. But no one was ever louder, more extreme, and for a short time more effective.

McCarthy began his crusade against the Communist conspiracy with a speech in Wheeling, West Virginia, on February 9, 1950. He horrified his audience with the accusation that the State Department was "thoroughly infested with Communists." He said that he had a list with the names of 205 State Department Communists on it. In later speeches he used other numbers, but that didn't make any difference. The figures were completely imaginary. What made the difference was that McCarthy spoke with such assurance and was so specific about the conspiracy that the press began to pay attention to what he was saying.

Very quickly this once-obscure senator with poor reelection prospects became a national celebrity. The press would report every charge he made no matter how outrageous they knew it to be. Right-wing groups that already believed the country was in the grip of the Communist conspiracy had found their champion. The money poured in. A lot of politicians who knew that McCarthy was talking nonsense and genuinely disliked his tactics began backing him because they were afraid of angering his devoted followers.

The more attention and support he got, the wilder and more extreme became the charges he made. He could destroy careers and entire branches of government with a single speech. A high point, or perhaps a low point, in his "anti-Communist crusade," and certainly a low point in American history, came in mid-June 1951 when McCarthy went to the floor of the U.S. Senate and delivered a two-hour-and-forty-five minute harangue that was part of a 169-page attack. The most memorable part of the speech was where he attacked a "mysterious, powerful" figure who was part of "a conspiracy on a scale so immense as to dwarf any previous such venture in the history of man. A conspiracy of infamy so black that, when it is finally exposed, its principals shall be forever deserving of the maledictions of all honest men."[1]

This "mysterious, powerful" figure was none other than the former secretary of defense, General George C. Marshall, a World War II hero, architect of the Marshall Plan (which many historians credit with saving Western Europe from communism after the war), and one of the most respected men in America. Marshall had his enemies and detractors, as everyone in public life does, but for McCarthy to stand on the floor of the Senate and charge that he was at the center of an immense Communist conspiracy was absolutely stunning. And McCarthy got away with it. Yes, he was denounced as "setting a new high for irresponsibility" and even as being "of unsound mind." But his millions of followers loved it. This is what they had believed all along, and now someone in the public spotlight was saying it for them. And many of those who didn't agree with everything McCarthy said assumed that there must be some truth in it. The notion that "where there is smoke there must be fire" is deeply embedded in our consciousness.

If McCarthy had been a clever politician, there is no telling how far he might have gone. But he wasn't very clever, and he alienated too many people, including the newly elected and immensely popular new president, General Dwight Eisenhower. Eisenhower had always hated McCarthy for attacking his old friend and former commanding officer General Marshall. Then McCarthy overreached himself by directly attacking the U.S. Army. The result was a long televised hearing of McCarthy's charges in 1954. It was the first major live television coverage of a political event. McCarthy, who was generally unkempt and untelegenic, looked and sounded downright thuggish during the hearings, and while no conclusion was

On March 16, 1955, when this photograph was taken, Joseph McCarthy was still a senator but losing favor with his colleagues and the American public. For years he had exercised great power and influence by charging that many of the most prominent and respected people in America were either dupes or agents of a vast Communist conspiracy.

reached the junior senator from Wisconsin was clearly the loser in the court of public opinion. By the end of the year he was censured by an overwhelming majority of his Senate colleagues. He became the only senator in Washington who was never invited to the White House.

Yet—and this is important—in spite of all the disapproval, and in spite of the many times that McCarthy's conspiracy charges had been demonstrated to be absolutely false, he never lost his core following. Polls showed that even after the censure by the Senate, fully one third of the American public still believed that McCarthy was right and thought he was a courageous hero for exposing the Communist conspiracy. McCarthy did not create this group, and it did not disappear with his fall from political grace.

McCarthy was never able to do anything with his still immense popular following because he lacked the skill and perhaps the ambition to lead an independent political movement, and because he was a chronic alcoholic whose drinking had begun to spiral completely out of control. He died on May 2, 1957, from the effects of his drinking. By the end of his life he apparently had begun to believe many of the conspiracy stories that he had previously told. He repeatedly told friends, "They're killing me."[2]

After his death some McCarthy partisans claimed that he had never been a heavy drinker and that his death had been due to infectious hepatitis or something else unconnected with alcoholism.

The most extreme of the McCarthyites found a more sinister explanation for his death. William Loeb, editor of the ultraconservative but very influential *Manchester Union Leader* of New Hampshire, wrote shortly after his hero's death:

> McCarthy was murdered by the communists because he was exposing them. When he began to arouse the United States to the extent of the communist conspiracy in our government, in our schools, in our newspapers, and in all branches of American life, the communist party realized that if it was to survive and succeed in its conspiracy to seize control of the United States it had to destroy McCarthy before he destroyed the party.[3]

Some even thought that the "assassination of Joe McCarthy" had been engineered by President Dwight Eisenhower and Vice President Richard Nixon. One dedicated McCarthyite insisted that the great man had been murdered not by the Communists but by the Illuminati!

In the minds and imaginations of the conspiracy theorists the Communists not only were going to take over our government, but our bodies as well. One of the more bizarre episodes of the Cold War era was the controversy over fluoridating the water supply to prevent tooth decay.

Putting fluorine, a pale yellow relative of chlorine gas, into the water supply was first tested in the 1940s. The tests showed quite conclusively that fluoridated water did help to prevent tooth decay in children. But some people complained that the fluorine also produced other effects, such as dizziness, nausea, and headaches. No scientific evidence of harmful side effects was ever found, but public-health controversies of this type are fairly common. Usually they are resolved quietly. Not so with fluoridation. Very quickly a large movement sprang up, claiming that the entire population was being force-fed a deadly poison. In high concentrations fluorine is a deadly poison. But so is chlorine.

Many who opposed fluoridation were motivated by a vague fear that their freedom was being eroded when the government introduced a chemical into their water supply. It was seen as a threat to their personal liberty; it was un-American. However, similar fears had not been expressed over the much more widespread use of chlorine to kill harmful bacteria in the water supply. To others fluoridation was a kind of "mass medication," a way of dosing the multitudes that might be the precursor of socialized medicine and a symptom of the looming Communist takeover.

To many, fluoridation was nothing less than an integral part of the Communist conspiracy, a "method of Red warfare"—a plot to drug Americans into submission. A speaker at an American Legion convention in New York claimed fluoridation was a "secret

Russian revolutionary technique to deaden our minds, slow our reflexes, and gradually kill our will to resist aggression." According to the *Americanism Bulletin*, fluoridation had been used by Germany's Weimar regime (the left-wing German government that fell to Hitler) and had also been used by the Russians to obtain phony confessions from prisoners. Fluoridation, the *Bulletin* went on, was "more dangerous than atomic bombs."

Today most of the country's major water supplies are fluoridated. Because of that, you probably have fewer cavities, and in case you didn't notice, the Communists have not taken over—yet.

THE NEW WORLD ORDER

The collapse of Soviet communism in the 1990s left many in America feeling abandoned and adrift. It wasn't just the former Communists who felt that way either. Many of those on the far right, the most fanatical of the anti-Communists, suddenly found themselves without a focus for their fears or an anchor for their anger.

For decades they had been able to blame practically everything that went wrong in the world or in their lives on the international Communist conspiracy. Suddenly the Russian Communists were no more, and even the most fanatical persons could not convince themselves, or anyone else, that the Communist collapse was just another clever Commie ploy to confuse the true patriots and weaken their resolve, while secretly underground the Communists were still there, more powerful and more sinister than ever. Somehow the Communists in China, the most populous nation on Earth, just couldn't take the place of the old Soviet Communists. There was no denying it, no escaping it, the Communist conspiracy, which seemed to explain so much, was dead and gone.

But in a very real and personal way, little had actually changed in America. Those who had blamed the Communists were no richer or more powerful than before. Taxes were still high. The government was still trying to take away their guns. The rampant immorality that they had seen as being promoted by the Communist conspiracy was, if anything, more rampant than ever. Something was still wrong. To some very nearly everything was still wrong. A conspiracy to deprive them of what they needed and wanted was still out there. But what was it?

It was President George Bush who inadvertently give this conspiracy its new name. Shortly after the victory over Iraq in the Persian Gulf War, President Bush said, "I hope that history will record that the Gulf Crisis was the crucible for a new world order."

The New World Order (or NWO) has become sort of a catch-all phrase. It means that some sort of one-world government or international control is to be forced on the United States, destroying the nation's sovereignty and the constitutional freedoms of its citizens. Those behind the conspiracy are a shadowy but immensely powerful group that might be called the "Establishment" or the "Elite." Whoever they are they do not represent the ordinary folk who should be represented in a democracy like America. In this belief or fear both right- and left-wing conspiracy theorists often agree. Sometimes it is difficult to tell the difference between them, and sometimes there is no difference.

George Bush himself was just the sort of man to set the conspiracy theorists' bells ringing. He was a wealthy member of the Eastern political establishment, the ultimate Washington insider. Never mind that he had moved to Texas and had attempted to portray himself as the quintessential Texan. That pose fooled no one. While at Yale, George Bush had even been a member of the secret Skull and Bones Society. This Yale student group is secretive and may be both snobbish and silly, but it is hardly sinister. To some conspiracy theorists, however, the Skull and Bones is right up there with the Freemasons and the Illuminati.

Bush had been a member of several highly suspect internationalist organizations like the Council on Foreign Relations (CFR) and the Trilateral Commission (Trilat). He had even been a CFR board director. And, most damning of all, he had been director of the Central Intelligence Agency, every conspiratologist's favorite bogeyman.

In their book, *50 Greatest Conspiracies of All Time,* authors Jonathan Vankin and John Whalen describe the New World Order this way:

"The champions of the NWO are indeed a cadre of powerful industrialists, bankers, academics and politicians who for three quarters of a century have been a gray eminence behind the governance of Britain and America. More to the point perhaps they *are* the governors of the Western world. Call them what you will they are the 'Establishment.' Through vastly influential organizations like the Council on Foreign Relations and the Trilateral Commission, these elites formulate tomorrow's public policy today and staff the ship of state with their own.

"If this network is something less than the Red Devil depicted in many a right wing conspiracy theory, it is none the less the kind of big business cabal that helps the elite of the private sector if not 'rule the world' then at least run it like a business."[1]

The most influential and respectable promoter of NWO conspiracy theory was the late Professor Carroll Quigley, a scholar from Georgetown University. In his massive book *Tragedy and Hope,* he wrote that there "does exist, and has existed for a generation, an international Anglophile [pro-British] network which operates, to some extent, in the way that the radical Right believes the Communists act."[2]

Quigley said that he had been close to this cabal of international manipulators, and that he even admired their goals—and had been allowed to examine "papers and secret records."

Quigley saw the international conspiracy as a relatively benevolent one whose goal is "nothing less than to create a world system of financial control in private hands able to dominate the political system of each country and the economy of the world as a whole." The result would be peace and prosperity, and of course great profit to those who pulled the strings.

Quigley represents a moderate, or centrist, conspiratorial view. The far right has adopted a much more menacing view. The John Birch Society, which during the 1960s and 1970s was considered the ultimate far-right conspiracy group in the United States, even thought that the internationalist elite controlled the Soviet Communists, and the Birchers hated the Communists. In the official John Birch Society ideology it was the internationalist capitalists who actually financed the Bolshevik revolution in Russia in 1917.

A popular John Birch Society book of the 1970s was Gary Allen's *None Dare Call It Conspiracy*. This was the sequel to the all-time Birch Society best-seller *None Dare Call It Treason*, which detailed the society's view of the Communist menace in America.

In Allen's opinion the first move that this internationalist elite made to control America and subvert the Constitution was to establish a central bank, the Federal Reserve System. Then came the income tax, and taking America off the gold standard. The 1929 stock market crash and the Great Depression that followed were "scientifically engineered" by the Establishment. So were the two world wars and the Vietnam War. The conspirators did very well for themselves by selling arms to both sides. Of course, the most fiendish creation was the United Nations—the hated "one world government" that will destroy America.

[84]

Right-wing conspiracy theorists have spent many hours compiling lists of powerful American political figures who are also members of the Council on Foreign Relations, the Trilateral Commission, or any of the other international establishment organizations. In President Clinton's administration, for example, the secretary of state, all five of his undersecretaries, and many of their subordinates as well as the national security advisor and head of the CIA were all members of the CFR.

Some conspiracy theorists with anti-Semitic leanings see an ever-threatening cabal of "international Jewish bankers" behind it all. Others look to the Illuminati, the Freemasons, or some even more esoteric, obscure, and probably quite imaginary secret society as the hidden hand controlling events.

While manipulation of the Federal Reserve system may be of compelling interest to some conspiracy theorists, it is not the sort of belief that gets most people excited. In truth, most people have absolutely no idea what the Federal Reserve system is and they don't really care very much. Invoking the Council on Foreign Relations and the Trilateral Commission is not going to create a great deal of excitement either. But fear of a New World Order does involve far more emotional issues—what the politicians call "red meat" issues.

The July 9, 1995, edition of *The Washington Post* contained a long article by staff writer Serge F. Kovaleski on the bombing of the Alfred P. Murrah Federal Building in Oklahoma City. Federal authori-

The north side of the Alfred Murrah Federal Building in Oklahoma City. Two people were eventually charged with detonating the bomb that destroyed the building and killed more than 150 people. One of them, Tim McVeigh, traveled the gun and weapon show circuit, at which dozens of books and pamphlets promoted the idea of governmental conspiracies.

ties indicted a couple of antigovernment ex-soldiers for the attack. For most of the public the evidence against the suspects seemed overwhelming. But Kovaleski wrote, "Conspiracy theories about the Oklahoma City bombing have been flooding the Internet, fax machines, talk radio and militia meetings around the country, spun by deeply distrustful minds that cast a broad net of blame. . . ."[3]

These theories generally blame the federal government itself for the bombing and say that the two men charged are either innocent scapegoats or government-controlled "zombies" who were set up in order to discredit the militia movement and other patriotic right-wing organizations.

Kovaleski writes, "A springboard for many of the Oklahoma City conspiracy theories is the contention that the federal government is engaged in a plot to destroy individual rights and liberties and hand over control of the country to the United Nations, which will oversee a 'New World Order.'

"Some theorists believe that proof of a planned U.N. takeover can be found on the back of a 1993 Kix cereal box which shows a map of the United States carved up into 11 regions. This, conspiracists say, is an illustration of the New World Order plot to reduce the country to departments after the conquest.

"By staging violent acts, like the bombing, and creating villains, the government can justify suspending the Constitution, declaring martial law and seizing people's weapons, the theory goes." [4]

[87]

The sinister and mysterious black helicopters, apparently the unofficial vehicles of the New World Order, were said to be seen hovering over the federal building at the time of the explosion. The most comprehensive book on this subject is Jim Keith's *Black Helicopters Over America*. The subtitle is *Strikeforce for the New World Order*.

Some analysts believe that conspiracy theories about the Oklahoma City bombing may soon eclipse the JFK assassination in conspiracy lore. True conspiracy theorists will of course dismiss Kovaleski's article because it appeared in *The Washington Post*, which, they assert, is an establishment paper controlled by the New World Order.

Televised interviews with some militia members after the Oklahoma City bombing give an indication of just how paranoid some of the conspiratorial thinking has become. Some expect an invasion of the United States by United Nations (usually African) troops who are now being trained in Mexico. They will be carried to the United States in the notorious black helicopters. Some also talk about mind-controlling drugs or mind-controlling computer chips that are being implanted in unsuspecting individuals during routine surgery.

For individuals who are immersed in conspiracy theories this extreme, the world is a terrifying place. And they are sometimes tempted to strike back at their imaginary enemies. That is what makes life just a little more frightening for the rest of us.

THE EXTRATERRESTRIAL CONSPIRACY

According to some polls more than half of the American public today think that the Earth may have been visited by spaceships from other planets. These ships have been called Flying Saucers, Unidentified Flying Objects, or most commonly by the abbreviation UFOs (pronounced U-FOHZ by insiders). In addition many people believe rumors that the government has known about these visits for more than half a century, and, for some reason, has been covering up this knowledge. In short, there has been a vast and sinister conspiracy of silence about an invasion from outer space!

This is not the sort of conspiracy theory that generally sends people running to the hills with their guns or even causes them to change the way they vote. On occasion, however, the belief can become dangerously obsessive. In June 1996, members of a UFO group on

Long Island, New York, were indicted for plotting to poison county officials with radioactive materials. According to the indictments the men believed that a UFO had crashed on Long Island and that county officials were trying to cover this up. The leader of the group also appeared to believe that government agents, including the local police, were plotting to kill him.

The firm conviction that there is some sort of a UFO conspiracy pops up regularly in books, on television and radio talk shows, and in films like the incredibly popular *Independence Day* (1996), which became one of the biggest moneymakers in Hollywood history. Many reasons have been given for the success of this film. One certainly is that many in the audience are thinking, "Well, it might be true." Belief in UFOs is part of our culture, part of our mental landscape. We can hardly imagine a time when we didn't believe in UFOs.

I know how it all began because I was an eyewitness and in a small way even a participant in the beginnings of the extraterrestrial conspiracy belief.

For many years there had been reports off and on of strange objects sighted in the sky. But what came to be regarded as the age of flying saucers began on June 24, 1947. On that day a man named Kenneth Arnold, a private pilot, was flying near the Cascade Mountains in the state of Washington when he sighted nine objects streaking through the sky toward Mount Rainier. The lead object looked like a dark crescent; the other eight were flat and disc-shaped. They disappeared from view after about two and a half minutes.

On the following day Arnold told his story to a couple of local reporters. One of them put it on the Associated Press wire, and it was picked up widely. The Arnold sighting stimulated other sighting stories. In general, however, the Arnold sighting was regarded as what journalists call a "silly season" item, a marginally newsworthy story that was printed during the summer months when there was relatively little "hard," or important, news.

In the late 1940s there was also a pervasive atmosphere of suspicion and fear. The United States had emerged victorious from World War II. Almost immediately it was plunged into the Cold War, that long period of confrontation with the Soviets. The United States had already developed an atomic bomb, and everyone knew it was only a matter of time before the Soviet Union had its own atomic bomb. The fear was that the next war would be even more terrible than the last, that the human race might actually annihilate itself.

This atmosphere affected the way people began to think about UFOs in several ways. The U.S. government and particularly the military began to wonder if the strange things that people reported seeing might not be some sort of Soviet "secret weapon." Some of the things that people reported were actually secret U.S. military projects, and these were to be kept secret.

Much of the general public thought or at least hoped that the spaceships had come to help save the human race from itself. That was a popular theme in a lot of science fiction.

Flying saucers also had an active and effective promoter. He was Ray Palmer, editor of the pulp science-fiction magazines *Amazing Stories* and *Fantastic Adventures*. The covers of these magazines regularly featured semiclad girls being menaced by a BEM (Bug Eyed Monster). Though these were clearly lurid fiction magazines, the eccentric Palmer often ran long editorials promoting any number of truly bizarre theories or beliefs.

While much of the press first regarded flying saucers as a sort of joke, Palmer took up the cause in his editorial columns. But the publishers got tired of Palmer's increasing use of the magazines as his personal soapbox. He quit or was fired over plans for an all-UFO issue. In the spring of 1948, Palmer began a new magazine, *FATE*, devoted to "true" tales of the strange and unknown. The cover story for the first issue was "The Truth About Flying Saucers" by Kenneth Arnold. Palmer himself probably wrote the article and a later Arnold book, *The Coming of the Saucers*. Palmer's breathless style was unmistakable.

Later, Ray Palmer edited a number of other flying-saucer magazines. He never became rich as a few UFO promoters have, but he stuck with the subject. Year in and year out, even at times when interest in UFOs seemed to have faded entirely, Palmer was still out there promoting. Astronomer Donald Menzel, an early critic of UFO theories, said that Palmer practically created flying saucers. That is an exaggeration, but he certainly helped to keep the interest alive.

Ray Palmer died in 1977. Right up to the end even his friends were not sure whether he believed anything he wrote.

In the late 1940s I was a young teen living in Chicago (where Palmer's magazines were first published), and I was a devotee of science fiction and "true mysteries." I was therefore an avid reader of Palmer's publications. Over the years I became disillusioned when the flying saucers I sincerely believed were going to land in some public place for all to see failed to do so.

Still, I can vividly remember the tremendous feeling of exhilaration of those early days. There was a small band of us who believed—no, we KNEW—an astonishing truth that the rest of the world was too blind to see. It made us feel very special, and it was a faith that was painful to give up. From personal experience I can say that the attraction of bizarre, even completely crazy, theories can be astonishingly powerful. I am never tempted to ask, "How can a sane person believe such nonsense?" I did and I like to think that I'm sane.

If an ordinary teen living in Chicago could know the truth about UFOs, then certainly the government with all its ability to monitor the skies should know it too. The only logical conclusion one could draw was that the government did know the truth but was covering it up. And in fact, the government was covering things up, but they were not the truths that I and my fellow flying-saucer buffs had imagined.

Once again the era of the Cold War must be kept in mind. While a few in the government and military were intrigued by the extraterrestrial possibilities of UFOs, that idea was not taken seriously for very long. What the U.S. government was really concerned about was that the Soviets might be developing some sort of "secret weapon," an aircraft or missile, and this was what people were seeing. A special panel was set up by the CIA to look into the possibility. The Soviet hypothesis was quickly discarded for total lack of evidence. However, the U.S. government itself was conducting some experiments that were mistaken for UFO sightings, and that *was* being covered up.

The Roswell incident, now far and away the most famous UFO event, is a case in point. In early July 1947, just a couple of weeks after the Arnold sighting, something crashed in a field of a remote ranch near Roswell, New Mexico. The owner of the ranch, William "Mac" Brazel, went into town a few days later and reported this to the local sheriff. The sheriff called nearby Roswell Air Base, and the Air Force sent out a team of officers to investigate.

The Air Force investigators picked up some of the debris from the ranch. It consisted mostly of highly flexible metallic-like fragments and pieces of a light but stiff material that appeared to be covered with strange writing or figures.

This photograph, dated July 8, 1947, shows Brigadier General Roger Ramey studying the remains of what the Air Force said in a press release was a "device used by air force and weather bureau(s) to determine wind velocity and direction" that had fallen near Roswell, New Mexico, a few days earlier.

On July 8 the public-relations officer at Roswell Army Air Base issued a press release stating that a "flying disc" had finally been found and that the debris was being sent to Fort Worth for examination. That story was a sensation, but a short-lived one. Within hours, in a news conference at Fort Worth, Army spokesmen dismissed the whole incident, saying what had fallen to Earth on the Brazel ranch were the remains of an ordinary weather balloon that had been destroyed in a thunderstorm.

Most people, including most UFO buffs, accepted the explanation. While interest in UFOs grew during the 1950s and 1960s, the Roswell story was almost entirely forgotten. It wasn't until the late 1980s that UFO enthusiasts rediscovered Roswell with a vengeance and began to reexamine the case.

Rancher Brazel was long dead, but others who were on the scene at the time or who now claimed that they had been on the scene, began telling their stories. Some of the stories indicated that the whole weather-balloon story was fraudulent and the government knew it. They said that Brazel and others actually had been told to keep quiet about what they had found or seen. "In 1947 when the government told you to shut up, you shut up," one witness recalled.[1]

The stories got wilder—much wilder. There were rumors of a much larger crash near Roswell and of the bodies of several space aliens found on the scene and hidden away by a fearful U.S. government. It was usually suggested that they were hidden at Wright-Patterson Air Force Base outside of Dayton, Ohio.

[96]

The story kept gaining momentum. There were several books on Roswell. It was the subject of a very popular made-for-TV movie. There was even what purported to be a film of an "alien autopsy." The film was an obvious phony. At least it was obvious to many of us. But it was so widely watched that the Fox TV network gave it a repeat showing almost immediately, and copies of the film are still available for sale or rent.

There are now two UFO museums in Roswell (and not much else since the air base closed down). They are places of pilgrimage for UFO believers and some nonbelievers.

Then, in September 1994, the Air Force finally admitted that, yes, there had been a cover-up at Roswell—sort of a cover-up anyway. While what fell to Earth on the Brazel ranch was a balloon, it wasn't an ordinary weather balloon as the Air Force had originally said. The balloon was part of a program called Project Mogul. It was aimed at putting sensors high into the atmosphere in order to detect possible Soviet nuclear tests. And in 1947 the project was top secret.

People had indeed been told to shut up—not about spaceships but about a top-secret project. "This won't lay it to rest," sighed Colonel Albert C. Trakowski, a retired Air Force officer who had run Project Mogul.

He was quite right. Said Walter G. Haut, who runs one of the Roswell UFO museums, "All they've done is given us a different kind of balloon. Then it was weather, and now it's Mogul. Basically I don't think anything has changed. Excuse my cynicism, but let's quit playing games."[2]

It is difficult to pinpoint just exactly where and when the government cover-up stories began. But they certainly started early in the flying-saucer era, and they were helped along enormously by something that happened about six months after the Kenneth Arnold sighting. This incident also involved a balloon, a cover-up, and tragically the death of an airman.

On January 7, 1948, Captain Thomas Mantell was killed when his National Guard F-51 crashed while pursuing what he believed was a flying saucer near Fort Knox, Kentucky.

Captain Mantell was leading a flight of four F-51s on orders to investigate a UFO sighted over Godman Air Force Base. Mantell radioed, "I'm closing in on it now to take a good look. It's directly ahead of me and still moving at about half my speed. . . . The thing looks metallic and of tremendous size."[3]

A short time later his plane crashed. The official explanation was that Captain Mantell had blacked out from lack of oxygen during the chase, which could have easily happened in a plane of that era. Of course, there were rumors that the wreckage of the plane showed that it had been shot full of holes or that the area of the crash had been found to be intensely radioactive. There were, however, no facts to back up such rumors.

But a vital question remained—what was Captain Mantell chasing? The initial Air Force explanation was that he was chasing the planet Venus. That is not as silly as it sounds. At certain times and under certain atmospheric conditions Venus can appear to be enormous, and it has fooled even experienced pilots. But at the time of the crash Venus was not in a part of the sky where it could possibly have fooled Captain Mantell. The explanation was quickly ridiculed, and the Air Force looked foolish or, worse, sinister.

It wasn't until 1951 that the Air Force admitted they knew what the pilot had been chasing, and they had known all along. He was chasing a giant Skyhook balloon. But in 1948, Project Skyhook was also top secret. Air Force officials deliberately misled investigators and suppressed reports from other observers who had identified the object as a balloon. By the time the Skyhook explanation became known, the damage had been done. Many assumed, quite reasonably, that if the Air Force had lied about an accident that killed one of its own pilots, it might still be lying, still covering up something more sensational than a secret balloon project.

It was impossible for the U.S. government not to respond to the widespread and growing public belief in UFOs and in a government conspiracy. But the response was clumsy and deceptive and simply fanned the fires of public disbelief and distrust.

After the death of Captain Mantell the Air Force initiated a string of "projects" that were ostensibly aimed at investigating and explaining the UFO phenomenon. They had names like Project Sign, Project

Grudge, and finally Project Blue Book. At the start some of those involved in the Air Force investigations took the extraterrestrial hypothesis seriously indeed. But by the time Project Blue Book, the last and longest lived of the Air Force UFO projects, was established, the investigation had become little more than a public-relations effort. For most of its twenty-year existence, Blue Book didn't have the personnel or the funding to investigate much of anything. The staff, which consisted of a major, two sergeants, and a secretary, could not possibly handle the thousands of UFO sightings that were reported annually. They didn't even try. UFO buffs denounced Blue Book as a cover-up, and in a sense it was. What the Air Force was really covering up, however, was not secret information about space aliens, but the fact that they didn't take the whole subject seriously and were doing as little as possible about it.

Another red flag for believers was the early involvement of the Central Intelligence Agency in UFO investigations. In fact the CIA had been monitoring the phenomenon since 1949, despite statements to the contrary. In January 1953, after a major UFO flap, the CIA convened a scientific panel on UFOs headed by Dr. H. P. Robertson, a well-known California physicist. The panel apparently took its job seriously but quickly concluded that UFOs themselves represented no national-security threat. However, the Robertson panel reported, the public was developing "a morbid national psychology" that might induce "hysterical behavior and harmful distrust of duly constituted authority." The panel concluded that "immediate steps to strip the Unidentified Flying Objects of the special status they have been given," should be undertaken.[5] In brief, tell people as little as possible and downplay UFOs.

In 1953 the CIA was just beginning to acquire its reputation of enormous, almost omniscient power, in some eyes attaining the status of an invisible government. When the report of the Robertson panel was declassified with its suggestions that UFOs essentially be buried as far as the public was concerned, it was cited as yet another example of the ongoing conspiracy of silence.

By 1966 the Air Force was thoroughly sick of its involvement in the UFO controversy. The U.S. government wanted to get out of the UFO business completely. The chosen method was to convene a committee under the direction of a distinguished scientist who would review what had been learned over the previous twenty years and issue a definitive report. At first no major scientist or university wanted to touch the study, though there was a sizable financial grant attached.

Finally the job was taken on by Dr. Edward U. Condon, a physicist from the University of Colorado. At first Condon appeared the perfect choice. In the late 1940s and early 1950s he had come under severe attack from the House Un-American Activities Committee and Representative Richard Nixon, then a young and ambitious congressman from California who was making a reputation for himself as a fire-breathing anti-Communist. Condon was accused of "consorting with Communists." As a result his security clearance was revoked, but Condon fought back and ultimately was vindicated. So he had a reputation for independence and taking on the government, in addition to being a well-known and well-respected scientist.

I attended the press conference at which Condon's appointment as head of the study was announced. Condon declared that he was quite neutral on the subject of UFOs. This, of course, was untrue. Like most scientists Condon thought the extraterrestrial hypothesis was silly at best, though he didn't know much about the subject at the time. But he seemed quite serene in his belief that he would be able to produce a study with such overwhelming evidence that the public would be persuaded.

I talked to him after the news conference and told him that unless he produced the little green men from Mars, the UFO believers would skin him alive. He thought I was exaggerating. Several years later, after controversies left Condon both shocked at the reaction to his work and deeply embittered, he sent me a note saying that during the controversy he had often thought of our brief conversation. I was no seer. I had just been with the UFO world long enough to know how thoroughly the belief in a government conspiracy had gripped the believers. For them there was no such thing as honest disagreement. There was only conspiracy and cover-up.

Condon's problems started early, particularly after a memorandum from project coordinator Robert Low, stating that while the committee had virtually no hope of finding a UFO they would have to appear as if they were looking for one, was leaked to the press. As attacks from the UFO community increased and became ever more virulent, Condon, who had seemed so calm and collected at the initial press conference, became angrier and angrier. His denunciations of the UFO believers and their supporters became louder and more intemperate. A rumor swept the Ufological community that Condon had gone mad. He was mad all right, but he had not gone mad.

The members of the Condon committee examined in detail the evidence for most of the well-known UFO cases, and found nothing sensational. While a few sightings could not be adequately explained, the committee assumed that this was because of lack of evidence. They found no evidence of alien spaceships. The UFO buffs had discounted the Condon report even before it was written. When the massive 1,465-page report was finally issued in January 1969, it may have served the purpose of giving the government an excuse to get out of the UFO business, but it had virtually no effect on public opinion. Those who cared assumed it was just part of the cover-up. It was the same reaction that had greeted the Warren Report about the JFK assassination a few years earlier.

Implications of a UFO conspiracy and cover-up often reached well beyond the Air Force, the CIA, and even beyond the planet Earth. One that has been enshrined in public consciousness is the tale of the "men in black."

The beginning of this story is almost ludicrously mundane. In September 1953, Albert K. Bender, head of the grandly named but really quite tiny International Flying Saucer Bureau, announced in his publication *Space Review* that the flying saucer "mystery" had been solved. "But any information about this is being withheld by orders from a higher source." [6]

Bender concluded his statement with these words: "We advise those engaged in saucer work to please be very cautious." He then shut down his organization, stopped publishing *Space Review,* and generally withdrew from the UFO field.

To his friends, Bender confided a few more details. He said that he had been visited by "three men in dark suits," later to be known as "three men in black," and that they had been "pretty rough" with him and essentially scared him off.

Generally his friends, most of whom were devoted UFO buffs, didn't believe Bender's story. They knew his organization had been losing money, and they figured that he was just looking for a dramatic excuse for abandoning UFOs. But the story of the men in black (MIB) began to take on a life of its own, and soon others who said they had UFO encounters reported that they too had been visited by the sinister and mysterious MIB.

Bender's original account makes the MIB sound like CIA or other government operatives. But in later accounts they take on a weirder and unworldly aura. They are sometimes said to have "glowing eyes," which are hidden by dark glasses. They arrive in large black Cadillacs that have a strange purple glow on the inside, and appear to be able to navigate dark roads without headlights. Or they show up suddenly at remote spots, apparently without the aid of any vehicle at all. Their speech is often strange and robotlike. But their universal aim seems to be to silence those who "know too much."

Despite the fact that there has never been a single bit of credible evidence to indicate that the MIBs even exist, much less what they are, they have become an integral part of the atmosphere of conspiracy that surrounds the UFO field.

Nor do all the conspiracy theories date from the early days of UFOs. In December 1984 a collection of what were supposed to be government documents surfaced revealing the existence of a super-secret group of scientists known as "Majestic 12" (MJ-12) that had been appointed by President Harry Truman to study the remains of aliens that had been found in a crashed UFO in 1947. The members of the group were all well-known scientists, many of whom had openly ridiculed the idea of spaceships. They were also all dead.

Initially the MJ-12 documents created quite a sensation. But on closer examination most people, including many UFO buffs, concluded that they were fraudulent. But the MJ-12 documents are still regularly cited as proof that the government "knows" and is "covering up." Like Roswell and the MIB, MJ-12 has become enshrined in UFO mythology.

A genuinely secret military facility in Nevada has now become the focus of conspiratorial speculation. The place is best known under the name Area 51. For a long time the military even denied that such a place existed at all. But it's there, and it's well guarded. Just exactly what is going on in Area 51 is unknown, but some of the more informed speculation is that one of the operations is disposal of extremely hazardous waste, which would certainly be a good reason for the military to want to keep the place secret. Until fairly recently, Area 51 has had no connection with UFOs. But there have been a fairly large number of UFO sightings in the area, and the connection between them and a secret government facility has proved irresistible. Somehow the two must be connected, though no one seems to know just how.

In 1995, Nevada State Route 375, a 100-mile (160-kilometer) stretch of secondary road that runs past Area 51, was officially designated the Extraterrestrial Highway. Nevada state officials cheerfully admit that this is kind of "a tourist ploy." And the tourists do come, and they buy souvenirs at the Little A'Le Inn, a combination gift shop, motel, and restaurant. Some of the more serious UFO buffs decry the commercialism and the frivolity.[7]

UFOs, government cover-ups, MIBs, secret facilities, and all the other conspiratorial trappings appear

The two stars of the enormously popular television show,
The X-Files. *Agents Dana Scully (Gillian Anderson)
and Fox Mulder (David Duchovny) regularly
investigate a dark and conspiracy-haunted world.*

regularly in newspapers, magazines, and on radio and television. Much of what is produced is avowedly fiction, like the enormously popular TV series *The X-Files*. But it all contributes to the general feeling that "something is out there" and we are not being told the truth about it.

And remember that all of this—all of it—began with an obscure little "silly season" article back in 1947.

THE FINAL CONSPIRACY

If you dig into practically any conspiracy theory, even the most skeptical person may find him or herself seriously wondering if there isn't "something to it" after all. Could all the apparent connections just be a series of coincidences? Could so much of the information simply be false? The answer to both questions is yes, but that can be a hard answer to accept.

A good conspiracy theory sounds reasonable. It appears to answer a lot of unanswered questions. It can also be exciting, far more interesting than mundane reality. For many, the conspiracy theory merely confirms what they already suspect or believe. And, of course, there is the fact that there have been conspiracies and cover-ups throughout history.

Two widely publicized conspiracy theories illustrate these points.

The first revolves around the death of President Bill Clinton's longtime friend and personal lawyer Vincent Foster. Foster had been a lawyer in Little Rock, Arkansas. He had worked closely with Hillary Clinton in the Rose law firm for nearly fifteen years, and he knew the Clintons well. After Bill Clinton was first elected president, Foster came to Washington to work as a deputy White House counsel and the Clintons' personal lawyer.

Between the time of Clinton's election and inauguration, Foster had helped negotiate the end of the Clintons' Whitewater partnership with Arkansas banker Jim McDougal. He was also involved with the White House's inept firing of the staff of the travel office. Both Whitewater and what came to be dubbed "Travelgate" became major problems for President Clinton, his wife, and his administration. Foster himself became the object of intense scrutiny.

Then on the afternoon of July 20, 1993, Vince Foster was found dead in Fort Marcy Park, Virginia, just a twenty-minute drive from the White House. Foster had been shot in the head. The fatal pistol was in his hand. His death seemed to be a suicide.

Immediately and inevitably, rumors began to spread. One rumor alleged that Foster's office had been sealed on orders of Hillary Clinton and his files purged of all incriminating material before investigators had a chance to look at them. Another, more sensational and persistent rumor was that Foster had not shot himself in the park, but had been killed elsewhere and his body had been transported to the park and arranged so that his death would look like a suicide. Here are what people have cited as evidence:

"Foster's whereabouts for a couple of hours before his body was discovered are unknown. No one saw or heard Foster shoot himself. No one even saw him enter the park." But Fort Marcy Park is an obscure and isolated spot that is often deserted. It is not surprising that he was not seen or heard.

"There was not enough blood at the scene." In fact, FBI investigators found a lot of blood at the scene.

"Foster's body was covered with carpet fibers . . . he had been rolled up in a carpet before his body was moved." Investigators concluded that the carpet fibers are unimportant. Carpet fibers are found nearly everywhere, and there were not enough fibers on Foster's body to indicate that he had been encased in a carpet.

"Foster was not suicidal." Though Foster had never openly talked about suicide, everyone knew he was a deeply troubled man. Moving from Little Rock to Washington apparently put him under pressures that he was unable to handle.

"Foster didn't leave a suicide note," or alternately, "his suicide note was a forgery." There is a common myth that every suicide leaves a note. This is not true. Some suicides leave a note, and some do not. Foster left no note. But a few days after his death, torn-up pieces of a note were found in his briefcase. It wasn't really a suicide note, but a sort of personal defense and complaint that he had written a little over a week before he died. In it he expressed his belief that no one in the White House had violated any laws. The last item said, "I was not meant for the job or spotlight of public life in Washington. Here ruining people is considered a sport."[1]

Some insist that the handwriting on this note was not Foster's and that the pieces were planted in his briefcase to bolster the suicide theory. Foster's wife insists that she knew he had written such a defense, and the handwriting most certainly was that of her husband.

While investigators and most of the mainstream media have concluded that Vincent Foster did indeed kill himself, the story of a murder conspiracy and cover-up has been kept alive by a small group of journalists, most of whom are working for a multimillionaire named Richard Mellon Scaife. Scaife had contributed hundreds of millions of dollars to fund conservative causes. He dislikes Democrats in general and Bill Clinton in particular. He owns a small newspaper that has printed most of the articles questioning the Foster suicide. He also supports the Western Journalism Center, which has produced a video called *Unanswered: The Death of Vincent Foster*. Foster's death is a regular feature of some radio talk shows, and a Vincent Foster home page is even available on the World Wide Web.

The campaign has worked. As this is being written, there remain genuine unanswered questions about Whitewater, the travel-office firings, and other activities about which Vincent Foster might have had knowledge. But there should be no question about how Foster died—he committed suicide. Yet polls taken in 1996 indicate that about three quarters of the American public are not convinced of this.[2] Most Americans appear to believe that Foster may indeed have been "the man who knew too much" and that a conspiracy and cover-up have obscured the facts surrounding his death.

An even more insidious conspiracy theory surfaced—or to be more accurate, resurfaced—in August 1996. A series of articles in the *San Jose Mercury News* said that the CIA played a key role in launching the crack-cocaine epidemic. The articles revived an old charge that the agency aided cocaine smugglers during the Reagan administration's covert war in Nicaragua.

The story runs like this: In the early 1980s the Reagan administration had a near obsession with the left-wing Sandinista government of Nicaragua. The CIA, at the strenuous urging of its director, the late William J. Casey, was covertly and sometimes illegally supporting the Contras, a collection of rebel groups attempting to overthrow the Sandinistas. Some of the Contras were dealing cocaine in order to get money to support their army. In other cases individuals who were nothing more than drug dealers may have operated under a Contra cover. That much has been fairly well known and accepted for a long time.

The question is, how much did the CIA know about the drug dealing at the time, and did they just look the other way or actually participate in trafficking cocaine? The CIA has always denied such charges, but with a secret agency such denials are routine and just as routinely disbelieved.

The newspaper's articles set off a firestorm in the African-American community. Starting in the early 1980s a devastating epidemic of a cheap, solid form of cocaine called crack swept through black neighborhoods. The epidemic had been fueled by the availability of massive quantities of relatively inexpensive cocaine from South America. Was it possible that the CIA or some of its operatives had actually allowed the deadly drug to be spread?

And there were even more ominous rumors. It was hinted that CIA involvement was not just the result of overzealousness in the cause of the Contras and indifference to the results, but part of a deliberate and genocidal conspiracy against African Americans.

On talk radio and across the Internet there was speculation about how the CIA first introduced crack cocaine into black areas and then had its agents spread the deadly drug across the country. It was said that this was a plot to subdue and ultimately destroy African Americans. These theories found a receptive audience in a community already deeply distrustful of government authority.

At the time of this writing, there were a number of ongoing investigations of the charges of CIA links to drug deals. So far no clear evidence of any such links has been found, but it is impossible to predict what future investigations might reveal. However, it is also impossible to imagine that evidence to support the grander conspiracy, that the CIA deliberately began the crack epidemic, will be ever be found, because it doesn't exist. The reality is that in the early 1980s huge quantities of cocaine were pouring into the country from many sources—most of which have never been linked to the CIA. Even if those drug dealers named in the *San Jose Mercury News* articles had never existed, the use of crack cocaine would have spread in the same way. There was just too much of it out there already.

But none of that makes any difference anymore. No investigations, no rational discussion, will remove the fear and the anger that have developed. People will believe in this conspiracy for the same reasons that people have always believed in conspiracies—they want to, because it seems to explain the terrible things that have happened. The ideas of conspiracies and cover-ups help people make sense out of events, indeed out of a world, that often seems senseless, indifferent, or cruel.

However, conspiracy theories are not a look at the real or "hidden" history, but a flight from reality. And a theory, no matter how deeply one believes it, will not change that reality.

The best thing that you can do when confronted with a grand conspiracy theory is to step back and get a little historical perspective. Try to remember all the other conspiracies you have read about in this book.

Have the Communists taken over America?

Have the Illuminati?

Was John Wilkes Booth found alive?

Have flying saucers really landed?

Of course not. Yet conspiracy theorists of the past have confidently predicted all these things. Their predictions about what is going to happen in the future are not going to be one bit more accurate.

Some conspiracy theorists try to pass the whole business off as sort of a harmless intellectual game. They put out publications with names like *Paranoia*. "We just want people to think," says the director of the Kennedy assassination museum in Dallas. The authors of a popular conspiracy book call themselves The National Insecurity Council. They tell their readers to find their book "entertaining." They add, "But we also hope you'll take it seriously." [3]

They warn their readers not to be "carried away" and see conspiracies everywhere.

"We don't encourage that."

"However," they continue ". . .conspiracies have existed throughout recorded history. When you consider that conspirators deposed six Caesars in a row (starting with Julius), one American president by a conspiracy in Dallas is not so hard to believe."

What about those six Caesars? Julius Caesar was indeed stabbed by conspirators, but in a public place and everybody knew who the conspirators were. His successor Augustus had one of the longest and most successful reigns in history. He was virtually worshiped by the people of Rome and died of natural causes when he was an old man. Augustus's successor Tiberius was not nearly as successful or popular, but he died in his bed at the age of seventy-three. The next Caesar, Caligula, was seriously insane and was killed by his officers. Claudius Caesar was an old man when he died. He may have been poisoned, but this is by no means certain. Nero was overthrown in a revolt by the army, and he killed himself. The next three Caesars died in quick succession in the civil wars that swept Rome. A revolt and a civil war are not conspiracies.

That business about six Caesars being deposed by conspiracies came out of the Robert Graves novel *I Claudius*, or more probably from the popular television series made from the novel. It's very good drama, but very bad history. Nevertheless, a lot of people, including those who wrote this particular conspiracy book, seem to think that it is real history.

History, be it ancient Roman history or modern American history, is too complicated and too chaotic to be smoothly manipulated by a single grand conspiracy. Small and seemingly trivial events, like small and trivial people, can sometimes have enormous effects. And well-laid plans often have totally unexpected consequences.

In conspiracy theory everything works smoothly for the conspirators. No one messes up the plan. There are no conflicts among conspirators. No one spills the beans. There are no unforeseen events. But the real world doesn't work that way.

Not long ago I talked to a retired CIA official. He said that since the CIA was a secret organization, people who didn't know anything about it could claim that it did practically anything and there was no effective way to refute the claim. He thought that by and large that had been good for the agency, "because people didn't know how often we messed up."

And then he said, a little wistfully I think, "If only we had been as powerful as people thought we were." [4]

Conspiracy theory can be fun. It is entertaining and essentially harmless to speculate about UFOs in the Nevada desert or who is really buried in John Wilkes Booth's grave. But conspiracy theories can also produce horrifying results. If people are convinced that their government has secretly been taken over by hostile and alien forces that are out to deprive them of their freedom and perhaps their very lives, we should not be surprised when some of these people get "carried away" and try to strike back by shooting agents of the government or blowing up government buildings. That is not "entertaining" at all.

Notes

Introduction

1. Charles Paul Freund, "From Satan to the Sphynx: The Mysteries of D.C.'s Map," *The Washington Post* (Nov. 5, 1995), p. C3.
2. Jonathan Vankin and John Whalen, *50 Greatest Conspiraces of All Time* (New York: Citadel, 1995), p. XII.

Chapter 1

1. David Barboza. "A Museum That Provides Conspiracies Rather Than Answer Questions," *The New York Times* (May 28, 1995), p. 22.
2. Gerald Posner, *Case Closed* (New York: Random House, 1993), p. 404.
3. Posner, p. 431.
4. Posner, p. 442.
5. Posner, p. 443.
6. *The New York Times*, p. 22.

Chapter 2

1. Vankin, p. 349.

Chapter 3
1. Editors of Time-Life Books, *Manias and Delusions* (Alexandria, VA: Time-Life Books, 1992), p. 11.
2. Editors of Time-Life Books, p. 12.
3. Nesta Webster, *Secret Societies and Subversive Movements* (first published 1924, republished by Christian Book Club), p. 405.
4. Personal communication to author.

Chapter 4
1. Sources give several slightly different versions of the message.
2. There is some dispute as to whether Lord Salisbury actually was a Freemason or just sympathetic to Masonry. However, the most influential conspiracy theorist on this subject insists that he was a Mason.
3. Martin Fido, *The Crimes, Detection and Death of Jack the Ripper* (New York: Barnes & Noble, 1993), p. 149.

Chapter 5
1. Ronald Radosh and Dennis King, "The World According to LaRouche," *The New Republic* (Nov. 19, 1984), p. 18.
2. Radosh, p. 18.
3. Radosh, p. 18.
4. Brian Siano, "Big-Head's Back," *The Humanist* (May-June 1992), p. 37.

Chapter 6
1. David Oshinsky, *A Conspiracy So Immense* (New York: Free Press, 1983), p. 146.
2. Oshinsky, p. 283.
3. Oshinsky, p. 367.
4. Editors of Time-Life Books, p. 14.

Chapter 7
1. Serge F. Kovaleski, "Oklahoma Bombing Conspiracy

Theories Ripple Across the Nation," *The Washington Post* (July 9, 1995), p. A3.
2. Kovaleski.
3. Vankin, p. 249.
4. Vankin, p. 250

Chapter 8
1. Kevin D. Randle and Donald R. Schmitt, *UFO Crash at Roswell* (New York: Avon, 1991), p. 116.
2. William J. Broad, "Wreckage of a Spaceship of This Earth (and U.S.)," *The New York Times* (Sept. 18, 1994), p. 1.
3. Jerome Clark, *UFO Encounters, Sightings, Visitations and Investigations* (Lincolnwood IL.: Publications International, Ltd., 1992), p. 34.
4. Ronald D. Story (ed.), *The Encyclopedia of UFO's* (Garden City, NY: Doubleday, 1980), p. 58.
5. Story, p. 286.
6. Clark, p. 94.
7. Trip Gabriel, "Strange Extraterrestrial Attraction Luring Tourists to a Desert Town," *The New York Times* (Aug. 13, 1996), p. A8.

Chapter 9
1. Tom Cornwall and Ambrose Evans-Pritchard, "The Suicide That Won't Die," *World Press Review,* Vol. 43, No. 2 (Feb. 1996), p. 36.
2. Cornwall, p. 37.
3. National Insecurity Council, *It's a Conspiracy* (Berkeley, CA: Earth Works Press, 1992), pp. 7-8.
4. Personal communication to author.

Bibliography

Balsiger, David, and Charles E. Sellier Jr. *The Lincoln Conspiracy*. Los Angeles: Schik Sunn Classic Books, 1977.

Cohen, Daniel. *UFOs: The Third Wave*. New York: M. Evans, 1984.

Davis, John H. *Mafia Kingfish: Carlos Marcello and the Assassination of John F. Kennedy*. New York: NAL, 1989.

Editors of Time-Life Books. *Manias and Delusions*. Alexandria, VA: Time-Life Books, 1992.

___. *The UFO Phenomenon*. Alexandria, VA: Time-Life Books, 1987.

Fido, Martin. *The Crimes, Detection and Death of Jack the Ripper*. New York: Barnes & Noble, 1993.

Garrison, Jim. *On the Trail of the Assassins*. New York: Sheridan Square, 1988.

Grant, Michael. *The Twelve Caesars*. New York: Scribners, 1975.

Hinckle, Warren, and William Turner. *Deadly Secrets: The CIA-Mafia War Against Castro and the Assassination of JFK*. San Francisco: Thunders Mouth Press, 1992.

Hougan, Jim. *Secret Agenda: Watergate, Deep Throat and the CIA*. New York: Random House, 1984.

Humes, Edward. *Buried Secrets: True Story of a Serial Murder*. New York: Dutton, 1991.

Hurt, Henry. *Reasonable Doubt: An Investigation into the Assassination of John F. Kennedy*. New York: Henry Holt, 1985.

Knight, Stephen. *The Brotherhood: The Secret World of the Freemasons*. New York: Dorset, 1984.

___. *Jack the Ripper: The Final Solution*. London: Grafton Books, 1977.

MacKenzie, Norman (Editor). *Secret Societies*. New York: Holt, Rinehart and Winston, 1967.

Marrs, Jim. *Crossfire: The Plot That Killed Kennedy*. New York: Carroll and Graf, 1989.

National Insecurity Council Staff. *It's a Conspiracy!* Berkeley, CA: Earth Works Press, 1992.

Oshinsky, David. *A Conspiracy So Immense*. New York: Free Press, 1983.

Posner, Gerald. *Case Closed: Lee Harvey Oswald and the Assassination of JFK*. New York: Random House, 1995.

Quigley, Carroll. *Tragedy and Hope: A History of the World in Our Time*. New York: Macmillan, 1966.

Randle, Kevin D., and Donald R. Schmitt. *UFO Crash at Roswell*. New York: Avon, 1991.

___. *The Truth About the UFO Crash at Roswell*. New York: M. Evans, 1993.

Reeves, Thomas C. *The Life and Times of Joe McCarthy*. New York: Stein & Day, 1982.

Robison, John. *Proofs of a Conspiracy*. Boston: Western Island Press, 1967.

Roscoe, Theodore. *The Web of Conspiracy: The Complete Story of the Men Who Murdered Abraham Lincoln*. Englewood Cliffs, NJ: Prentice-Hall, 1959.

Rovere, Richard. *Senator Joe McCarthy*. New York: Harcourt Brace, 1959.

Speliglo, Milo. *The Marilyn Conspiracy*. New York: The Birch Lane Press, 1993.

Vankin, Jonathan. *Conspiracies, Cover-ups and Crimes*. New York: Paragon Press, 1991.

Vankin, Jonathan, and John Whalen. *50 Greatest Conspiracies of All Time*. New York: Citadel Press, 1995.

Webster, Nesta H. *Secret Societies and Subversive Movements*. Christian Book Club of America, first published 1924.

Index